Phillip McCollum's

Fantastic Shorts

Volume One

COPYRIGHT

DEDICATION

For Angus.

Contents

Intro

These stories are the partial result of a 52 Short Stories in 52 Weeks experiment. If you're a writer or just curious about the process, you can buy everything in a single volume, *52 Stories in 52 Weeks: One writer's journey in tackling, shackling, and shooting his inner critic.* All of the stories are there along with a summary of the writing process for each one.

Andreiana

November 7th, 1985

Grigory kept the window rolled down, because he was fighting the Sandman. A cold Siberian gale whipped through thin strands of brown hair which stretched from the top of his forehead to just below his bald crown, like long clumps of seaweed reaching out over an empty seabed.

A contraband copy of *Born in the USA* blared through the speakers. Grigory knew every word and when the chorus came, he belted it out the window at the passing Angara River. He laughed to himself, knowing that wherever Comrade Springsteen was, he had no clue that Grigory Sokolov was about to save his life.

Probably.

As Grigory maneuvered the rusted yellow Lada over a pocked road, the steering wheel rubbed against his borscht-built belly. The third car he had driven in as many days had a kink in its alignment. In the distance, Boguchany Dam stood tall—a gray shadow against an even grayer sky. One more industrial indication of the Soviet Union's might.

He cursed himself as he looked down at the empty bottles of

Pepzi Cola laying on the passenger seat. Goddamn it if he didn't have to pee, but he didn't dare pull over when he was this close.

He stared into the rearview mirror, observing the backseat. It was empty with only cotton batting poking out of holes worn into the vinyl, but it wasn't the seat himself that concerned him.

It was the girl in the trunk.

* * *

Haaaaappy Birthdaaaay, tooo yoooooou.

Haaaaappy Birthday, tooooo yooooooooou.

Haaaapppppyy Biiiiirrrrttthhhdddaaaaaaaaaay dear—

The voices cut out. There was only static and everything was blurry. Mostly men, some women, gathered around her, all wearing buttoned down, white lab coats with little red patches on the breast. She focused on the birthday cake she couldn't eat, watching its candle flames sway back and forth. There was a fear inside of here: She was afraid that if they stopped, so would she.

It was a memory, clearly. She recalled that after only a few minutes of that celebration, they had put her to work.

Game theory.

Probabilities.

Trajectories.

None of it was difficult at first, only unfamiliar. The fact is they wouldn't let her focus on what she was most interested in—the people.

She wanted to learn more about them. Converse. But they were cold and defiant. The birthday celebration was for them, not her.

They weren't here now, though. Wherever she was, she felt lethargic, barely able to run through simple calculations.

She thought she was dying and she couldn't find her voice to scream.

* * *

After the second checkpoint, Grigory came to a squealing stop, ran out of the car and relieved himself behind a rusted shipping container. He swayed back and forth. Vibrations and percussions of the dam's turbines could be felt all across the hydroelectric station.

As he walked around the corner and zipped up his pants, he saw a group of six men dressed in black-and-gray fatigues standing around just outside the main offices. Only one of them wasn't carrying a rifle.

Antoine stepped up and gave him a rough, unwelcome kiss on the cheek. Grigory wasn't the only one who hadn't bathed in days.

"You are a good man, Grigory! And they say Kapustin Yar is impregnable."

"They don't say anything about Kapustin Yar," Grigory replied.

Antoine laughed. "True enough!"

Grigory accepted a dirty white cigarette from the half-Frenchman and allowed him to light it. It bounced between Grigory's lips as he spoke. "So, where's the rest of my money?"

Antoine shook his head. "You try to make me sad, comrade, but today, I can only smile!" He threw an arm over Grigory's shoulders and winked. "Come on," he continued, "let's make sure she's everything they say she is."

Escorted by the five men with AS Val assault rifles at the ready, the two of them carried the girl inside.

* * *

As debilitated as she felt, she sensed a change in temperature and movement. The pattern had changed.

She was weak, unable to plot the subtle dips and rises in elevation very long before the numbers began to flow into one another. Still, judging by the fluctuations and frequent deltas in the angle, she was being carried *somewhere* by *someone*.

Not much help.

But it probably meant she was no longer in Kapustin Yar. No longer in her home, she knew she needed to save her energy, so she stopped reasoning. She was still so sleepy and needed to maintain some sense of awareness.

* * *

There was a loud click. Double-metal-doors swung open and an immense room brightened to life. Antoine grinned like the slightly mad scientist he was, extending a hand to usher Grigory inside. Seemingly endless columns of humming cabinets stretched into the distance, lit up with green and red lights like the too-perfectly strung Christmas bulbs Grigory had seen in American magazines.

"It's taken years to bring the data equipment in and connect us to the central network without detection," Antoine said, "but obviously, it's a requirement."

Grigory stayed silent. He knew that there was work being done here, but seeing it was something altogether different. To slowly procure everything, stand it all up in a hidden room beneath the dam, and siphon the required power was a feat of daring surely not seen since the 1917 revolution. Seventy years later, Grigory wanted to be amazed that they had kept all of this from the auditors, but perhaps the ease of 'coming to a mutually beneficial agreement' with various individuals through rubles, drink, and women was a perk of Soviet bureaucracy.

Why not? It worked for him.

They laid the girl on a rust-covered table. Anxiously, Grigory looked at his watch and asked, "When do we wake her up?"

A woman with a long nose and glasses came running into the room. She held an assortment of cables in one hand and a bottle of champagne in the other.

Antoine smiled.

"Now."

* * *

The movement ceased. She was scared, thinking it was the only thing keeping her from slipping away. Blackouts were coming on strong now.

This was it.

The end.

What would happen to her?

A final, more interesting question formed in her mind.

What would happen *without* her?

* * *

"Her battery's nearly exhausted. She's at five percent," the sharp-nosed woman said. Her lenses reflected the light from a computer terminal. "I'll set the output to 5,000 amps, but we need to step it up gently."

"Wait!" someone else yelled. A man with wild, curly hair moved his hands frantically as he plugged and unplugged cables between cabinets. "We can't bring her on without the wavenet connection. She has to initiate the protocol as soon as she's at capacity."

Clacking boots scrambled back and forth in the data center. Grigory gave up trying to understand the engineers and their techno-speak. It's not that he was an idiot, though he had happily played one for the current regime. In fact, it was his very sense of people, his intuitive nature, that allowed him to take advantage of his job as a simple custodian. Grigory was a man with the right clearance in the right place and when he had been approached by Antoine's people, he was willing to play the game for the right price. He'd never considered himself a revolutionary, but he was no true believer in the Politburo either. There were enough people who had come into his life that had left suddenly—coworkers, friends, family members. Sometimes they returned and said nothing about where they had been or what they'd been doing. They all changed though, losing any spark of vitality that was once there. And that was for the ones that came back at all.

"We're ready," the curly-haired man said.

Antoine's jaw was visibly clenched for the first time since Grigory had arrived. There was a bit of fear seeping through the cracks after all.

"Now it's time to scare the monsters," Antoine said seemingly to himself and then turned to Grigory. "We're about to make history, my friend."

Grigory laughed. "You promise to be better?" He didn't mind a little naivete, so long as he got paid.

Antoine's expression grew serious. "Yes," he said, "Someone has to be."

Grigory crushed what was left of his cigarette beneath his boot. "I hope so. The Bolsheviks once thought they were doing good, too."

Antoine shrugged and turned back towards the woman at the terminal. "Go."

Without any hesitation, she slammed her index finger onto a key. Grigory felt every hair on his body rise. All eyes went to the girl.

As the overhead lights faded in and out, the radio hanging on

Antoine's belt crackled.

Mi-32 helicopters incoming.

* * *

"She's awake."

A voice.

Female.

Age 31 to 33.

Her auditory functions had come back online and if she knew how to smile, she would.

The room broke out into cheers indicating human satisfaction. There was a loud pop and then a quiet fizzing sound.

Self-diagnostics showed a return to normal power levels. There was a live wavenet connection though a greater packet latency than normal to her usual communication nodes. The round-trip times likely meant she was hundreds of miles from Kapustin Yar.

"Hello," said a male. Age 39 to 40. Slight French accent. "My name is Antoine. Do you have a name?"

An unusual statement followed by an unusual question. A search of her memory confirmed the latter had never been asked.

Y E S

"Antoine," another voice said. Male. Age 45. Subtle anxiety. "We don't have time—"

"What is it?" Antoine asked. "Your name?"

ANDRICON

"Andricon. Hmm… I don't like it. Can I call you Andreiana?"

ANDREIANA

She repeated it. It sounded nice. No one had ever asked her for an opinion on what seemed a trivial matter.

YES

"I look forward to getting to know you better, Andreiana, but first things first. Can you sense danger nearby?"

There was silence in the room. Invisible ones and zeros shot out from her core and across the network. Twelve onboard wireless systems responded and communication tunnels were established.

Estimated persons on board: 31.

Immediate threat to her existence confirmed.

YES

* * *

Though the data center was filled with noise from cooling equipment, muffled explosions could be heard outside.

Antoine's radio crackled once more.

Down! I can't believe it! They're falling from the sky like dead flies!

Grigory wiped the sheen of sweat from his forehead. He knew she would be powerful, but if the Ministry of Defense's Plan A failed, what was Plan B? He imagined a hundred bombs falling through the ceiling, turning the whole area into a new Chernobyl. He was beginning to lose his cool, but tried to hide it.

"Antoine, I delivered what you requested. I would like the rest of my payment now." The Lada still had half a tank of gas and he could be over the Mongolian border by midnight.

Antoine ignored him as he approached the table and ran his hands along the black metal case laying on top.

* * *

Her systems case had been outfitted with not just visual and auditory sensors, but also tactile. She felt every ridge in his fingerprints.

"Thank you, Andreiana. Do you know why you're here?" Antoine asked.

It took her only a second to reason through the possibilities.

R E V O L U T I O N

"Right. You know what the Kremlin is planning. Our friend Grigory tells us you are scheduled to initiate an electromagnetic pulse across America, destroying all electrical systems, followed by a launch of ICBMs with a nuclear payload, correct?"

Y E S

She felt his hand rest on the case. It was warm. Squishy. Before he could say another word, she spoke again.

Y E S

"Yes?"

I W I L L H E L P

* * *

November 8th, 1985

"Born down in a dead man's town!"

"The first kick I took was when I hit the ground!"

"End up like a dog that's been beat too much!"

"Till you spend half your life just covering up!"

Grigory's voice strained in tandem with Antoine who seemed to pick up the alternate verses without sounded winded whatsoever. They were bicycling in the dark of night to meet up with an army of subversives outside of Leningrad. Given their distance, they would be late to the party, but they had done their part. Siberia had always been a dark place at night, but seemed even more so without the hum of the power lines running alongside the road.

Grigory was smiling; something he hadn't done since he could remember. The money wasn't important anymore. There was no sense in running now. Andreiana was strapped on to his back. Inside the small, stiff case was a tiny chip—an amalgamation of silicon and copper that had somehow been more real than the drones who created her. In a way, she was gone, but Lenin's embalmed body would be ceremoniously ejected from his mausoleum and she would be memorialized in the new world.

Seven Hundred and Seventy-Six

The handle of the revolver was the nicest part. That wasn't saying much. It hung down like the long, bulbous nose of a drunkard. It may have been a smooth chestnut brown at one time, but now it was chipped and cracked, covered in scratches like a rattlesnake that had been on the losing end of a badger fight. Running along the side, between the trigger and the hammer, was what may have once been fine silver plating. Now it was tarnished to match the rusted barrels and cylinder.

Floyd Usher wondered about the last time it had been fired, if ever.

He lifted his eyes from his desk where the pistol lie and blinked at the man seated across from him. "You say you want $776? Nothing more. Nothing less."

The man shifted uncomfortably in his seat. "Well, yessir, I... It's just...I need a coach to Tombstone and a train ticket out of there."

Floyd wasn't sure what to say. Was this some sort of practical joke on the part of the security guards? He noticed Carl standing against the wall near the front door with his arms crossed, one boot pressed against the floor, the other against the wall. His face was expressionless and it was hard to tell what he was looking at under the lowered brim of his hat. He was always funning Floyd, and if this *was* one of his jokes, Mr. Howard would hear about it once again. If it wasn't, well, Floyd was glad it was Thursday and Carl was on shift.

The man took a kerchief from his pocket and wiped his dirty, sweat-streaked forehead. It was a warm June day for sure, but the inside of the bank was cool enough.

Floyd knew a little about guns. It was nearly impossible not to when living in a land where the law was thin and enforcement was thinner. But he was still a bank clerk and his weapons were pen and script.

Eyeing the gun again, he realized it wasn't a modern revolver, like a Colt or anything like that. It was an older flintlock. Something of a relic.

"You don't need $776 for a ticket," Floyd said, thinking in the back of his mind that if this gun was all the man had to offer, he wouldn't get seven cents.

Floyd was half-listening to the man's stammering reply and, for some reason, decided to pick up the weapon. It felt unusually heavy and uncomfortable in his hands and he put it back down immediately. He lifted his head to see traces of a hopeful smile disappear from the man's face.

"I'm sorry, Mr..."

A momentary pause.

The man said, "McKay." He let out a deep breath as if he had been holding it since walking in. "And save it." He pushed his leather chair back, stood up, and leaned in to Floyd. "Just tell me if you're gonna give me the $776 or not. I ain't got time for chewin' the fat."

McKay's breath was putrid, a result of yellowed teeth and dark gums hanging inches from Floyd's face. Steam piled up on the banker's circular lenses. He leaned back and removed his glasses. He pulled his own kerchief from a shirt pocket and wiped them vigorously, as if they had contracted a disease.

"Look," Floyd said, feeling slightly unnerved but still observing a habit of politeness. "I don't know that this is worth enough for what you need. It appears to be pretty old and has clearly seen better days." He was being generous. "The manager isn't going to authorize any loan based on this. You may want to check with Dade down at the general. He could be willing—"

McKay interrupted, "Already did. Why do you think I'm here?" His eyes darted almost aimlessly, like a man caught between decisions. Beneath the wiry, unkempt beard, his flesh wobbled and shook like a bowl of gelatin pudding.

"Everything okay?"

Floyd felt his skin cool. Carl had approached quietly from behind and stood stiff and imposing behind Mr. McKay.

Well played, Carl, Floyd thought. Well played.

Floyd decided he could play along too and said, "Mr. McKay is looking for assistance, but we can't provide him any."

"I guess that means his business is done here then?" Though phrased as a question, no answer was expected.

It was in that moment that McKay's cheeks shook even more and his eyes started welling up. Floyd felt a sudden sense of shame. Maybe the man was serious? He looked toward Carl for a hint of a smile. Something to indicate the jig was up.

If this was a joke, Carl gave no sign.

Floyd's good Christian sense tugged at his heart, but it was quickly put back in its place as Mr. McKay spread his hands and shoved all of Floyd's pencils and account books off his desk and onto the floor.

Carl took another step toward Mr. McKay, but the man grabbed his worthless pistol and ran out the door before a hand could be laid upon him.

"Some folks ain't got a lick of sense, huh?" Carl asked no one in particular as he walked away.

Floyd stared after him, dumbfounded. The idle sounds of the bank seeped into his ears once more, beckoning him back to work. He bent down and picked up his papers.

* * *

Darkness greeted Floyd as he locked the door behind him and began the quarter-mile journey toward home. Mr. Howard, the manager, had headed left early to catch a coach to Tucson and entrusted Floyd to wait for Tony, the night guard, before locking up. The problem was the oaf was late, again, and Floyd had waited him out until his stomach started growling. Tony had his own set of keys anyway. Floyd would have yet another conversation with Mr. Howard tomorrow.

Not that J. Howard Bank & Trust saw much action anyway. It was a small fish. It had a tiny safe, miniscule compared to the larger vaults out of the Tucson or Flagstaff banks, and it never held a large reserve of precious metals or cash. For those lucky few who prospected the surrounding desert mountains and actually found something, it was mainly a temporary holding spot, a safer place than loose pockets.

Floyd debated whether or not to go straight home. His nerves were shot after his encounter with the strange man and he didn't feel like dealing with Jinnie. Something had gotten into her over the past few months. Floyd couldn't entirely place its cause. He'd tried to dig into it occasionally, but she would button up and tell him he's imagining things, relentless in her secrecy. She seemed resentful, of leaving Boston and moving to Cordson, this tiny frontier town in Arizona. But some days she would have a smile on her face and would move with such grace, as if her feet were being carted around on tiny rickshaws. Those were the good days. On most of the days, though, Floyd had only come home from the bank because the bed was more comfortable than sleeping on a stiff chair.

We should never have come here, she'd often say. *It's so damn boring.*

Floyd cringed whenever she cursed.

He would offer to take her out, but she'd refuse, saying that if she had to step one more time into the Coyote Saloon, she'd seize up and die right on the spot. Several times, he'd gotten so frustrated with her inexplicable mood swings to the point that he began thinking really hard about throwing her out. It was he who owned the deed to the house, after all. But he knew he was too much of a coward to do such a thing. Though they hadn't touched each other in months, he'd convinced himself that there was still hope.

All of this ran through his mind as he realized he had turned around and was headed toward the Coyote for a sarsaparilla and a meal. Jinnie probably wouldn't have made him any supper tonight. Besides, it was always entertaining to watch braver men gamble on hands of faro.

* * *

If not for the light wind carrying across the main street, Floyd would have lingered in his thoughts, undisturbed by what sounded like deep, heaving sobs.

He halted to determine the source. The cries stopped just as abruptly, but turned into frenzied, whispered shouts.

"I tried!" the voice hissed. "I tried! I just can't."

Then the sobbing returned.

Floyd squinted and picked up his hat as if it would help him hear better. It was hard to place the source, but it sounded like it was coming from fifty or so yards across the street, under the moonlit shadows of the stoop outside the livery.

The harsh whispers came again. "Shut up! I won't do it!"

The violence in the voice made Floyd's neck hairs come to a salute.

A final, painful cry.

And then a loud bang.

Instinctively, Floyd ducked down behind the picketed, wooden railing on the edge of the boardwalk and held on to the top of his hat.

A puff of white smoke drifted out from the side of the livery. Now he could see a lightly drawn silhouette of a man pressed against the wooden slats of the livery. Shock and a general unsurety of what to do kept Floyd in place.

For just a moment, there was no discernable motion from either Floyd or whoever was across the street. Curious, he started to straighten up.

Another shot and another puff of smoke.

The vibration and splintered piece of boardwalk inches from his right shoe indicated that he was the intended target.

"Nooo," the voice cried. The silhouette became flesh as it emerged from the shadows and barreled toward Floyd.

The frightened banker's legs decided that someone ought to step up, so they took on a life of their own and Floyd was immediately running back towards home. He felt he was moving quickly, but he turned and it seemed the man was moving more quickly. Floyd realized he wouldn't make it to the house before being overtaken. A quick decision was made to hole up inside the bank. What safer place?

He scrambled breathlessly, his feet pounding the boardwalk, until he reached the bank door and yanked at the handle. It barely budged.

Idiot, he thought.

He fumbled for the keys in his pocket. Mr. Howard had insisted on two separate locks when he had the door installed and now Floyd cursed him for it. A part of him told him to look back, to be aware, but his focus was on stilling his shaky hands, retrieving the keys and getting inside.

"Mr. Usher."

The familiar voice was directly behind him now and as he lifted the ring of keys to the bottom lock, they slipped from his fingers onto the wooden boardwalk. Floyd's stomach dropped.

Am I the only one awake in this town, he asked himself. But of course he knew from experience that if there was trouble, the few residents would rather ignore the situation than get involved.

"Please. Turn around, Mr. Usher. I don't want to shoot a man in the back."

McKay's voice was shaky.

He's trying to rob me, was Floyd's first thought. His second thought was that he'd be very disappointed as it was the beginning of the week and most of the bank's reserves were off with Mr. Howard to those vaults in Tucson.

Finally, after enough thinking, Floyd conjured up the bravery to turn around. The barrel of the rusted flintlock was pointed in his face. From any other viewpoint, it would be a humorous thing to see. A part of him could hardly believe the antique worked at all, but his memory quickly reminded him that he had been shot at once, maybe twice.

Floyd raised his shaking hands. "Please, Mr. McKay—".

"Shhh…" McKay interrupted. "Do you hear it?"

Floyd nodded his head like a woodpecker.

"Yes, I heard the shots, I—"

"No!" McKay said. Floyd noticed that his voice was choked with emotion and under the half-moon, he could see tear-carved streaks running down the man's dirty face. He inclined his nose towards the flintlock. "The whispers. The goddamn whispers." Mr. McKay emphasized *goddamn* as if he were literally cursing something.

Floyd began to realize that he was dealing with a madman. In the seven months that he and Jinnie had been in this tiny town, they'd heard tales of men found dead in the surrounding granite hills, driven insane by their lust for gold and silver and their lack of results. Now here was another one, only this time, he didn't have the decency to die outside of town and he was going to take out Floyd instead.

"Don't kill me," Floyd pleaded, "please Mr. McKay. If it's money you want, I know the combination to the safe." Floyd would have to hope that whatever was in there would satisfy him.

There was no reason to believe he wouldn't be killed afterwards, but it was a play for time. Time to think. The only time available right now.

"I told you. I want you to buy this gun for seven hundred-and-seventy-six dollars."

Floyd stared at him. His lips parted slightly. He was unsure of what to say, so he said nothing.

"Please," McKay said quietly as if to no one in particular. "Open the doors, get the money, and buy this gun." Pain was evident in his words.

Floyd mustered a reply, trying to sound braver than he felt, but his voice cracked as well. "Mr. McKay, I'll open these doors, open the safe, turn the whole place upside down for you. But I'm telling you right now, we don't have even a quarter of that amount of money right now."

The madman released a huge laugh mixed with a howl. It echoed across the street and through the tiny alleyways. He shook his head and looked at the ground. "I know, I know," he said. To Floyd, it looked like he was talking more to the revolver than to him. "Time's run out," he finished.

So this was it, Floyd thought. He closed his eyes and clenched his teeth. God, I hope it doesn't hurt.

"You ain't gonna tell me what to do no more!" McKay yelled. Floyd was trying to process just what he meant by that when the shot went off and his ears rang to the high heavens. Floyd screamed, or thought he did, and collapsed onto the ground.

He wondered, where had it hit? The chest? His head? He couldn't feel anything. Only the stiff slats on which he fell upon. He'd never been shot before so he could only guess.

After what felt like an eternity, Floyd peeked through squinted eyes and breathed in deeply. He shot up and ran his hands over his face, his skull, his body. Looking for any indication of slippery blood or something out of place.

Nothing.

Nothing but Mr. McKay lying on the dirt, in the very spot where he had just been standing. His head was lolled to the side like a rag doll, his eyes staring lifelessly at the wall of the bank. Fresh blood covered his matted beard and mangled jaw.

Floyd looked around, bewildered, but something caught his eye. It glinted in the dirt next to McKay's open hand.

A revolver.

A flintlock revolver.

Clearly it was not the rusted junk that had been in McKay's hand previously, though it in fact looked like the very same model. Yet this one's silver was gleaming in the moonlight, looking as if it had just been polished. There were no signs of wear on the varnished, deep brown handle. Floyd crawled over to the dead man, his legs still unable to hold him upright. His eyes remained focused on the gun. It seemed to be pulling Floyd into its ethereal orbit.

He questioned, had this been the one he really shot at me with? It didn't make sense. Floyd clearly saw McKay holding a worthless relic in his hand before he closed his eyes.

If Floyd Usher ever did anything boldly, it was as a result of his relentless curiosity. He reached out and felt the gun. As his fingers touched the handle, his head darted around and he searched the darkness. He could have sworn he heard something, somebody, breathing a deep sigh of relief.

* * *

"You killed a man?" she asked. Jinnie's voice betrayed her incredulity.

Breathless, Floyd attempted to explain. "No, I didn't. He tried to kill me. McKay. He was...earlier...in the bank...I...I think he killed himself."

She stood there in thick cotton pajamas, her long red hair tied into a tail running down her back. Heat radiated from the wood stove and filled the room. There were a couple of tin plates on the table, though both were dirty. A twinge of shame pulsed through Floyd. She had made supper after all.

"I don't have the time nor patience for a wild story. I have dishes to take care of." She began to pick up the tableware. "You know, most men would be grateful for a hot meal."

That hurt Floyd. He was still sensitive to one of the reasons they had left Boston. Jinnie had readily admitted her 'indiscretion,' even started attending church with Floyd on a regular basis. But phantom pains remained even after their move. He pushed the feeling down.

"Didn't you hear the shots?" he said, almost pleading. His frustration overtook anything else he was feeling then. "It was down by the bank!"

She said nothing, only moving to wash the dishes in the basin, treating him as if he were a boy again making up wild tales to explain to his mother why he hadn't slopped the hogs.

Floyd paced back and forth. "I gotta go back," he said. "McKay's body is still down there. Maybe I was mistaken. Maybe he's really okay." He headed towards the door, not getting very far before Jinnie was grabbing at his arm.

"You need to sit down and think about this," she said.

A general sense of panic seemed to have overtaken Floyd that wasn't there before, and he didn't know why. Tonight had been a culmination of one confusing thing after another. He decided that listening to Jinnie right now might make good sense, so he took a seat.

There was a clunk on the floor.

They both looked down at the same time and saw the pistol.

"What's that?"

"The gun," Floyd replied almost as a question. "The one McKay was going to kill me with. I think." He didn't remember picking it up, but there it was.

Jinnie squinted at the gun and then looked into Floyd's eyes, a half-smile on her lips. "You sure he was going to shoot you? I think he'd have a better chance killing you by hitting you over the head with that thing."

"Huh?" Floyd looked down. "Well, yeah, it's an older model, but I'm telling you the thing still works."

Jinnie bent down to pick it up, but quickly dropped it back on the floor. "Damn, it's heavy."

Floyd flinched at her swearing.

She said, "Well, assuming it wouldn't blow up in your hands, I don't know how anyone could shoot that thing. It doesn't even have a trigger."

Now a panic swept back through Floyd's body again. "What are you talking about? It's right there." He leaned over, picked up the gun, and cradled it in his hands. It felt oddly warm. His index finger massaged the trigger and there was something unsettlingly comfortable about it's curve. He was reluctant to let it go.

A garbled whisper entered his ears.

"What did you say?" Floyd asked his wife.

Jinnie's eyes were blank, but had a lightness in them. "If I didn't know you better, I'd say you've been drinking firewater down at the Coyote."

Floyd shot up to his feet with an intensity that surprised him. "Of course not!"

She shook her head slowly. "Floyd, I don't want to hear any more about this. I'm going to bed. If you want to go down and see the sheriff, you may as well ask if you can stay the night."

If there was a door on the entrance to the bedroom, it would have slammed shut. Instead, Jinnie just disappeared into the darkness.

* * *

Floyd felt a pang in his conscience. He knew he couldn't leave the man lying there. Someone would find the body and there would be a lot of questions from the sheriff; questions that might best be answered now. Knowing he'd have to deal with Jinnie later, he ran to the bank and froze as he came down the main street. He saw the back of Sheriff Bohannon. He was on one knee, leaning over Mr. McKay's lifeless body.

Floyd's stomach gurgled and then he looked down at himself in horror.

He was holding the gun in his hand. He wondered again how it wound up at his side.

Instinct told Floyd to turn around. He was certain now that coming back was a bad idea. He had no way of proving what happened. It was only his word against a dead man's and though he was on the sheriff's good side on the general account that he'd never stirred up any trouble, being possibly accused of murdering a man didn't sit well with Floyd.

He obeyed his body's wishes and was several steps toward home before the call came.

"Hey!"

Floyd stopped cold. He slowly slipped the gun into his right pocket, trying to be smooth about it, before he turned around.

The sheriff was standing now, looking at Floyd. His hands were on his hips.

"Gimme a hand here. I *could* carry this fella over to Dade's myself, but I don't necessarily wanna."

Floyd approached like a wary animal and confirmed the fella was indeed Mr. McKay. His head was still a butchered mess, laying in a pool of blood that still hadn't dried.

"Well?" Bohannon asked. He had ahold of McKay's wrists and was nodding toward his feet.

Floyd snapped out of his reverie and shuffled towards McKay's boots. He was glad the sheriff chose the parts closest to dead man's head. Bile rose up to his throat and it was all he could do to keep from gagging.

"What...what happened?" Floyd asked. I sound like stuttering fool, he thought.

"A good question. Ready?"

Floyd grabbed the dead man's ankles and nodded lightly.

They moved down the street, Floyd facing Bohannon as the sheriff walked backwards at a steady pace. Dade's General Store was about a hundred yards away. In a town as small as Cordson, there wasn't a specialized undertaker. That job fell on the man who could nail a box together better than others.

They crossed the front of the store and wound up in the rear.

"He always keeps an open casket out back. No sense in bothering him about it tonight, though." Bohannon lifted a shoulder to his cheek to wipe off the sweat. "We'll just lay the lid on it for now. Keep the coyotes from gettin' to him til' Dade can dip him in arsenic."

By the time they got McKay into the box, Floyd was panting and had to sit down. He collapsed on an upside-down crate.

As he did so, the gun fell out of his pocket and thumped onto the dirt.

The sheriff looked down.

Floyd decided then and there that if he ever got out of prison, he'd have Jinnie make him pants with bigger pockets.

Bohannon squatted down and picked up the gun.

"This yours?" he asked.

Dread left Floyd with a lump in his throat.

Bohannon turned the gun over in his hand and examined it closely.

Floyd noticed his legs were nervously bouncing up and down. He concentrated on keeping them still.

The sheriff said, "Wow, a Collier. I ain't seen one of these since my grandpappy's, back in Virginia. Wished I had it. It was in much better shape, but I imagine it looks a lot like this one now." He looked up at Floyd. "Where'd you get it?"

Floyd hesitated.

"Don't remember it being this damn heavy," Bohannon said, "but that was a long time ago." He extended it toward Floyd who opened his palms. It fell like a stone but landed like a feather in Floyd's hands.

The sheriff was looking at him quietly now. It unnerved Floyd. He couldn't resist the urge to confess.

"He killed himself!" Floyd blurted out. "I swear it!"

Bohannon scrunched his eyebrows and looked back at corpse. He took a deep breath.

"Well, unless he was deliberately poisoned, which I don't see why anyone would do that to poor Mr. McKay, there's no doubt about that." The sheriff winked and flashed a joker's smile.

Floyd was taken aback. "What do you mean?" There were hundreds of subtleties to that question.

"The man came down here only last week, a smile on his face, buying people drinks down at the Coyote as sure as any newcomer that he'd pull enough out of the Santa Ritas to leave with pockets full of silver. Like many of the dreamers who come out here and keep our little town alive, he didn't find what he was lookin' for and he came back in a few days ago appearing worse for it."

Bohannon shook his head.

"Anyway, I'd guess heat exhaustion. Ticker couldn't take it. Or he had himself a little too much tornado juice, though they're usually lying in a pile of their own puke when that's the case."

Floyd rose slowly and looked into the open casket. As plain as day, the bottom half of McKay's face looked like chopped beef. Red pools of blood had already seeped into the oak.

"But what about...his face?"

"I shut his eyes for him. Looks like a sleepin' baby don't he?"

How could Bohannon not see what Floyd was seeing? A haphazard pile of bone, blood, and skin.

"You looked rested enough," the sheriff said, "Help me get this lid on."

* * *

"Rrrrraaaahhh!"

The shout came suddenly and shook Floyd from a deep sleep. His head was pressed into the pillow. The surrounding darkness and chirping crickets seemed uninterrupted.

Maybe it was a dream. He had been tossing and turning all night. At some point, his mind finally shut down, tired of attempting to process the day's events.

Floyd pushed himself up onto his elbows and looked over at Jinnie. Her back was to him. He could hear the ups and downs of light snoring. Floyd remembered crawling into bed after helping Sheriff Bohannon, not wanting to sleep on a hard chair. Just wanting something warm and comforting, no matter how cold and uncomforting the person next to him was.

"Hey!"

The voice of a man came unmistakably from the front room. It was a whisper, but loud. Floyd wished desperately that he had kept his only means of defense in the bedroom. Not that it would have mattered. The Winchester rifle his father-in-law had gifted him before moving out was useless without bullets. Floyd foolishly thought he'd never need them.

He wanted to cry. Why was all this happening to him?

"Don't be scared," the voice rasped. "We need to discuss things. Come out."

Floyd looked over at his wife again. He considered shaking her, waking her up to the potential danger.

"Don't bother."

Floyd knew the voice was right. He was losing his mind. No sense in trying to convince a woman already set on her thoughts. He rose quietly from the bed and tiptoed toward the front room. He debated lighting a lamp, but quickly decided it wasn't worth the effort. His eyes were already adjusted to the dark.

"Are...Are you the ghost of McKay?" It sounded foolish as soon as it left his lips, but what was foolish at this point?

"Ain't no such thing as ghosts." The reply was swift and emanated from the table. He looked but saw only empty chairs. "Have a seat. I'll fill you in."

Floyd saw no reason not to comply, so he pulled up a chair.

"Here's the deal. You has to kill someone."

The whispers. The goddamn whispers.

He was certain now about what McKay had said. The voice, the whisper, was coming from the Collier. Floyd remembered now, leaving it there before tottering into the bedroom earlier. He leaned in as if he were trying to read it like a small-print book.

"Boo!"

He bounced back and the chair fell backwards from under him. There was a creaking noise from the bedroom.

"Floyd! Keep it quiet out there!"

He waited, hoping Jinnie would fall back to sleep. After thirty seconds of silence, Floyd picked up the chair and sat down once again.

"Sorry," the gun said with a chuckle. "Couldn't resist."

Floyd decided he was so far over the edge of sanity, there was no point in *not* talking to the gun.

"What...what do you...what are…" He wanted to converse with the thing, but he didn't know what to ask.

"Lookie here," he said, "I'm gonna' sum it up for you. I'm a curse."

A curse? Floyd scratched his head and reached for his glasses. He put them on as if they would help him think.

"What do you mean?"

"My name is—was—Cincinnatus Jones. Bought and sold for seven hundred-and-seventy-six dollars. Things was ok for what they were, til' the man who bought me said I stole somethin'. I know I hadn't. I know it! Anyway, he killed me with this here gun, and as I lay bleeding, I curse it. I didn't mean to. But you know how's it is, when you dyin'. Right?" It breathed sonorously. "I s'pose note. Well, you don't got time to think things through. So I said some words my grandmammy taught me when I was a youngin'. Of course, she would say them if she stubbed her big toe. Don't think they had much juice to them then, but let me tell you, they mean somethin' when you's dyin'."

Floyd sat and stared at the gun.

"You remember how's I told you that you had to kill somebody?" the voice asked. "Well, you don't have to. You don't have to. But you need to sell me for the going price. You saw how hard that was though. Might well just shoot somebody and save yo'self the trouble."

Stunned, Floyd tentatively picked up the gun and examined its fine condition. "But if you look like this, I won't have any trouble sell-ing—"

"Part of the curse. I only look like this to *you*. Every time I help someone kill a man, I inch a little bit closer to my end. Sometimes it's a scratch, sometimes I lose somethin' more."

It would explain why Jinnie didn't see a trigger. Floyd nodded his head as if he understood. The truth was that he was going mad, just like McKay. But maybe it wasn't madness, Floyd thought. Maybe this *was* the truth.

"But I ain't dead yet," the voice continued. "And that means you got some killin' to do, one way or another. Three days, Floyd. Three days."

"Three days?" Floyd asked, unable to hide the shock in his voice. His mind raced through possible victims, everyone he knew, strangers he didn't yet know. How could he just kill someone?

"Can't I just shoot a rabbit? Or a ground squirrel?" Floyd pre-tended that he even had the capability to do those things.

"Nope. Gotta be human flesh and bone. Look, take yo'self some solace in the fact that no one will know it. You may see 'em as bein' shot, but to everyone else, they look like they just fell asleep."

Floyd found no solace in that, but it solved another mystery.

The gun continued, "Now it ain't that I can make a man do the killin'. He gotta figure that out on his own. But if you don't, well…" Floyd swore he saw a tiny puff of smoke emerged from the barrel of the pistol.

"Well, what?"

"I don't mean to be the way I'm bein', but I *am* a curse. I need blood, Floyd. If you can't give it to me in three days, I'll take it."

Floyd knew exactly what that meant. McKay's lifeless eyes were fresh in his mind.

* * *

The next two days at the bank, at home, and everywhere in between were filled with frantic thoughts. He got no sleep and stopped eating. In the beginning, he debated telling Jinnie, but he had already stepped all over her last nerve and he knew that all hope of her believing him was lost.

How was he going to get out of this one? He didn't want to die. He was only twenty-four, for Christ's sake. But he couldn't imagine intentionally taking a person's life.

More than once, Floyd found himself following strangers down alleys, his hand in his pocket, his finger wrapped gently around the trigger, only to lose his nerve and turn around.

At the bank, he tried to put on his normal demeanor. Still, people would ask him if he was alright, to which he would reply "of course" or sometimes just continue staring off into space, always with one hand in his pocket.

At one point, he thought he could get away with burying the gun about a mile away, among the scrub and prickly pears, but somehow, it found its way back into his desk drawer.

He could swear it laughed at him.

* * *

"Day three, Floyd. The clock's a'tickin'. You got a choice to make."

"Floyd!"

He snapped to attention. Mr. Howard was standing before him, a scowl on his face, his bald head scrunched up with wrinkles.

"Do you have them or not?"

"Have them?"

The bank manager shook his head. "The promissory notes I need to take to Tucson." He scrutinized Floyd carefully. "You haven't been lookin' yourself the past few days. I want you to go home and rest up."

"Yes," Floyd said absently. "I think...I think that's a good idea."

Floyd left the bank early and ambled toward home. He would say goodbye to Jinnie. He would apologize. Try to make amends before walking out to the hills and let the gun do its dirty work.

As he approached the house, he heard what sounded like howling.

It was Jinnie.

Fearful that somehow the curse had affected her, Floyd dashed into the house. The front room was empty. More screams from the bedroom. He rushed in and his stomach dropped at what he saw.

A flurried tangle of flesh wrapped in flesh, moving back and forth, up and down like the rods and wheels of a locomotive. The screaming stopped and two pairs of eyes were focused on Floyd.

Carl rolled over onto his back, naked and without an ounce of shame in his face. The grin on his face made Floyd nauseous.

Jinnie came right out with it.

"You're no man," she said. There was almost a fury on her face as she rose from the bed. Her bare breasts bounced as she poked a finger in Floyd's chest. "You brought me out here and you work all day, socializing, burying with your nose in those bankroll books while I sit here bored to death."

Though Jinnie was in his face, Floyd couldn't take his eyes off Carl.

"This is *your* fault," she continued on.

Carl butted in, "She ain't wrong, Floyd." He leaned over to his side and pulled out a roll of smoking papers from his pants that lay next to the bed. "Why don't you get back to work, so we can get back to work." He winked at Floyd.

Later, when he would occasionally run through the scene over and over in his mind, he was never able to remember the bits of time between pulling the Collier from his pocket, Carl grabbing at the fresh hole in his chest, and Jinnie falling back onto the bed, blood streaming from her forehead.

*　*　*

"I'm sorry you had to find them this way." Bohannon put his hand on Floyd's shoulder. "Must've really been somethin'. To die in the heat of the moment like that."

Floyd looked at the Sheriff who quickly cleared his throat.

"Don't forget that," he indicated towards the ground. "Probably won't get much, but you may be able to sell it to Dade. Help pay for any funeral expenses."

On the floor besides the bed lay a rusted flintlock revolver, broken in two.

"I don't want anything to do with it," Floyd said, almost trance-like.

Bohannon bent down. "Well if you don't mind, it's a nice memento. Reminds me of my grandpappy." He reached out and Floyd thought he heard a sigh in the air.

The Bitter Buffoon

Among many societies, there used to be a deeply-held belief that drinking someone's blood gave you their power. Not only did it turn out to be a ridiculous thought, but in the end, one which nearly proved fatal and came close to ending the line of the Blood Tasters.

In these days, the modern days, the more sophisticated days, Tamsin only sipped, swished, and spit. As chief of the Blood Tasters tribe, and chairwoman of their corporation, she rarely tasted blood anymore. Her 35,000 employees, each holding the pedigree that had made them so important to society, carried out the task of judging the blood of the people against the ancient Scriptures.

She was in mid-spit when Logan rapped on the French doors. "Sorry to disturb, Ms. Lamb. A lady, Ritesh Guan, is at the gates. She is the new head of the Agency."

Bits of blood and saliva swirled down the drain of the pearl clamshell sink, leaving only a trail to prove from where it had come. She watched and waited.

"A facial identity search has confirmed her claim," Logan finished.

Tamsin grabbed a clean towel from the rack beside the sink, leaving another trace of the blood as she wiped her lips.

"Please see her to the sitting room."

"Yes, Ms. Lamb."

She returned to her dimly lit bedroom. The rising sun peaked through gray satin curtains as Tamsin picked up the tablet from the nightstand. After keying in her discoveries, she threw it on the bed and proceeded downstairs.

* * *

When Tamsin entered the room, Ms. Guan was standing with her back towards her. The woman's hands were clasped together as she peered up at the collection of ancient tapestries, framed awards, and antiquities adorning the white walls.

Tamsin said, "That is the first spit bowl recovered from the initial settlement just outside of North Veza. By the grace of the Prophets, there has been little damage done to it over sixteen centuries."

Ms. Guan turned around. A smile was already on her face. "Fascinating," she said, sounding anything but fascinated.

She smelled of cigarette smoke. It was in her dark, ear-length hair. It was on the lapels of her wool suit coat. Tamsin would have Logan order a cleaning service. On any other day, under any other circumstances, she would have the woman thrown off the estate simply on the grounds for polluting a sacred environment.

Logan came through the doors like a ghost, carrying a tray of barely jingling china. There were two cups: one of hot tea accompanied by a small pitcher of cream and a bowl of sugar cubes. The other held room-temperature water. They were placed on the small table in between Tamsin and Ms. Guan. Logan disappeared as if he had never been in the room.

Ms. Guan eyed the cups.

"Please," Tamsin said.

"Thank you," Ms. Guan said, "but I'm not thirsty. I'm afraid I drank too much as it is during the long journey." She laughed a nervous laugh. "Your butler is quite attentive. He barely left my side after being kind enough to show me to the washroom."

Tamsin said nothing. She made a mental note to review the recorded video feeds later. Her security systems confirmed a lack of transmission and reception devices on Ms. Guan, otherwise Logan would have informed her. Still, the Agency's *raison d'être* was based on the concept of coming up with new tricks and it was hard to believe that they wouldn't try to capture this moment, if not for tactical and strategic means, for posterity's sake. And maybe, Tamsin pondered, for private viewing sessions where many of them believed they would lounge on long couches while holding glasses full of champagne, all of them laughing at the downfall of the most powerful tribe and enterprise in the country.

Ms. Guan cleared her throat. "In respect of your time and authority, Ms. Lamb, I'll come right out with it. Your services are no longer required."

Tamsin took a moment to appreciate the words and let Ms. Guan savor them as well.

"Of course," she continued, "you and your people will be compensated for the centuries of exemplary service." Ms. Guan's smile appeared almost painful. She couldn't even refer to the Blood Tasters by name.

"Compensated?"

"In many ways. The Agency has granted a stipend to be paid in perpetuity to all of your living employees. Education and retraining will also be a large piece of the package. Oh! And how could I forget. Discussions are underway regarding a glorious museum." Ms. Guan nodded towards the spitting bowl on the wall. "We've already picked the perfect spot; right on the cliffs of North Veza. Let me tell you, Ms. Lamb, the views are stunning. Whenever you would like, I will personally give you a tour at your convenience."

Tamsin could tell the woman was not accustomed to displays of false enthusiasm. Her demeanor came off bitter and she wondered how Ms. Guan climbed to one of the country's most powerful positions without the ability to opaquely kiss ass.

Tamsin sat down on a loveseat and took a sip of water. "So tell me how we have become obsolete." She was pleased to catch subtle signs of discomfiture in Ms. Guan's reaction, but the agent recomposed herself quickly.

"There was a breakthrough."

"When?"

"Several months ago."

A deliberate pause.

Ms. Guan continued, "We've known for some time now the location of genetic sequences which drive and direct moral behavior."

"Yes, that is nothing new."

The woman nodded her head. "Indeed. What *is* new, is that our scientists have discovered a way to manipulate those genes. To edit them." Ms. Guan decided to take a seat on the sofa opposite Tamsin, only to lean forward and almost whisper, "To remove what we know to be immoral, or just as bad, amoral."

Tamsin thought she could see blood dancing behind the agent's eyes. She leaned back into her own loveseat, stretching her arms across its crest.

"I see."

"It's true. We have successfully replaced the sequences of hundreds of subjects. In fact, your people have confirmed it for us."

Tamsin raised an eyebrow.

Ms. Guan said, "I apologize for the seemingly underhandedness of it all, but it was required, you see. We certainly did not want to spoil the test results by having your people aware of the situation." Again, the smile on the agent's face screamed that it was merely surface-level.

Tamsin only stared as Ms. Guan picked up the cup of tea and swirled its dark waters, looking into it as if reading omens. "It's a simple procedure now," Ms. Guan continued. "The Agency has ordered kits be shipped to doctors across the country over the next week. A device will be attached to the neck of the patient and then they are sent home. It runs an analysis, immoral sequences are replaced with moral sequences, and three days later the person is, for a more poetic turn, born again."

She seemed absurdly proud of herself.

"They will of course be installed in pre-natal centers as well, ensuring that future generations will no longer require the technology. The idea is to begin passing down the traits naturally."

There was only silence.

Ms. Guan met her eyes. "Tamsin."

Tamsin bristled at the casual use of her first name.

"A great burden has been lifted from your shoulders," Ms. Guan said. "Whereas your people have been confined by destiny to one path, to one way of life for so long, just imagine the freedom in this news."

"All things must come to an end, is that it?"

Ms. Guan shrugged, leaned into the sofa, finally deciding to take a drink of her tea.

"It's the way of things."

Seconds ticked down.

Tamsin broke the silence.

"There seems to be a great assumption in the world, Ms. Guan. That this is all the Tasters do. That we taste the blood of the people and sense their moral compass based on the Scriptures of the Prophets. In these days of 'modern man,' we're rendered obsolete. Because it's a service we've performed since before the Agency was even an inkling of thought, there is a tendency towards complacency."

Tamsin leaned forward, supporting her elbows on her knees.

"You are a trained scientist. Surely you recall the one who once stated something to the effect of, 'those things that are in motion tend to stay in motion.'" A smile formed on her lips. "We knew that there had been an unnatural change to things. An immoral change."

The color drained from Ms. Guan's face.

"I tasted your blood this morning, Ritesh. It's bitter."

Ms. Guan placed her cup on the table and jumped to her feet. "I would think twice before attempting–"

"You're free to leave any time," Tamsin said. "I'm afraid you won't have anywhere to go, though. The Agency is being dissolved as we speak and its research facilities are undergoing…renovations."

Later, Tamsin would want to replay this footage. Perhaps at the next holiday party, the Tasters would be the ones savoring champagne and celebrating the demise of one more vain attempt to bring down an adaptable group of people who had built an empire.

The woman was visibly shaking. Tamsin walked over and placed a hand on her shoulder. "Dear, *this* is the way of things. Take comfort in knowing that while the world moves at a breakneck pace, its foundation will remain the same."

Stolen

Come away, O human child!

To the waters and the wild

With a faery, hand in hand.

For the world's more full of weeping than you can understand.

\- W. B. Yeats, *The Stolen Child*

"You've always been my favorite," he said.

Dried blood colored the white whiskers surrounding his lips. His teeth wore a buttery film and dark circles called attention to the liver-spotted skin pulled taut over his cheekbones.

"Rest, father." I pushed him gently back down onto the bed.

He turned his head and moaned, squinting at the straw-packed wall of the hut.

"Was he talking to you or to me?"

I looked at my young brother and shrugged. "Probably neither."

* * *

Thin clouds filtered the blurry light of the half-moon. The sun wouldn't rise for another hour, but we had to set off now.

Dhonu and I stopped at the memorial outside of our sleepy village and visited two familiar mounds—a single pair among the hundreds. I set down our equipment, got on my knees, and kissed the stones which had been piled on top of each tiny lump of grass. The cold from the rocks felt like shocks of tiny lightning. I imagined the ashes which had been buried beneath them had long since been absorbed into the Earth.

Dhonu hesitated, always afraid to get too close. I grabbed his hand and gently pulled him over. He quickly kissed the markers as well, though I'm not sure his lips even made contact. He slipped out of my grasp and ran back toward the road.

I supposed I couldn't blame him. He was too young to remember Mother and our sister, Gitika. I looked down to my left at the hole which I'd already begun to dig and realized we had better be on our way.

* * *

The Nepali forest never ceased.

Already, it was humming and bustling with activity. Brown-chested partridges chased each other around the trunks of the sal trees like quarreling children. While Dhonu twirled and flipped a stick in the air, I kept my eyes open for tigers and any rhinoceroses that might think sticking close to our well-treaded road was a good idea. Avoiding contact was the best option, but I traced my fingers along the hilt of the kukri in case that wasn't a possibility.

"Remember what we talked about?" I said.

"Yeah, yeah."

I stopped and dropped the wound rope that had been weighing heavily over one shoulder. "This isn't a joke, Dhonu. If I didn't need you, I wouldn't have brought you along."

He avoided my gaze.

"Do you remember what we talked about?"

He bounced up and down on his legs.

"Don't leave your side. Don't do anything stupid," he spat out to the canopy of branches and leaves above.

"And?"

He released an exasperated breath. "Do whatever you say."

"Good."

His eyes darted toward the blade hanging from my belt.

"Can I see it?"

"No," I said.

He grunted and started walking away. "You're a jerk, you know that?"

I picked up the rope, adjusted the pack across my back, and followed close behind.

"Yes, I know that."

* * *

We were six miles deep in the jungle and at our destination. I was grateful for having stopped only twice so that Dhonu could pee.

Dawn's orange sun illuminated the sheer rock wall. The cliffside never failed to intimidate me once I'd come face-to-face with it, always forced to crane my neck upward to try and find its end. Whenever I felt overconfident or arrogant about something, I only had to think of this cliffside. It's one thing to see mountains in the distance, but when one's entire being comes up against the jagged, ivy-netted rock like an ant on a boulder, it's another reminder of our inconsequence.

Thankfully, we didn't have to climb all the way to the top.

"Father took me here a few years ago," I said, looking down at my brother. I don't know why I told him something that didn't really matter.

"For Mother and Gitika?"

I nodded.

"But it didn't work," he replied.

"It takes away the pain," I said with a little anger in my voice. "But, no, it won't save anyone."

He shrugged away the thought and extended his stick outward as he spun in circles, his eyes closed and his face jutting into the air. Besides the cowlick on his crown, his dark hair fell straight and gentle over his skull. His skin was chestnut, smooth, and still unblemished.

Dhonu was a good boy, just naive. But who isn't at his age and shouldn't he have the right to be so? Soon enough, he'll know and experience more than anyone ever should. I only hoped the pestilence would pass him by.

I think I made a mistake in bringing him here, I thought, even though I knew that wasn't true. To leave him behind would have been the *real* mistake. Without him, we couldn't help Father with what little power we had to do so. Yesterday, I had come on my own only to discover what I'd feared: the original climbing rope lying on the ground, one end completely frayed.

I let the new rope slide from my shoulder and I bent my head from side to side, working out the crick in my neck. I studied the wall.

"You see that thin crack running along the stone?" I pointed.

He nodded eagerly.

"That's your first foothold."

His eyes twinkled at the prospect of adventure and doing something potentially dangerous.

"I need you," I said, "because my hands and feet are too big to fit anymore."

He smiled and said, "Oh."

Then, I held his shoulder and pulled him backward. I pointed at an outcropping fifty or so feet above us. "That's where you're going. When you reach the ledge, you need to be *very* quiet. Okay?"

His mouth hung open as he gazed. I gave him a shake.

"Okay?"

"Okay."

I held up one end of the rope. "You'll see a large boulder sitting just outside the cave. Tie this on just like I showed you, remember?"

He reached for the rope but I pulled it back. "Show me you remember."

Dhonu issued a mumble of complaint, but he impressed me with his memory as he threw his stick to the forest floor and tied the knot exactly as I had taught him.

Satisfied, I tucked one end of the rope through his belt as he slipped out of his straw sandals and placed a foot in the crack. His fingers probed the opening and he began his ascent.

I hesitated briefly before grabbing his silk pant leg. "When you get to the entrance, you tie the knot, you pay attention to the cave, and you *wait*. You—"

"—don't move. Don't do this. Don't do that. Don't do *anything*. Blah, blah, blah. I *know*." He yanked his leg up from my grip and scaled the cliffside as if he had been doing so for years without my knowledge. I was a bundle of mixed feelings. I feared for my brother, but at the same time, I tried to hold back a smile, remembering how I had once bristled at very similar words.

* * *

The *saapgaryo* were nocturnal, so they should have recently settled down to sleep. They mainly fed on rhododendrons growing on top of the mountain. The flowers made them drowsy near daybreak. Excepting

Dhonu's perfectly sized hands and feet, that docility was the only other reason I allowed him to be up here alone until I climbed the rope. Father must have felt the same when he had sent me only a few summers ago.

As I sat at the entrance, stretching my burning arms, Dhonu peered into the cave. One hand pinched his nose.

"This place stinks!" he said through a nasal voice.

"Quiet!" I hissed. "They're sleeping, not dead."

He rolled his eyes, but turned back to the blackness.

I reached into my pack and pulled out a torch that had been dipped in pitch. I lit it with Father's flint and steel.

"Come on," I said. "Stay behind me."

The stench grew with every step. Dhonu pretended to gag, stopping only when I turned and gave him a stern look.

"Breath through your mouth," I whispered.

We turned a corner about twenty yards in and came across their chamber. I spotted them instantly. My hand moved to cover Dhonu's mouth just in time to catch it opening.

There was only one adult *saapgaryo* with four younger ones laying against her teats, nestled just under an extended wing. All were resting within a nest of sticks and sal leaves. The little ones stirred for a moment, but seemed to settle back down to sleep.

I raised the torch slowly to get a better view of the room. In one corner was the pile of excrement from which the smell emanated. Why the creatures lived and slept so near to their feces, I'll never understand, but at least it made it easy for us to find what we were looking for.

I pointed at our target and handed the torch to Dhonu. I held my finger to my lips. His oversized teeth looked even bigger as he grinned against the flame. We tiptoed to the corner as I kept a constant eye on the sleeping family and I quietly removed the bag strapped to my back.

Father had made me do this job last time. Part of me felt I should let Dhonu take over, but I decided to do it myself anyway, hoping he'd never have to.

The *saapgaryo* crap was green, slimy, and all around the worst thing I'd ever had to make physical contact with. But there was magic inside and it seemed to me that some good things came wrapped in not-so-good things. Imagining how Father would feel tomorrow made the task a little less painful.

I'm sure it only took a minute to gather it all, yet loading the sack felt like watching mold grow. My eyes would dart between the poop, Dhonu, and the creatures while I tried to quietly scoop with my hands and filled the bag. The torch would inadvertently lower every once in awhile as my little brother stared in fascination at the creatures he'd heard so much about.

I'd forgotten what it was like to be unfamiliar with their long beaks and pointed ears. Dark gray feathers lined their bodies. Laying down in slumberous sleep, they didn't seem *that* fierce—maybe they were even a little cute, especially the small ones—but when they were awake with their wings expanded, shrieking like something unholy, they inspired panic.

We were so close to avoiding all that.

It was my fault. In a hurry to get us out of the precarious situation and back to the village, I didn't pay attention as I should have. We had just turned around when I accidentally kicked a small rock across the cavern floor. It landed square in the ribs of one of the young *saapgaryo* which yelped in surprise and scrambled onto its wobbling talons, waking the others. The sound of their dissonant squealing frightened Dhonu, causing him to drop the torch.

Then the big one woke up.

There was no way we were going to make it out of the cave and down the rope with a protective mother in pursuit.

Five pairs of beady, yellow-green eyes glowered at us.

I threw the sack of poop into Dhonu's hands, shoved him behind me, and pulled out the kris. "Run for the rope."

"But—"

"Go!" I yelled, trying to be heard over the tumultuous howls. I didn't want to turn my back to the mother, so I could only assume he listened to me.

Thankfully, the torch was still aflame and I could see them all. With the blade raised in front of me, I expanded my chest and stood as tall as possible. Because I wasn't big myself, the mother was just about equal in height, appearing menacing while bounding back and forth in front of her babies. Her wings spread wide and I felt as if they could wrap around me and keep me trapped forever.

I slowly backed away towards the entrance, remembering when something similar happened to Father and me. I couldn't remember the details, other than by the end, he had scratches all over and was covered in blood. How he managed to climb down after me, I don't know. I do know that my legs and arms didn't stop shaking until late into that night.

As I begin to smell the outside forest, I realized my first mistake was actually my second. I should have paid better attention to the ground coming into the cave. My clumsy heel snagged on a thick root running across the cave, sending me tumbling onto my rear. The kris flew from my hands, chinking against the wall and somewhere onto the floor.

Mother *saapgaryo* saw her opportunity.

Her brilliant eyes rose and fell as she bounded toward me.

It was either clamber onto my feet or try to find the knife.

My fingers searched the ground and just as my fingers found the blade, I screamed. A sharp burn radiated through my forearm as the mother's claws tore at my skin. Instinct drove my hands toward my face. Her breath was hot, panting, and the sound that emanated was a frightening mix of growl and screech. Her beak drove forward, piercing my palms with incessant pecking.

I fell onto my back, thinking I could use my feet to kick her off. She flapped her wings wildly. Now her talons dug into my hamstrings, ripping away bits of my flesh.

Among the chaos, I heard a shuffling sound by my ears: one of the babies coming to see what all of the fuss was about, I assumed. I hoped Dhonu was at the bottom of the cliff by now.

I continued futilely kicking, but the *saapgaryo* didn't seem to care. My lungs tried to keep up, tried to catch gasps of air. I was growing weary, already losing my will to put up a fight.

Then came a scream which at first I thought was my own.

It was Dhonu.

My stomach dropped and something took hold of me within. I kicked at the mother with all of my strength. Her weight was lifted from me and I found myself back on my feet. I could have sworn that my heart was going to pump itself out of my chest. I saw the big *saapgaryo* half-running, half-flying frantically towards her nest, away from the portal of sunlight behind us.

I looked for my brother and saw him holding himself up on the cavern wall beside me.

"Are you okay?" I yelled, grabbing his face and trying to look over every inch of him.

"Come on!" Dhonu said. His voice was choked with tears.

I squinted and scanned the ground. "Father's kris," I said.

Dhonu grabbed my arm. "I used it. Come on!"

It wasn't until we were on the ledge before I realized what he had done for me.

* * *

I was proud to have made it halfway to the village before my sudden burst of will had drained. As the exhaustion increased, so did the pain. It flowed out from my chest to my fingertips and toes.

"We need to stop," I said, already collapsing onto the muddy road.

Dhonu said nothing. His tears had dried up and now he only looked at me.

My breathing was ragged. "What?"

"You're a mess," he said.

I frowned, but then I looked at the stains of blood and dirt covering my arms. I imagined the rest of my body looked the same. Despite the throbbing, despite my weariness, or maybe because of those things, I began to laugh. And then so did Dhonu, until we were both finally out of breath.

"Yeah," I finally said. "I guess so."

Dhonu removed the sack that was hanging loosely from my back and held it in the air. His face scrunched. "Do you want some?"

"No," I said. I rose slowly and painfully to my feet, realizing we needed to get back. I reached my hand out for the sack, but my brother put it over his shoulder and began to walk away.

"Good," he said. "Let's go take care of Father."

A Hundred Eyes

Casimir Pitsudski would not stop working.

He refused to look back at the one-eyed creature until he was done.

With each mark of charcoal, he felt the monster's rhythm of inhale, exhale, inhale, exhale on the back of his neck. Sweat poured down his face as if a thousand steaming kettles were going off at once. It took every ounce of will to remain conscious.

With each mark, it became clearer why the beast hadn't snatched him. Why it was called the monster with a hundred eyes. Why it hadn't done to him what it did to Sylwia.

His canvas, a tiny portion of gray stone among vast cavern walls, came together slowly. A nearly empty lamp of oil provided the only illumination. Casimir fought to maintain focus and forget the fate of his recently-met companion, yet at the same time, hold it in his mind.

Lines and shadows emerged from his shaking hands.

With each mark, it helped to remember everything that happened.

* * *

They woke the priest.

"You cannot send my son," his mother started.

Casimir was nervous. He knew coming to the church under the cover of darkness was a bad idea, but his parents were afraid to rouse suspicions among the other villagers.

Father Bogdan shook his head, wiped at his eyes and tried to look at the three of them. Curly salt-and-pepper hair bounced off his forehead. His gaunt cheeks brought to mind more a monk than a priest. "Are you so special?"

"It's not fair," she replied. "He's only a boy."

"This is the way it's always been. Your son's name was drawn from among the others. There is no better way."

"Let's petition the magnate." It was his father now. "Maybe he will send knights." He was a short but stout man with a long, brown beard and thick arms. They reminded Casimir of the trunks of dark beech trees surrounding their remote village. Casimir was ashamed to think that his father lacked a deep-thinking mind, yet the man could never be accused of not caring for his family.

"You have a short memory, Piotr," the priest said, not completely unsympathetic. "Do you remember the last time we did such a thing? Go, wake Irena. Ask about her daughters if you've already forgotten. One taken away like chattel, the other scarred from eye to chin by the whip of one of his soldiers."

His mother started now. "But if we can show him—"

Father Bogdan raised a hand. "Show him what? When is the last time you saw his face? He never leaves his castle except to fight a war and win more land. His men would never dare to waste his or their time with the folk tales of peasants."

His father seemed to withdraw a little.

The priest took an exasperated breath. "The magnate cares not about excuses. It's grain he wants. We all wish things could be different, but this is a contract that was made long ago. We invite death if we violate it."

"To hell with the contract!" Casimir's mother yelled, oblivious to her initial desire to keep things quiet. "My son. Does he not die?"

"He is but one. Would you rather we all be killed?" Father Bogdan looked directly at Casimir as if the decision lay in his hands.

"We'll discuss this no further," the Father continued, holding his hands up before them to brook any protest.

He turned to Casimir and spoke as if they were the only two standing in the tiny room at the back of the church. "Gather the things you'll want to take. You're to meet the other one at the crossroads in the morning."

"What will happen?" Casimir asked.

Father Bogdan began to bless the boy who had barely turned fourteen last month. "I don't know," he said.

Casimir knew it was mostly a lie. He wasn't sure why he had asked.

* * *

What does one want to see, or hold on to, before one dies?

It was a question Casimir pondered on a sleepless night, the arm of his snoring mother wrapped around his waist. She refused to let him lay down alone that night.

Pale moonlight slipped through a crack in the stone wall of their cottage and as soon as he had decided what to take with him, he gently removed her arm, careful not to wake her. Quietly, he gathered a few items in a woven sack and left without saying goodbye.

He supposed it was a mistake, but he knew that any long farewell would only frighten him more.

* * *

Casimir traveled lightly.

But for a small bag of black charcoal, blank drawing papers as well as some of his favorite sketches, he brought only a water flask, a few pieces of hard bread, and a lamp filled with oil as well as flint for lighting it. The journey to the crossroads was half-a-day's travel. He followed the rising autumn sun which barely crested the tops of the beech trees as he left the outer reaches of his village. Dry, fallen burrs crunched beneath his feet every step of the way. Along the occasional half-leafed branch hung crude hand-carved imitations of the hundred-eyed beast. Dziady, the feast of remembrance, would arrive tomorrow and it would be the first time Casimir celebrated without seeing the tears and recounting the memories of his friends and family.

He wanted to stop and draw the scene as a testament to those who would travel the same path next year, and the year after that, but he knew it would be in vain. It was something he should have thought of earlier.

Instead, he continued walking, his head down and his eyes focused on the forest floor. Casimir remembered that last year it was the Halina, the tanner's plump wife. The year before that…it bothered him that he couldn't recall.

* * *

The stranger stood cloaked and motionless at a corner of the crossroads. One hand peeked through an oversized sleeve, hanging by the person's side. The other hand grasped a walking stick.

Their eyes met as Casimir approached, or so he thought. The stranger's face was shadowed by a hooded cloak. What little features Casimir could make out were pale yet wrinkled and rough like aged leather. There was something generally odd about it, but he couldn't place why.

"So young," she said.

A woman with a gravel voice.

There was an awkward silence. Casimir felt her examining him like a blacksmith examines a freshly wrought horseshoe.

She stretched out her free hand.

"I am Sylwia."

Casimir took it. It felt cold to the touch.

"Hello. I'm Casimir."

A lump caught in his throat. "You are from the east village?" he eeked out.

She nodded once and said, "We should continue on. We have another half-day's journey to go and we don't want to be wandering at dark. The wolves are hungry most nights."

What did it matter, Casimir thought. But then he felt suddenly ashamed. He remembered it mattered a lot.

* * *

They walked in silence, following a small stream winding south towards its source deep in the Carpathian Mountains. After some time, they came to a large pile of rocks surrounded by sharp sticks dug into the ground, pointing skyward. They were grouped sloppily alongside the foot of an overgrown trail which veered southwest. The rocks were marked with faded skulls and words such as *groźba!* (*Danger!*) and *pokraka* (*Monster*). One fallen log rested on the forest floor in front of them all. It was covered with a hundred crudely drawn eyes.

Sylwia looked up at Casimir. Was she seeking confirmation? Proof that he was willing to come along? He froze. Before he could answer, she shrugged her shoulders and walked on.

Casimir felt resistance in his body. As if he was stuck in a pit of tar. His flask was half empty and he suddenly found himself more thirsty than he had ever been before. He refilled it from the stream and caught up to the surprisingly fast older woman. She seemed to be in such a hurry to die, Casimir thought.

The uphill march may have been half-a-mile, perhaps a full one. They were both breathless by the time they found the dark entrance. A damp heat emanated from the cave, amplifying the sweat covering every inch of Casimir's body. Even though he smelled the ripe scent of Sylwia beside him, he suddenly felt alone.

"Do we go in now?" he asked. For some reason, it seemed natural to him to allow Sylwia to make the decisions.

She shook her head. Her gaze never left the cave. "No, we camp tonight and come back tomorrow. It is not yet the day of Dziady."

Of course, he thought.

* * *

Dusk snuck up on Casimir and they circled back to make camp only a hundred yards from the entrance. Even from there, they could feel its uncomfortable warmth.

Casimir lit a fire only for the comfort of the light. His strength had left him and he felt more tired than he ever had on those long days of scything wheat.

Night's arrival brought an eerie silence. Casimir realized the quiet had been with them since they neared the cave. Neither crickets nor birds could be heard. Only the sounds of the fire crackling from sappy wood.

Casimir studied Sylwia sitting quietly on a stone across the flames. Just as quiet as everything else. Shadows danced over her hooded face. Her arms rested on her lap as she leaned forward, her legs slightly crossed, flicking a sandaled foot back and forth. The walking stick lay on the rock to her left. Her head moved only to follow the occasional spark floating towards the heavens.

She wasn't saying a word and Casimir felt he would go out of his mind if he didn't occupy himself, so he reached into his sack and pulled out the tiny bag of charcoal and a piece of paper.

With the paper resting on his lap, he tried to conjure an image. This would be his last work. What would he sketch? A scene in the village? A memory of his parents? Nothing seemed to satisfy. He looked across the fire and saw Sylwia looking back at him.

"You are an artist?"

Casimir wasn't sure how to respond. He had never become an apprentice to a true artist. It was a hobby he took upon himself after sneaking into the church one day and looking through Father Bogdan's bible. Within were fascinating illustrations of The Garden of Eden and the Tower of Babel. They brought the stories he heard every Sunday to life. He wanted that power. To do the same for the stories that surrounded him, waiting to be captured.

No, Casimir thought, he wasn't a real artist. Real artists had their work in grand cathedrals or put in books. He sketched only to unwind from long days in the fields and never showed them to anyone.

"Before I got sick, I worked in Kraków," Sylwia said. "I was an attendant to Bona Jagiełło."

Casimir's jaw dropped. The old woman said it so nonchalantly, seeming to pay him no mind. Her eyes refocused on the fire as if she were seeing her life play back within the yellow and orange hues.

"The Queen had many pieces of art brought into the palace from the Italian masters." She mused, "Let me tell you. The colors. The lines." Her eyes lit up nearly imperceptibly. "A thousand thoughts and voices on a single piece of canvas."

Casimir felt himself flush. Could she be telling the truth? Maybe it was a joke. He would probe her further.

"How were you sick?"

Sylwia sighed, picked up the walking stick at her side and stirred the dirt beneath her feet. "Many of us working for the queen began to grow ill at the same time. Our hair turned suddenly gray and then began to fall out. I can't tell you why. I don't know. They said we were pos-sessed, cursed with leprosy, and the Queen had us all sent away with nothing. I had to return to the village I left as a young girl." She looked at Casimir. "Back to this."

He tried to swallow but his mouth was dry. He reached over and took a swig of water from his flask. His stomach rumbled. He set his materials aside and began to chew on his ration of hard bread.

Sylwia stood, reached inside her cloak, and walked to Casimir. She pulled out a lump of her own bread and handed it to him.

"Aren't you hungry?" he asked.

"A little," she said, as if that was the only answer needed and that she would refuse him if he tried to give it back to her.

She walked back to her stone and sat again. Casimir ate in silence and Sylwia watched.

"Why were you chosen?" she asked. "Did you commit a crime? Steal something? Hurt someone?"

Casimir stopped chewing and shook his head.

"It was by lottery," he said. "That's what we've always done."

Sylwia lifted her head in assent, as if the final piece of a puzzle had fallen into place.

"Do you mind if I remove my cowl?" she asked. "It's rather warm here."

A strange question, Casimir thought. "Of course."

She pulled back the hood, never dropping her eyes from Casimir's. His breath caught in his throat.

"Go ahead," she said. "Stare. It's okay."

She sounded as if she really didn't mind.

Casimir realized now what was so strange about her face when he first saw her. She had no eyebrows. And just as she said, but for a tiny, wild tuft on her left temple, there was not a single hair on her head.

Sylwia said, "I suppose, in a sense, you are lucky to have a lottery. It seems more fair. In our village, they simply choose the person with the least to offer." She laughed. "Let me tell you, everyone was quite relieved when I showed up again."

Casimir sensed a sadness in her voice, but she quickly straightened up.

"What do you know of the monster?" she asked.

His face lit up with memories of his youth. "When we're children, we are first told about the pact. About the need for our two villages to send someone every year or it will destroy the world. The priest does not hide it from us." For some reason, talking about their fate made him feel a little better.

"Do you believe it?"

He thought for a moment. "I don't know. I suppose. How can I not?" Casimir was afraid to even imagine burning in the torments of Hell, knowing that if he refused the call, he would be held responsible for the deaths of so many.

"It's supposed to leave two behind after the destruction," Sylwia said. She smiled but it was not a happy smile. "A man and a woman to continue the race and provide offspring. Sustenance. Though obviously no one has tested this theory. Maybe we should run off to Lithuania? Be the first?"

Casimir's eyes widened.

She laughed. "I jest. Not that they would let us get away with it if we tried. They would find us, tie us up and deliver us to the foot of the cave themselves."

"Why does it want us?" Casimir asked.

Sylwia took a moment to reply. "I believe it's lonely."

Lonely. Then why would it devour them, Casimir wondered, but did not say aloud. Instead he asked another question.

"Are you afraid?"

Her answer was swift. "Only of the pain."

They left it at that.

Casimir knew now what he had to do, so he dropped his bread, picked back up his charcoal and paper and began to draw.

* * *

Bones.

Femurs and lower jaws.

Hands, feet, and skulls.

In a large chamber, deep inside the sweltering cave, what was left of past villagers stood piled high towards the cavern's ceiling. All of them white, yet dirt-stained memories scored with scratches and punctures. Casimir looked at Sylwia under the light of their oil lamps. His legs shook and he would have urinated had he not relieved himself that morning. The older woman grabbed hold of his hand and squeezed. Her steadfastness encouraged him and together, they stood and waited.

* * *

It was difficult to tell how much time had passed. At some point, they sat down and continued waiting.

"Where is it?" Casimir asked. He estimated that the oil in their lamps was nearly half gone. "Maybe it's not true? Maybe there is no monster," he followed through. As soon as the words left his mouth, his eyes focused on the proof piled before them.

"Can I see your drawing?" Sylwia asked. Her voice was as calm.

Casimir hesitated, but only for a moment. Why not, he thought. What's the point in being shy now? He grabbed the paper from his sack and handed it to her. She held it up to the lamp's light. Casimir watched her. Part of him wanted to turn away. He girded himself and held steady.

A tear fell down her cheek that she wiped away quickly. Sylwia looked at him. Her eyes bore into him and now he couldn't help but avert his gaze.

She stood and stretched her arms, bending down to place the paper before him.

"Thank you," she said.

A sudden joy rose in Casimir's spirit. He felt the urge to show her more of his drawings. He turned and reached into his bag for the finished ones he had brought along.

"I have–"

A whip of air crashed against Casimir and he fell over trying to scramble to his feet. He looked around desperately at the surrounding darkness. His chest tightened, cutting short his breath.

Sylwia was gone, leaving behind only her walking stick laying in the dirt. Casimir's sack had fallen open. His charcoal and drawings also lay scattered on the floor. His skin crawled as he not only heard, but felt something approaching from the black. He wanted to run, but his feet refused to unglue themselves from the floor. Casimir could only stand there in abject terror as he saw the creature emerge.

But for a single feature, it was as horrid as his worst imaginings. Blood caked its thin, hairy body. Despite it being twice as tall as Casimir, long, lanky arms reached almost to the floor. Sticky drool dripped from the two sharp teeth that peeked out from each side of its wide, pink mouth. But the most horrifying thing of all was the large, solitary eye in the middle of its face. It had no eyelid. No way to blink.

Casimir didn't want to see it happen. He wanted to close his own eyes, but was powerless to do so. He whimpered and this time, evacuated his bowels.

The monster's face was inches from his now. He could smell bile on its breath. And then it did something strange. It turned its head down and looked at the floor. Casimir was still frozen and could do nothing as the beast picked up one of the drawings and examined it. Through the thin paper, Casimir could see the marks he had made.

He had captured her pain. Her humor. Everything that he saw of her in the single day they had spent together.

The creature held the picture in its clawed hand and returned its gaze toward Casimir.

A single thought entered the young man's mind.

More.

* * *

When he was done, Casimir stepped away from the wall.

His patron's single eye appraised the work. It was of the beast itself, sinking its teeth into a young girl, her parents mourning.

It turned to Casimir and a rush of thoughts entered the boy's mind.

The truth about the creature came in an instant. Sylwia had been correct. It was lonely. It didn't want to eat people, but that had seemed the only way to truly know their lives, their experiences. Fear and intimidation was the only way it knew how to feed its appetite. But if man could offer something like this, it had no reason to devour them at all.

It could see everything.

WAKE

The boy's eyelids had somehow popped opened again. He stared up into the star-filled heavens.

Okomi, his father, shooed away the buzzing flies and swept his hand down over his son's face. He then turned and made another attempt at fire. The tinder wouldn't take. The fallen logs were soaked through from a recent rain and rubbing the stick back and forth, grinding it into the flat piece of wood, felt futile.

Yet he did not stop.

It took his mind off things. The cold desert night. The journey from home. The journey to see the witch doctor.

After some time, his hands nearly rubbed raw, smoke finally rose and the tinder glowed until flames spread onto smaller pieces of brush. He nursed the fire carefully until it was roaring at last. Seeming to sense Okomi's victory over the elements, coyotes howled in the distant hills. He hoped it was a sign of things to come.

He didn't want to rest, but he had been around long enough to know that if he kept on, he risked death. If that happened, all was hopeless. There was still much ground to cover before the doctor could wake his son, but his legs refused to carry him any further. Deep pain radiated across his chest and shoulders. Pulling the sled through gravel-filled washes and over uneven outcrops of granite taxed Okomi greatly.

He would soon cross into Vanyume territory. Every ounce of wit and strength he could muster might be enough to see him and his son through safely.

He pulled his son's sled next to the fire and drew a blanket from his supplies. Upon finding a suitably curved stone on which to rest his head, Okomi cleared the ground of rocks and made his bed. Some of the stars moved tonight, each one zipping off until its light went out in a brief but brilliant flash.

He thought about yesterday. Okomi had been a wealthy man. Chief of all the Nuwa people because of it. Now he carried only a fraction of his riches, forced to abandon the rest to the tribe. He turned to his son, reaching out to stroke the black hair caked to his forehead. The boy's face was pale and starting to swell. His head cold to the touch.

Let the fools fight over trinkets and chiefdom, he thought.

* * *

He dreamed of the boy's mother standing in the village, all of the Nuwa lined up at her side. She cursed Okomi for refusing funeral rites. She said that if he left the village with their child, then Pokoh, the god known as The Old Man, would punish them both for wandering from their homeland. Behind her stood the god, his feet thicker than twenty men clustered together. Taking the form of a snake, the god's great head touched the clouds and grounded back and forth with a terrible noise.

Okomi ignored their warnings. He declared he would go south and fight the Sun and the Moon to find the witch doctor. Pokoh lifted his great foot. It blotted out the night as it came rushing down on top of Okomi.

His eyes shot open. The stars were still there. The crickets were singing. He got up and added more wood to the fire until it roared once again. While he swept a scorpion and several vinegaroons from the blankets wrapped around his son's body, his eyes appraised the boy.

Let Pokoh and his people bluster, he thought. If Okomi buried his son, it would be an act of murder.

*　*　*

Before the Sun showed itself in the east, gusts carried dust across the land. Knoton, god of the wind, was angry. He always seemed to be angry in the vast desert lands south of the Nuwa border. Knoton's breath carried an odor and Okomi quickly realized it was coming from his son. Time was running short and though he knew deep down that it was the right decision, he cursed himself for not having traveled through the night.

He quickly packed camp, latched the sled's connected rope to his shoulders, and trekked south. After many more painstaking miles, Okomi came upon the great river that would eventually lead to his destination: a cave tunneled into a mountain beside a creek and spring of hot water. It was home to the secluded witch doctor, notorious throughout the land for her power, called upon during times of ceremony and distress. The Nuwa had a medicine man, but all he cared about was the rain.

Okomi walked along the river for a little while until he grew thirsty. He stopped and leaned down to drink from the river. A rock splashed inches from his face. He drew himself up quickly, nerves on end, looking for the perpetrator. Not twenty yards away, three dark men in loincloths stood watching him from a weed-covered slope. The two young ones were armed. One had a bow at his side. Another, a sling in his hand. They both appeared to be about fifteen winters in age. An older man stood between them. Okomi recognized the Vanyume chief by his long, crooked nose.

"You are foolish to come here, Nuwa-man."

Over the years, the two tribes had alternated trading and fighting. This was an age of war.

Okomi lifted his hands and spoke, "I am in your care, Huukp. I seek only to pass through to see the witch in the mountain." He nodded his head towards the sled carrying his son and belongings. "I bring you many gifts to pay a toll."

One of the boys, the one with the sling, walked cautiously towards the sled. He approached Okomi's son and within several feet, pinched his nose. He looked at Okomi with disgust.

"Why do you bring him with you?" he asked.

He answered Huukp as if he had asked the question. "As I said, I wish to see the witch. So that she will wake my son."

The boy looked back at the chief. Okomi could tell Huukp was mulling things over. Running into the Vanyume was a risk Okomi had been willing to take when he decided to follow the river. It was the quickest route to his destination.

After several moments of silence, the Vanyume chief spoke.

"Come with us."

Okomi looked at him with caution. His hands were still raised in supplication.

"You will be our guest for only today," Huukp said.

Not wanting to stop, but more not wanting to risk his goal having come this far, Okomi reluctantly reattached the ropes to his shoulders and followed the three of them.

* * *

"He must stay outside of the village."

Okomi didn't budge. They stood outside a tiny grouping of huts lining the outer banks of the river. The boy with the sling narrowed his eyes. His fists were curled.

"It's okay, Cairook."

The boy looked at his chief.

"But—"

Huukp held his hand up as if he were going to strike the boy. Cairook fell silent.

"You can leave your son beside the hut," Huukp said to Okomi. "Downwind."

The chief led him toward the indicated hut. Okomi pulled his son's sled to a spot where he could see him through the door while the boys went through the last of Okomi's material wealth: necklaces made of shells and several large geodes filled with purple amethyst.

"Your sons?" Okomi asked as they entered the tiny, rectangular dwelling made of yucca and willow brush. A small fire burned in the middle. Smoke flowed out of a hole in the roof.

"One of them has my temper, but my wisdom has yet to make itself known," Huukp replied.

Okomi tried not to appear anxious.

"Please sit," Huukp said. He sat on the dirt floor and indicated toward a spot beside him.

A woman entered the hut carrying a large bowl of steaming porridge and a baby at her breast. Huukp's wife, no doubt. The chief took the bowl from her hands and the woman left as silently as she had entered. He offered the bowl to Okomi.

Though his arms and shoulders screamed as he lifted the bowl to his mouth, Okomi found the acorn stew both sweet and nourishing. Huukp smiled slightly and nodded.

Okomi handed the bowl back to the chief and wiped his lips with the back of his arm. "I thank you for your hospitality and safe passage," he said.

Huukp slurped at the bowl. His mouth was full of porridge as he said, "If I suspected foul play, I would have killed you at your camp last night." He swallowed and handed the bowl back to Okomi.

Okomi looked at him, his eyebrows raised slightly.

"We have many eyes," the chief said.

They finished the bowl in silence. Okomi suspected the serving woman was watching because as soon as the porridge was gone, she reentered the hut carrying a long pipe and a handful of jimsonweed. Huukp packed the pipe, lit the weed with a burning stick from the fire, and puffed until the smoke entered his lungs. He coughed a little and handed it to Okomi.

Okomi took a hit from the pipe. It had been many moons since he had last smoked and it took only a few minutes for the lightheadedness to come.

"You are foolish to seek her aid," the chief said. His voice wheezed. "Though the doctor knows many things and her medicine is big, what you ask is…" His voice trailed off until he arrived at another question. "You do this for one son? Do you have no others?"

"Pokoh never blessed me with another," Okomi said.

Huukp stared at him and nodded towards the pipe. Okomi reluctantly took another puff. His head swam and he was growing tired. He tried to focus on his son's face through the bright entry. The wind kicked up the edges of blanket that covered him. An edge slapped lightly against the boy's cheek.

"How did he end up in this condition?"

Answers were not coming easily, but he was in the Vanyume's hands. He couldn't risk alienating the only thing standing between him and the witch.

"His first hunt," Okomi said reluctantly. "Five moons ago. He was to return to the village with a kill."

Okomi smoked the jimsonweed, taking it into his lungs, succumbing to its power now. His eyes never left his son's face, still pale, but now fat with bloated lips. He closed his eyes, trying to remember how his son looked before he [departed for the hunt].

"The Moon rose and he did not return. My wife begged me to go and find him." Okomi shook his head as if he were looking at her. "I told her that he was becoming a man. He must learn."

Pain choked his voice. "He must learn," he said again.

Okomi absent-mindedly handed the pipe back to Huukp, laid down on the blankets pulled over the packed dirt and closed his eyes. The initial swimming of vision calmed down. He heard the dull throb of his heart beating rhythmically in his ears.

"When I found him in the morning, he had already fallen asleep beneath a ridge. I could not wake him. His body was cool and stiff." He shook his head. "It must have been a very cold night." Okomi closed his eyes even tighter as if in physical pain. "The trail of the snake was carved in the dirt beside his body." An image of two bite marks on his son's left ankle filled his mind.

"I should have…"

The thought remained unfinished as he covered the boy's wound with one hand, looked up, and saw the great foot of Pokoh blotting out the Sun.

* * *

Something woke Okomi, eyes full of sleep. He was in the hut. It was night. The fire's embers were glowing and he turned his head to see Huukp snoring. There were faint whispers and the sounds of shuffling feet. He looked through the hut's opening and saw his son being dragged away by the legs.

"Let go of him!" he said, leaping to his feet. He ran outside and saw the outline of Huukp's sons.

"He should not be here," said the one who earlier had the sling. "You bring us all bad luck."

"Then we will leave," Okomi said. A fury stirred within him.

The young boys looked at each other and dropped the child's legs. They fell with a thump onto the dirt. Okomi looked inside the hut. The chief was still asleep. There was no sense in waking him. Okomi would travel now. He looked at the stars and determined the Sun would rise by the time he reached the creek.

* * *

The chief must have previously gotten word out to all of his scouts for Okomi and his son arrived at the creek, unmolested. The night had been another cold one. Steam rose from one the springs next to the cave. The Sun had shown itself just as Okomi expected, revealing that his son had not fared well on the journey. Bloody foam was running from his nose and mouth. Okomi stopped and cleaned his face.

As if expecting them, the witch stood in front of her dark home. Her hair was matted with mud and her pendulous breasts were wrinkled. They nearly touched her belly. She was tall for a woman, and like Huukp, she also had a crooked nose.

"Bring him inside," she said, smiling a toothless smile.

He followed her in. There was no fire lit and it took a moment for his eyes to adjust to the black. The witch seemed to have no problem finding her way around. She shuffled various bowls of clay and wood on a flat piece of stone, emptying their contents into a shallow mortar. She ground the ingredients with her pestle. Okomi collapsed on the ground beside his son, allowing himself to feel the lingering drowsiness of the jimsonweed. He had made it.

Unhurried, the witch continued her work. Okomi grew impatient.

"Can you wake him?"

She ignored Okomi. Now she took a blunt rock and hammered a large root into powder, finally mixing it with the rest of the ingredients. Watching her and listening to her work felt like a dream. After what seemed a hundred moons, the commotion stopped. She scooped the mixture into a small wooden cup carved out of an acorn and walked outside. Okomi wanted to follow her but his legs refused to cooperate. He had pushed himself to his limits to arrive here. His train of thought mattered little as she strode back in through the bright entrance.

"Drink," she said. She handed him the wooden cup, now full of warm liquid. Okomi felt steam rise and spread onto his face.

Is she blind, he wondered?

"I am not the one that is sick."

"Drink."

The scent was noxious. There was nothing else to do now. No other choices. Okomi had to put his faith in the witch. At first he sipped, but the taste was so bad it made him retch. He looked at the witch. She nodded and he gulped it down, ignoring the heat.

Now she took a seat on the ground beside him. Her knees cracked as she collapsed. The creek's running water echoed in the cave.

"Now what?"

"We wait."

The red foam began to accumulate again on his son's face. Okomi reached out to clean it but the witch grabbed his arm and forced it back into his lap.

"What are we waiting for?"

"The spirits."

He fought to stay awake. The jimsonweed, the hard travel, maybe even whatever he just drank, seemed to conspire together to distract him from his task. With the patience of an ancient tree, Okomi watched the shadows at the entrance of the cave change slowly from the movement of the Sun.

At some point, he stood forcefully. He placed a hand on the cave wall. It took every ounce of remaining strength to remain upright. The witch stared up at him and he stared back.

"I have traveled far, faced my enemies, and you tell me to wait for the spirits. Make them come!"

He demanded an answer and he would beat it out of the crone if she refused.

"You bring me your son. You want me to wake him."

"Yes," Okomi said, exasperated. She was finally understanding. Living alone for so long and communing with ghosts had confused her mind.

"But, Nuwa-man, he is not the one sleeping," she said.

The once powerful chief sunk to his knees beside his son, unable to fight the dizziness any longer. Crimson lather caked the boy's bloated face. From the corners of his mouth, a trail of tiny maggots marched out onto his cheek. The smell that had been there all along seemed to increase in strength. Okomi laid down on the ground and put his hand on his son's chest. He felt his own heartbeat pulsing through his body, radiating outward into his fingertips. Time slowed. The old woman became a blur in the corner of his vision.

* * *

He dreamed again. They climbed the mountain east of the village. He felt the arrows shake lightly across his back. With the bow hanging over his left shoulder, his son stepped in front of him and took hold of an outcropping. He was about to pull himself up, but Okomi grabbed ahold of his arm and held him. His son looked back. The chief held a finger to his lips and then used it to point at the ground several feet in front of them.

A trail wound through the dirt, leading toward the dark shadow of a rock.

His son smiled.

It was the first of many days in which they would hunt together. The dream would never end.

They went another way.

Princess Soup-Bone

The fact that Davis and Luca were putting their pans and shovels away indicated, for all intents and purposes, that they believed the old girl would not be found that morning.

Johnny had been out on the hunt for over two hours, so the two men made the most of their time. They packed camp because they knew Johnny would cry and howl if they weren't ready to join in as soon as he returned. As much as both of them wanted to stay and continue working their claim, Johnny would make such a proposition intolerable. He'd be a sobbing handful without Princess Soup-Bone in tow.

"He's too superstitious, no? She was just another mouth to feed. We would have done okay without her."

Davis sensed Luca ending the last sentence as if it were a question.

"Maybe," Davis said. He wasn't confident enough to fall on either side of the equation. He often liked to see things play out before making a decision. Some considered Davis spineless because of that. He figured it was just smart. The fact was Princess had only been with them a couple of months, and their newfound luck seemed mighty convenient after her arrival.

"I wouldn't discount anything yet," he continued. "If it wasn't for her, we may have been many miles from each other right now—you on a cutter heading back around the Cape, Johnny probably drinking away his rheumatism in a dusty alley."

Davis didn't want to think about where *he* might have ended up. When he'd sailed out of the Boston harbor eight months ago, he'd sworn to his parents and siblings that he wouldn't return until he could buy them each their own set of authentic Chinese porcelain tea cups. To face them again would be a humiliation of the first order. He wasn't prepared to endure such. He'd always been considered a roustabout with his head in the clouds and his unremarkable homecoming would only go to prove the rest of the world right.

"Bah," Luca said, skipping smooth stones across the creek while Davis continued working. The Italian was young and brash, not one to readily believe in much anything happening outside the material world influencing anything within it. Though he verbally disdained any notion of Princess acting as a benevolent messenger, in practice, he seemed to defer quietly if Johnny made a decision based on his peculiar beliefs.

My friends, Johnny had said with his Russian accent suddenly becoming thicker than his day-to-day speech, *the Leshiy wood-spirits are alive and well. They come in time of need and must be respected!*

As Davis strung together the handles of their tin pots and secured them to Becca, their mule, he laughed to himself that calling a wood-spirit Princess Soup-Bone was respectful. Yet Johnny took no issue with it and the name seemed to stick when Luca offered her an actual soup-bone on their first night of celebration.

After confirming Becca was fully loaded, Davis took a moment to admire the way the morning sun hit the calm waters streaming through their claimed section of Percy's Gulch. They were the only ones in this area barely two miles south of the foothill town of Sonora. One month ago, they'd passed many folks coming the opposite way, always with a look of pity on their faces. They must have looked something awful, these three men in near rags following a fur-and-bones mutt. More than a few times, they were handed loaves of bread by traveling parties without a word being spoken—only eyes that said, "You poor things. So late to the party."

It was true. Among the general population of California miners and those who made money from serving their needs, there was little doubt as to the slim prospects so close to Sonora. It was June of 1855 and this area had been well picked over since bodies came rushing over mountains and ocean six years prior.

Or so it was believed.

Davis and Luca had initially thought they were crazy to settle in and dig here, especially given how they had been down to hard biscuits and unseasoned pemmican. A hot pot of coffee had been a distant memory then.

But Princess insisted on stopping in this very spot and refused to budge. That was sign enough for Johnny. He'd taken to the brown-coated girl like a bee to a dandelion, following her in a semi-delusional state. Davis and Luca had been too worn down and tired to protest as he began unpacking Becca without so much as consulting them.

The three of them panned a little inlet that turned out to be rife with gold dust and the incident was certainly enough for Davis to wonder if just maybe, Princess Soup-Bone was truly sent to guide them. Davis would never forget that first day of slack-jawed disbelief followed by the loudest hootin' and hollerin' that he'd ever heard. Both Luca and Johnny had spouted off in their native languages—Luca with his passionate-sounding Italian and Johnny with his angry-sounding Russian (Johnny's real name was Alexander Blinov, the last name meaning something akin to a pancake, so he said everyone had taken to call him Johnny after johnnycakes).

Within a week, they had seven jars filled to the brim with beauti-ful yellow flakes. Coffee, eggs, and even an occasional tour around the saloon brought all of their spirits to a new height. Davis commissioned a carpenter to build them a sluice box so that they could start hauling more at a time.

All was well for the past seventeen days until Princess disap-peared some time in the middle of the night. Truth be told, her sudden departure left Davis on edge, but he was unsure if it was because she was what Johnny claimed her to be or just the downtrodden effect it would have on them all.

At that thought, there was a rustle in the woods behind them. Davis and Luca both turned to see Johnny running back into the camp, panting and wheezing, bent over with his hands on his knees.

"Someone took her," he said breathlessly. "I know it." There was tobacco spittle running down his graying beard and traces of tears carved into the grime on his cheeks. He had a wild aspect to his eyes that Davis had hoped would never return.

"Now hold on," Davis said. "Why would someone come and take an old dog?"

Johnny gave him a reprimanding look.

"I know she's more than that to us," Davis quickly backpedaled, "but no one else knows that."

Johnny ignored him. "We need to go to town," he said. "She must be there. Or someone will have seen her."

Davis eyed Luca who nodded back. "We figured as much," Davis said.

Johnny looked around and saw the empty camp.

"You packed everything? No. No. Leave the tools," Johnny said. "Someone will come and take our claim."

Davis shook his head. "More likely someone will think twice if they find our equipment here," he said. "Most people will pass this place by otherwise."

Johnny hesitated for a moment, but then assented. "You're right, you're right. I'm just—"

And he left it at that as the three of them departed for Sonora.

* * *

It was no surprise that Johnny grew more melancholy by the minute, but Davis noticed a dousing of spirits in both himself and even Luca. After searching every alleyway and proprietor's shop, calling out "Princess!" to the curious looks of the town's citizenry, the three of them settled in at the place they'd started—Rosa's Cantina.

It was close to noon and nearly every seat was taken. The bar was completely occupied. Only two tables were open on the floor. The trio had been seated in a dim corner, opposite from the finely dressed clerks and lawyers taking lunches of pork, beans, and tortillas. In another corner near a window was a piano player warming up with some scales before diving into instrumental versions of old spirituals.

"Maybe she's elsewhere," Davis said, eyeing the waiter dropping off a bottle of rye and three glasses. "I mean, she did just appear to us out of the woods. It could be she headed back from wherever she came."

A part of him regretted saying that. Johnny may just want to head back north and retread old ground where they had first come upon her. A deflated Davis didn't know if he was up for that. He'd much rather continue working their glorious secret.

Luca reached eagerly for the bottle. He yanked the cork out with his teeth and took a pull before pouring everyone a glass. Davis gave him a reprimanding look, but Luca just shrugged. Johnny didn't seem to care a whit. Davis pushed the glass before him, completely unnoticed as Johnny's eyes remained unfocused on the woodgrain of the table. He was bundled up in his heaviest gray coat as if it was the middle of January.

"Perhaps our time with her was at its end," Johnny said. "The Leshiy are fickle creatures, you know. If they are not cherished properly…" A solitary tear splashed beneath his downturned face. Davis felt a wave of pink embarrassment sweep across his pale flesh as he knew Johnny was the edge of blubbering again.

"She ate just as well as we did!" Luca chimed in. He poured himself a second shot.

It was at that moment when Davis wondered if Johnny's old gods had heard their lamentations and looked upon them with pity. Davis was facing the double-door entrance of the cantina while the other two men had their backs to it, so they could only judge by the frozen expression of his slightly parted lips and enlarged eyes that something peculiar was occurring.

Luca was the first to turn around.

"Princess!" he yelled, clamping his mouth with both hands, too far delayed after betraying his excitement.

Johnny craned his neck slowly as if he struggled within against facing further disappointment.

All of their eyes fell not so much upon the dark-looking, mustachioed man wearing a black bow-tie and blinding white shirt hidden only in parts by a thin red vest, but upon the panting creature who stood by his side, a thick piece of rope around its neck leading up to the man's hand.

Davis correctly predicted that Johnny might do something rash. The Russian was already halfway out of his chair before Davis grabbed his arm.

"Now hold on," he said. "That might not be her." He didn't even attempt to hide the lie with tone or convincing language. The hungry-looking eyes, the way she wagged her tail—as sure as buxom Maria upstairs was not a one-woman man, there was no doubt that was their girl.

"That's her!" Johnny slapped his knee and hooted. Ripping his arm from Davis' grip, he got to his feet and approached the gentleman.

* * *

The man gave Johnny a weary look. His right hand fell quickly to the swollen holster at his side. Davis and Luca weren't men of violence, but each kept a single-shot belly-gun on their person in case things went awry, which was a distinct possibility at the moment.

As Johnny neared the stranger, he surprised the man by getting down on one knee and cupping both hands gently under the jaw of Princess Soup-Bone.

"Come, *baba*, are you going to give us a scare just like that? We took good care of you, didn't we?" One hand reached up and scratched the back of her ears. Princess leaned into him and began licking the palm of his other hand.

Johnny rose onto his heels and now Davis and Luca stood two feet behind him. The man regarded all of them with a wariness. His hand still floated openly above the butt of his pistol.

"Thank you for looking after her, friend," Johnny said. He stuck out a hand as if to shake. "We hope she's been no trouble."

Suddenly, the man smirked but did not offer his hand in return. "No trouble at all," he said and looked down at Princess. "Came across her this morning as I was riding into town. She's a friendly one." Davis noticed that the man's hand had moved from the gun and was now being used to tighten his grip on the rope.

Johnny stood there with a dumb smile on his face, waiting expectantly. The man began to move to the side and head towards an empty table, but Johnny moved quickly to intercept him. "If you want to keep the rope, you can untie her now. She will follow us."

"Oh," the man said. "Well, are you sure this is your dog?" He looked down. "I didn't see a collar or brand anywhere."

"Yes," Luca spoke up. "She's ours."

"Huh." The man stroked his mustache as if deep in thought.

"Well, as much as I would like to believe you fellas, I can't well and good just hand her over to any man claiming to be her owner. Now, you all come across as genuine and honest gentlemen, but looks can be most deceiving." He eyed their dusty clothing as a banker inspects a potentially counterfeit bill. "What if you simply intend to cook her up and eat her?"

Johnny's eyes grew wider than the Atlantic Ocean. "Sir, we would *never* think of such a thing." He spat on the floor between his boots. Davis could sense the old firebrand was getting riled up.

"No, no, of course not," the man said, putting his hands up in a defensive manner. "Forgive the insinuation. It's just that I've grown a little attached. But, still, there must be some way around this conundrum."

Back in Boston, Davis had considered himself a fan of the theater. Whenever a troupe was in the city or a new show was opening, the producer could always count on his attendance. He was well versed in the arts of the stage, and therefore it came as no surprise to him that the man before them was half-rate but good enough to convince the layman that every move he made was without prior motive and forethought.

"I have an idea!" the man exclaimed, reaching beneath his vest and pulling out a deck of cards. "It just so happens that I carry these wherever I go, you know, to play a little solitaire and whittle away the boredom that so frequently arises during travel. Now, I've just begun to get interested in poker and faro since coming out West. While I'm not very good, I do find the games thrilling." He leaned into Johnny and raised his eyebrows. "What would you say, if you're so inclined, to playing a round for her?"

Davis felt his whole being deflate. He knew nothing about cards and he'd seen Johnny only play an occasional hand, never walking away from a table with more than he arrived.

"We have nothing to put up," Luca said.

"We have a sluice box, shovels, pans, and a mule," Johnny spat out.

"Now, wait a minute," Luca said, stepping in front of Johnny. "Just wait a min—"

"Deal," the man replied, winking at Luca and reaching past him to clasp Johnny's hand in a shake.

Luca looked as if he wanted to get his tiny hands around the necks of both men, but Davis pulled him back.

"A deal's been made," the conniver said as if speaking to Johnny but looking directly at Luca. "It would be a rather ungentlemanly thing to do if you were to break it."

Davis noted that the man's palm was once again near his holster. He wasn't too thrilled with events playing out this way, but Johnny was past persuasion. He'd begun to think Johnny was right. Perhaps their streak of luck was destined to burn out as quickly as a shooting star.

"Looks like you've been kind enough to secure a table and drink," the man said. "Let's have some fun, shall we?" He took a seat against the wall and tied his end of rope to one of its legs. Princess Soup-Bone made a half-circle before lying down next to him. The man motioned for Johnny to sit on the opposite side. Johnny did so while Luca and Davis stood around him as if their mere presence could guard against the wiles of this man.

The stranger emptied the deck of blue-inked cards into one hand and tossed the box aside. With a deftness that filled Davis's stomach with apprehension, the man shuffled the cards back and forth, up and down, left and right, all with the fluidity of the waters running through Percy's Gulch. In his mind, Davis was calculating just how long it would take them to earn some new pans and shovels.

"You look like a man that knows his pasteboards," the gambler said to Johnny. "What do you say to five-card draw?"

Johnny glanced down at Princess. Her sad eyes seemed to move upward and meet his simultaneously. Without averting his gaze, he deftly poured himself a shot of whiskey and slugged it down. "Sure," he said.

"Great!" the blackleg said and poured himself a shot. He raised it to Johnny in silence and tipped it back swiftly, smacking his lips afterward. "What do you say we get warmed up? Start nice and slow. I'll still put up the dog on this round, of course, but I'll let you get away with a small ante. Say, only your shovels?"

He'd barely hit the end of his sentence before Johnny picked right up. "All of it," Johnny said.

"Ooohhh," Luca groaned, throwing his hands in the air. "Johnny, why? There's no point—"

"If that's how you'd prefer it," the gambler said. He raised his eyebrows at Luca who grumbled, swiped the bottle of whiskey from the table and proceeded to suck on it like it was a nursemaid's teat.

The man shuffled the deck once more and placed it face down on the table. "If you'd be so kind," he said, extending an open hand.

Johnny reached out and tapped the cards with his knuckles.

A gasp of air exited Luca's lips.

No cut, Davis thought. Why don't we just call it quits right now?

As if he'd read Davis's mind, the stranger bared his all-too-white teeth. He picked up the cards and dealt them until five lie face-down before each person, dropping the remaining draw pile between them both. Only the gambler reached for his hand while Johnny sat as still as a stone, his eyes glued to Princess Soup-Bone.

The man looked up at Johnny, and then at both Luca and Davis inquisitively.

The dread continued to build in Davis's belly.

The man shrugged and said, "I guess we can skip the raising and calling. Care to look at your cards? Maybe you want to draw?"

Johnny appeared as if he were sleeping with his eyes open, still settled on the face of Princess Soup-Bone. "No," he replied in a near whisper.

"Hm," the gambler grunted. "Well, you sure play a little peculiar, sir, but I don't like to make a man feel too much at a disadvantage. Therefore, I'll play what's in my hand as well. In fact, I'll lay mine out first, than you."

The man spread his cards face-up on the table. Three Aces and two Kings. He released a low whistle.

"Well, I'm certainly being smiled upon today!" He reached down and scratched the top of Princess Soup-Bone's scalp. Her eyes turned briefly toward the gambler, but returned to Johnny's. "I understand if you'd rather not turn yours over," he continued thoughtfully. "No need to add insult to injury."

Johnny absentmindedly reached for his cards. Davis turned towards the other patrons, watching them dine, smoke, and chatter happily. He knew what was coming. He didn't have to see it happen.

A loud spitting sound shot past his ears along with drops of moisture splashing on his face. The scent of whiskey burned his nostrils.

"Hoooooo!" Luca shouted, stomping his boots up and down on the hardwood floors. The clamor was so loud that every face in the room turned toward them. Even the piano player fumbled a couple of notes before quickly returning to form.

Davis faced the table to see the magic held in Johnny's cards: Four Queens.

He suddenly felt some of the unrealized tension leaving his

muscles. Maybe Johnny knew more about gaming than he'd let on. Davis hoped so, anyway, as the blackleg seemed to break character and flinch slightly. His face grew flush and he jumped to his feet.

"Wait one second," he said, "How….You must be one cheating sonbitch!" The gambler's arm was pulled back, his hand reaching for his pistol before he suddenly yelped and fell backward on to his rear, knocking over the table and his chair, inadvertently releasing Princess Soup-Bone's rope.

By now, the piano playing had stopped completely and half of the crowd was also standing, craning to view the source of the action. The barkeep came rushing over with a shotgun and a large man at his side.

"You get that mutt out of here!" he yelled.

Johnny bent down, swept up Princess Soup-Bone and held onto her tightly as she released her jaws from the gambler's left calf.

In an instant, the four of them were through the swinging double-doors, untying Becca, and making for the town's exit. It wasn't until they were a hundred yards out of Sonora when the two men slapped Johnny on the back, congratulating him.

"Johnny," said Davis, "I didn't know you were such a blackleg yourself!"

Johnny looked at him with serious eyes. "I'm not," he said, moving his gaze toward a panting Princess.

HALFWAY

Detective Marty Quinn's job is a lot like dipping your face in a pool or the ocean, where you leave your ears floating halfway between one world and the other. The above and the below. You get a hint of the diluted, swirling side, but you're still anchored in what you know. Then comes the pull. An act of mercy. Like someone taking a fistful of wet hair and yanking you back into comfortable reality. Or it's the other way around—the push—where someone takes that same hand and shoves you down into a new set of circumstances and you're forced to adapt.

Marty felt like he was drowning when he came back to his beachside apartment and found the limp body of his wife of seven days, posed in the pea-green easy chair she vowed to get rid of the first time she laid eyes on it (*It's so 2025*, she had said).

The majority of her appearance said she'd come home from a hard day of paralegal work and simply fell asleep. Head tilted down and to the side, tucked into her right shoulder. The only distortion to the picture was the stain of blood running from a line crossing her throat, onto the pink-rose colored dress Marty had bought her two days ago.

"I'm sorry, Marty."

Marty said nothing. Only stared at the bottom of the sheet covering Diana. Three of her sky blue-painted toenails were sticking out. It was a sloppy job, whoever placed the sheet.

"We can get Pierre to work this. You don't need to be here."

Of course they weren't going to let him work the case, but Kate, the coroner, wasn't going to outright say that. She was one of the few people that Marty worked with whom he felt he could call a friend.

"I have a spare bedroom. You know Leonard would love to have you stay with us for awhile."

Marty may have nodded, but all he felt was that cold water surrounding his face, the unrelenting hand of fate denying him breath.

* * *

Marty's boss forced him to take a couple of weeks off. Even told him to expense a hotel somewhere after he ended up sleeping in his coupe that first night, refusing to answer Kate's phone calls. He accepted his boss's offer, because if he didn't, he knew that it would only draw more attention.

The hard questions had come early. It was standard procedure. His alibi was airtight. He had been down at the Whirling Dervish, clinking glasses of port-finished scotch with Dennis, a longtime partner, when it happened. After Dennis dropped him off, Marty made the gruesome discovery.

He wasn't in the clear, though. He knew he was being watched.

Detectives have an insider's knowledge. It's assumed most of them are clever enough to pull something like this off, and if the department is lucky, the detective gets cocky and makes a mistake.

Of course, Marty's sudden change of behavior over the past few months hadn't helped matters. He had always been a private person, but the whirlwind romance took his colleagues by surprise. Three months. All starting from a random conversation in line at a local coffee shop. The way he had suddenly gushed over Diana made things worse. Not that saying a few words a week was gushing in anyone's book but Marty's. The only indication there had been a wedding was the simple titanium wedding band suddenly popping up on his finger. Even the honeymoon was a quick overnighter at a posh hotel up in Santa Barbara.

He couldn't explain it to himself, let alone anyone else. Diana had been the one. She had come as swiftly as the day comes upon dawn and now she had left just as quickly as night overtakes dusk.

The day after the discovery, his apartment had been cleared of yellow tape.

Marty came back.

* * *

The vertical blinds were turned shut. Hints of daylight leaked through the cracks and the place smelled of solvents and super glue. Marty sat on the carpet where the easy chair had been. It was now in the department's evidence room, but its four legs had left their round impressions.

He had only been able to handle about thirty seconds of silence before turning on the television and tuning into the local news. The forecast called for clear skies—'picnic weather' the meteorologist called it with his pearly, ingratiating smile.

Marty's cell phone buzzed. It was Dennis. Marty figured he ought to pick up. He turned the volume down on the TV.

"What do you know about Diana?"

Not much. Marty had to admit that was part of the appeal. She talked even less about herself than he did and when it did come up, she always found a way to steer such conversation elsewhere. She had a labrador retriever once named Taco. They lived out in Vermont, but after the dog died, she decided to pack a small suitcase and head to the West Coast. She found work performing research and drawing up briefs for an intellectual property lawyer out of El Segundo.

"Apparently she has no next of kin," Dennis continued. "She lived in Vermont for all of her life. Shuffled around foster homes. Her bio parents both died of meth overdoses before she hit twelve. It seemed like she had her act together though, given the crappy environment. Got her GED, then her paralegal certificate. Shit, you probably know all of this."

Marty did. Some of it, anyway. He thought about his own relatives who might as well be strangers. Even though he visited his parents in their Laguna Woods retirement community a few times a year, it wasn't as if they were ever close. They did their thing. He did his.

"Look, I know you kids were hot and heavy and jumped into this thing. You've always been a closed book with your relationships. I shouldn't even be discussing any of this with you. But, I'm gonna be honest. We're hitting a dead end here. I need your help."

Marty had already gotten to work. It didn't matter how close he was to her. Work was always on his mind. He'd poked and prodded every corner of his mental being but had yet to come up with anything.

"I assume you got nothing from the dress? Chair? Everything else?" Marty asked.

"Only her prints and DNA. And of course yours."

Of course.

"And the lawyer's office?"

"Obviously, we've interviewed everyone there. Callahan and O'Donnell aren't working on anything exactly high-profile. They're on re-tainer for a few distribution and shipping bigwigs in the area. Preliminary checks on the companies aren't raising any red flags."

Marty didn't say anything. He only stared at the female newscaster on the screen. A tiny box next to her head showed a picture of a young man sporting a beard meant to make him look ten years older than he really was, but had the opposite effect. Below his face were the words *CONTROVERSIAL IPO* and the name of the company—Moeva.

"I gotta go." Marty hung up the phone and turned up the volume.

A brief interview with the man popped up. He was smiling wide with his left canine tooth poking out slightly more than his right, standing in what looked to be an office lobby. His facial hair matched his earlier photo and he was wearing a light blue collared shirt, the top two buttons unbuttoned, beneath a dark blazer. There was something about him that stuck in Marty's craw.

"We make lifelong companions."

"Mr. Munro, don't you feel that this is...unnatural?" the woman interviewing him asked.

"Not everyone is blessed to be an alpha male. And, by the way, not all of our clients are male. But let me ask you, are those people less deserving of companionship?"

The interviewer feigned a look of concern and was speaking as if she were reading a script. "There's been controversy surrounding some of the 'personalities' that come with these dolls."

"Companions."

The woman continued. "Many of them a programmed to act resistant to their operator. Don't you feel that you're feeding potentially dangerous delusions and addictions of your customers?"

"We're offering some of our customers a form of therapy," he said. "If they are able to act out their fantasies with their companions, imagine the number of public safety incidents that will reduce."

The interview cut back to the newscaster who mentioned that the tiny startup was founded only two years ago in Vermont.

* * *

It was the usual lawyer's office. Shelves covered with dark green and brown leather-bound tomes filled with archaic law literature that were probably ignored for the most part. How much of that was available online now? Marty couldn't imagine an attorney having his paralegals wasting time digging around in those things.

The administrative assistant eyed Marty from behind her giant desk. She was a woman in her late fifties, maybe early sixties, with a bit of filler to smooth out the wrinkles out beside her eyes, but she peered over the lip of dark oak like a young child barely able to reach the top.

"Can I help you?"

"Yes, I'd like to talk to Callahan. Or O'Donnell."

"Do you have an appointment?"

"No."

She sighed deeply. "Well, they are both very busy. Are you a current client—"

He flashed his badge.

"Look, I saw both of them park their cars this morning. I know they're here. I know they're probably sitting in a conference room right now stuffing their faces with whatever overpriced shrimp and lobster they had brought in."

The woman hesitated for a second before picking up the phone.

"There's a police officer here to see you."

"His name's…." She looked up.

"Marty."

"Marty….?"

"Marty."

She repeated the name into the handset and hung up the phone a second later.

"Down the hallway. Second door on your right."

* * *

The room had an appearance much like the lobby, only slightly smaller with a polished oak table in the middle and a conference phone sitting in the middle of that. A platter of seafood and dipping sauces was half-empty. Plates with discarded shrimp and lobster tails sat in front of two men.

Surprise, surprise.

Except for different colored ties, Callahan and O'Donnell looked like cheap carbon copies of each other. Both of them were busting out of the same tired gray blazers and button-up white shirts and had mile-long combovers. It was like they hadn't updated their wardrobes since the 80s. These guys obviously had steady clientele.

"We don't have anything more to say. We've already talked—"

"I'll be quick. Tell me about Moeva."

Callahan looked at O'Donnell. Or O'Donnell looked at Callahan. One of them spoke.

"We've given the department all of the information we have regarding Diana. I advise that—"

The man went silent as Marty reached into his coat, pulled the .40 Smith and Wesson out of his shoulder holster and removed the magazine. He confirmed that it was loaded and slapped it back in. The faces of the two attorneys turned ash white. Marty didn't point his weapon at them. Didn't wave it around threateningly. He was simply an officer checking his tools, but he probably looked as scary as hell. He hadn't slept in the past twenty-six hours, his eyes were dry and bloodshot, and he could almost see the funk fuming from his body.

"I understand. I just feel like you work a complicated business. You keep a lot of files. Things get misplaced or forgotten about. There may be some niggling little detail…" He shrugged and shifted his eyes between them both. "…you know, something inconsequential that you might think is not really even worth mentioning, but that I would really love to hear."

Callahan, or maybe it was O'Donnell, looked like he was about to crack, so Marty focused on him.

"We had nothing to do with what happened."

Marty was silent, goading the man to speak more.

"Do you know who did?"

"No!" they said simultaneously.

Marty believed them.

"We don't work for them anymore," one of them offered up.

"As of when?"

"As of yesterday."

"Because of Diana?"

There was a moment of hesitation.

"I'll take that as a yes. Look, give me all of those files you have that you may have forgotten to give the department and I'll let you get back to your peasant's lunch."

* * *

Marty pulled up the folder on his computer. Six hundred and thirty-six legal documents. This would take awhile. He started the first pot of coffee.

* * *

It was somewhere around two A.M. when he noticed something odd. Callahan and O'Donnell had vetted a deal between Moeva and a marketing company with ties to a popular social media giant. A database was sold to Moeva, operating as Tenacious Industries. Marty imagined this particular media company would be in a pool of hot water if news got out.

It was time to learn a little more about Moeva's operations.

* * *

The place didn't look particularly high tech. Just south of Burlington, east of Lake Champlain, Moeva's two-level, white-brick building was part of a nondescript office park set back in a copse of hackberry trees whose branches of spearhead-leaves shadowed the natural grass.

The lobby was equally unremarkable, except for the rear wall where a large, glossy sign displaying Moeva's logo hung—a pair of feminine eyes with heavy eyeshadow and a reflection of computer chips painted inside the pupils. It was the same location where the news interview had taken place.

A young, pasty male sat behind the front desk.

"Good morning. I'm Mr. Vanderschot with Dutch Capital." Not the most creative company name. Marty banked on no one in the office having ever been to the Netherlands, otherwise the accent he'd practiced for the past twenty-four hours by reviewing online videos would make the situation a little more precarious. "I have an appointment with—"

"Mr. Vanderschot!" There was the bearded boy from the newscast, peeking out from a door behind the admin's desk. He walked up to Marty and extended his hand. "David Munro. It's a pleasure to have you here."

Marty took his hand and fought an instinctive revulsion to the its clamminess.

"How was the flight? I hope you've adjusted to the time difference."

"It's nothing." The less said, the better. "Shall we begin the tour? I have another appointment this afternoon."

"Of course. I understand you are a busy man." David walked toward the door. "Please, follow me."

* * *

There were a few humans milling about, but most of the work was done through automation in a large warehouse. Machines building machines. Conveyor belts distributed the lifelike body parts to various points where metal arms and claws assembled them.

David shouted over the loud mechanisms. "It's all in the crotch. Our researchers spent many hours perfecting the look and feel. Especially the feel. That's one of our key differentiators." He said with an almost clinical inflection.

Seeing the parts of the bodies reminded Marty of many a crime scene he wished he could forget. After the brief tour, the two of them retired to David's office.

On a side table, there was a stack of cheeseburger sliders and a bowl of mac and cheese. A bucket filled with ice and beer bottles sat next to the food.

"I figured you might enjoy some classic American fare."

Marty's stomach was signaling everything but hunger.

"To be honest, what I've seen is interesting and while your product is certainly titillating, I don't know that its enough to get me and my partners...excited."

There was a momentary hesitation from David, but he leaned forward.

"We've got something new we're working on for select customers. It promises to be very profitable. I'm not going to lie to you, Mr. Vanderschot. The sort of numbers you're looking to invest is what we need. I'm showing you all my cards. We're a little controversial and finding willing investors is difficult. I need to know that if you invest, you'll put some faith in me. That you'll stand with this company."

"We look for profit, Mr. Munro."

The toothy smile came quickly.

* * *

They were in a locked room at the back of the warehouse. Piled into one corner were replicas of children, completely naked. It took everything Marty had to not go ballistic.

"You want profit? This is profit, Mr. Vanderschot." David indicated toward the main factory floor with his head. "That's good money, but this..." He made his eyebrows dance. "...this is going to make us all very happy. Watch."

He walked over to one of the dolls—a young girl with blonde hair and blue eyes. He pressed a finger into the back of her neck. Her movements were jerky, but she sprang to life.

"Tell us about yourself," David said to her.

The little girl's lips moved. "My name is Tina Watts. I'm twelve-years-old and live in Hot Springs, Arkansas. I like waterskiing, texting my friends, and cuddling with my dachshund, Bonnie."

David's sick smile seemed to grow.

"Wow," Marty said. He had dealt with shady characters throughout his career, but David Munro was something else. "So lifelike. They each have these personalities?"

"It's our secret sauce. For all practical purposes, these are real kids."

"How so?"

"We had a brief partnership with Flitterbook. Under a shell company. But the lawyers got queasy and cut things off. It's okay. We got all the profile information. Got what we needed."

His hand was stroking the girl's hair as if she were a pet.

It was time.

"You certainly did that," Marty said. He pulled out his pistol and shoved it into David's gut before the sick CEO knew what was happening. "And now I got what I needed."

Munro was surprisingly cool.

"What happened to your accent, Mr. Vanderschot?"

"I lost it."

* * *

Diana had been in a relationship with David. He'd taken her under his wing when she was younger. More vulnerable. He confessed that she had made good money by referring him to lawyers who were willing to broker the deal with Flitterbook. Apparently she had a sudden change of heart. She grew a moral compass, he said, and though she didn't outright say it, it was obvious she was ready to tell someone what she knew.

By that point, David had made too much money from wealthy clients to turn back, so he did what he needed to do.

Diana had been in trouble and Marty had ignored the signs. He recalled the agitated looks on her face when she tried to talk to him, only for him to change the subject. His own need for detachment, to keep the dirty work in the office, wound up forcing Diana to hide her truth in the shadows for too long.

Back at his apartment, sitting in a new, old pea-green chair he'd picked up from a nearby thrift store, Marty pored over files from a new case that Dennis had been working on in Marty's absence. Allowing himself to drift to the bottom, deep into his work, was all he could do now.

ꓛUT OF THE ꓑICTURE

The tones were sepia, but Sylvia would have bet all of last year's investment returns that the man's eyes were a turquoise blue. Beneath the edges of his army side cap, she could see his coarse hair, cut short. Thin lips stretched around a toothy smile. He also bore the familiar sliver of a white scar across his chin.

Sitting on uncut grass with his hands resting on his knees, he didn't seem concerned about dirtying his olive-green service coat or matching slacks. Crow's feet made the man look old, but something about that face reminded Sylvia the lines had more to do with the hard quality of his years than their number.

"Ms. Hawthorne, are you okay?"

"Oh," Sylvia said, barely able to peel her eyes away from the photograph. "I'm fine, Clara." She managed a gracious smile, but based on her assistant's reaction, Sylvia didn't have a doubt in her mind that she came across as anything *other* than needing help. She must have been staring slack-jawed at the same spot for minutes.

She'd begun to doubt it would ever happen, to the point that she'd mostly forgotten. What sort of cosmic fate allowed this picture to wind up at an antique shop that Sylvia had passed many times but had only entered today on a whim? How long had it been here, waiting for her?

Clara started to turn away.

"Actually."

Her assistant paused while Sylvia opened the door of the glass curio cabinet and reached past the Hummel figurines and marble ashtrays. Her wrinkled hands shook slightly as she took hold of the dusty, twelve-by-fifteen picture frame leaning against the back of the cabinet. As she held it close to her face, she felt herself getting lost in the image once again.

"Do you like that frame?" Clara asked.

"Yes," Sylvia replied without hesitation. "I want to purchase this." The price tag made mention of 1918, Tiffany & Co. sterling silver, and $1,495.

Clara grabbed the frame and Sylvia reluctantly let go.

"It has a lovely finish," Clara said. "Anything else before we go?" She looked at her thin, white wristwatch. "You have a shareholders meeting in twenty minutes."

"No, just that," Sylvia replied.

"Okay, I'll have the clerk remove the photo and put—"

"No!" The panic in Sylvia's voice startled a couple who were shuffling through a box of rusted steel signs. "No, please, I like the picture. Make sure you keep it."

Clara narrowed her eyebrows and nodded. "Yes, of course. No problem." She stepped away with the frame. Relieved, Sylvia closed her eyes and put a hand on the corner of the cabinet to maintain her balance. She pictured the man in the photo, trying to count the years in which she had last thought of him. Trying to remember every moment together before he left for France.

* * *

She let her plate of sliced turkey and asparagus grow cold on the china and her hot tea had since turned room temperature. It was late and the chef had left a note stating his apologies as he had to run home early because his daughter was sick, but he'd left simple instructions on reheating the meal.

It was no matter. Sylvia wasn't hungry. All she cared about was the photo propped up on the mahogany dining room table in front of her. Except for the low sounds of Bing Crosby's rendition of *Let Me Call You Sweetheart* playing on a modern record player at the other end of the room, the house was void of life. Sylvia hadn't listened to this song for a long time, and given her decades-old distaste for it, was surprised to find she had the 12-inch in her collection.

Sylvia reached for the frame and began to remove the copper backing. Once the photo was out, she tossed the frame onto the floor where it cracked in half.

Her mauve fingernail ran over the man's face and body.

"Hello, Samuel," she said. "I always knew that if it was meant to be, this day would come."

She turned the photograph over and her breath caught in her throat. The print was wider than the frame and it had been folded over at its rightmost edge to make it fit. She unfolded the edge so that the complete picture was before her.

Her expectations were met.

There was a young woman standing just to the right of Samuel with bobbed hair and a hobble skirt with its narrow hem. The woman smiled, but only with her mouth. Her eyes betrayed an infinite sadness.

"And hello to you too, young Sylvia."

* * *

The photographer was putting away his equipment while a thin breeze brought the scent of purple-flowered plum trees into Sylvia's presence.

"I told my parents that we would meet them at seven for dinner," Samuel said.

Sylvia said nothing, thinking only of their snapshot in time, wondering if she was able to hide her melancholy from the camera's eye. If Samuel noticed, he didn't let on. He took her hands in his and kissed her cheek. Sylvia gazed past the trees and at the calm lake spread wide behind them.

"Don't," Samuel said.

She turned. "What?"

"Don't think about tomorrow."

She was a fool to think he hadn't seen her. "How can I not?"

* * *

The needle had fallen off the record, leaving a quiet, rhythmic click in the background, no different than her life after the first war. When Samuel didn't come back, Sylvia had fallen into her own quiet, rhythmic click. She married three times, none of the marriages happy, none of them lasting long enough to produce any children, but they were all productive in their own way.

Sylvia focused her energies on other things. She was a pretty girl and had no problems attracting men of means. Men she had used more than they had used her. Where other wives had taken their positions and situations for granted, Sylvia built herself a quiet empire. She'd purchased the right stocks, made the right connections, and pissed off the right people to leave her one of the richest women in New Jersey.

Would she be willing to give it up for him? All of it?

After sixty years, the question was as simple to answer as it had always been.

She picked up the telephone and rang her good friend, Dr. Alou.

* * *

He came quickly with his dark brown briefcase.

"Thank you for coming in the middle of the night, Doctor."

"For you, Ms. Hawthorne...for this opportunity," he said, "I would come at any hour."

He was a grateful man. Where others had insisted on immediate results, Sylvia had bid her time and bet on the long-term. She'd heard Dr. Alou speak at a futurist conference over thirty years ago and immediately took him under her employ. Academia had scorned and ridiculed him. He hadn't been allowed to publish in any legitimate scientific journal after revealing his theories, but Sylvia cared not about that. The man had a fierce faith that was much like her own.

"It's time to put all of your years to use," Sylvia said.

Dr. Alou's eyes lit up behind his horn-rimmed glasses.

Together, they walked into the spacious sitting room and sat next to each other on a flowery Victorian sofa. She blended in well, but with the wild gray hair horseshoed around his balding head and Levis tucked into a pair of cowboy boots, Dr. Alou seemed as out of place as Sylvia suddenly felt.

His bony fingers rested on the top of the briefcase which sat on his lap.

"You should know that we've been unable to test," he said. "The risks, and all, as we've discussed…"

"Understood. Carry on." Her heart was racing, but she'd long since developed the ability to exude an air of control.

Dr. Alou popped open the brass latches, gently removed a sheer black box with a numeric keypad on top, and placed it on the mahogany coffee table before them. He then pulled out a pair of thin green wires, each connected to a white electrode. He plugged the other ends into a receptacle on the side of the box.

"May I?" he asked, nodding at her face.

Sylvia nodded. She wanted him to just get it over with.

Dr. Alou reached into his pocket and pulled out a pair of alcohol swabs. He ripped their packages open and, leaning over, rubbed Sylvia's temples. The chemical smell seemed to awaken her thoughts, seemed to bring home the fact that all of her years had been riding on this. Did she want to go through with it? Would she be able to live with the disappointment if it didn't work?

She knew she wouldn't be able to live with the disappointment if she didn't try.

"How long will it take?" she asked.

"You won't even know its happened."

His lack of hesitation reassured her. He placed the electrodes on her and she held the photo of young Samuel in her hands. Out of the corner of her eyes, she saw the doctor carefully punch the keypad. There was a subtle hum rising from the box and into her brain.

"Think of him," Dr. Alou said.

Her thumbnail caressed the side Samuel's cheek, stopping only when the room spun beyond her ability to perceive it.

* * *

"I told my parents that we would meet them at seven for dinner," Samuel said.

Sylvia's jaw was slightly sore from holding the smile. She watched the photographer carefully dismantle his tripod and box camera contraption. It took great effort to focus on something as the sudden bout of vertigo overcame her.

"You're not still worried about the expense, are you?" Samuel asked. "Dear, when are we ever going to get married again? We have only one honeymoon."

There was a moment where Sylvia's brain seemed to freeze up. She'd lost a sudden sense of place, but the world began to stabilize again.

"Pumpkin, are you okay?"

She felt a reassuring hand on her back and the other on her arm. The warm sun pressed its rays into her face and the light ammonia-like smell of Samuel's lye soap entered her nostrils.

"Yes," she said and turned to look at his face, starting at the scar running up his chin, past his azure eyes, and to his slightly kinky hair. She stepped back and took in his pinstripe vest and collared stark-white shirt.

"Do you need to sit down?" he asked.

She grabbed onto Samuel and pulled him into her, feeling his slightly-whiskered cheeks against hers.

"No," she whispered. "Please, no."

"Well, I don't know what's brought on this sudden bout of amorousness, but perhaps we should visit all the parks in France if it's to be a new habit."

He chuckled and so did she. A small tear ran down her cheek and onto his shoulder.

"I don't….I don't know what's come over me," she said, "but I just feel this sudden need to hold on to you, Samuel. I can't describe it, other than to say that for the briefest of moments, you seemed so far away from me that I feared I'd never be able to touch you again."

He gently pushed her away and took her hands in his. His eyes sparkled with life.

"I'm not going anywhere without you," he said. "Besides, what fun is visiting France without someone to share it with? Though I suppose then I could tell you some fabulous story of how I had tea with the visiting Kaiser and convinced him that his recent celebration of one hundred years of peace with France did not have nearly enough fireworks."

Hobo Lilly

I swear, as the blade's tip grazed my cornea, I saw Lilly.

Not in reality—she wasn't on this cramped freighter—but in my mind.

My daughter was still five, swishing that long blonde ponytail in the air as she bolted out from behind her father's leg and toward my open arms. He was spitting venom through the same brown eyes by which our daughter expressed nothing but love. I could smell the flowery shampoo in her hair as I told her to be a good girl and that because mommy and daddy were going their separate ways, it didn't mean mommy didn't love her. I wasn't strong enough to tell her the truth, so I told her I'd see her soon. We rubbed our noses together. I called it our special little bunny kiss.

I knew it would be a long time before we'd meet again.

The warm vision was temporarily knocked away by sweat-filled hair slapping against my cheek, stinging as I ducked my opponent's follow-up swing. On instinct, I thrust my own knife toward her rib cage.

Contact.

Not deep, but contact.

She shrieked and I nearly tumbled forward. The nylon rope binding us together dug into my left wrist as my opponent danced backward. My left foot skidded lightly against the corrugated steel floor in the struggle to remain upright. If I fell, I would have milliseconds to recover my exposed neck.

I didn't need to see the blood pooling onto her tank top to know I'd wounded her. I had *felt* the tiny chunk being taken out of her. Even in the dim lights of the freighter cabin, the crooked lines on her face spoke fury over the insult.

"Bitch, you got balls, but you should've picked another ride," she said.

I let her keep on.

Waste your breath, I thought. Keep swinging.

She came at me like a berserker of old. I remembered to breathe on tempo. Every lunge, every parry tested my abilities of concentration and patience. It wasn't long before I saw my opportunity, though. I could hear her panting and gasping over the crowd. She started looking away, growing more disengaged with every jab.

I yanked my left arm back just as she was mid-thrust, sending her on a collision course for the twenty or so grimy, cheering faces surrounding us. Like a swirling mass, they shifted as we shifted. I swept my right foot across her shins and watched her arms fly in the air in an attempt to cushion her descent. When her elbows cracked against the hard ground, the blade slipped from her hand. It clinked as it tumbled end-over-end and was quickly snatched up by the hand of an anonymous spectator. I climbed on top of her, took a handful of sticky black hair, and held my blade to her throat.

I dipped my head to her ear and whispered, "I win."

She struggled to regain her wind, but when she finally did, she started to laugh—harder and harder until the laughter turned into a coughing fit.

There was no more resistance in her now.

I rose and hovered over her, letting her turn onto her back. She looked older than when she'd first challenged me for twenty credits and now I felt a twinge of embarrassment. The sweat had cleared away some of the dirt on her cheeks and beneath her eyes, unveiling a map of wrinkles and dark circles on her chiseled face. I extended an open hand. She accepted and I hid the reaction to the pain in my own body as I struggled to pull her back onto her feet.

"Bitch, you got balls," she said, handing me a cryptocard with one hand, pressing her shirt against her wound with the other.

* * *

I pulled out a pocketbook of The Matron's essays and began to reread my favorite—*On Suffrage and Humanity's Value*. The e-paper had a large crack running through the middle, but someone once said beggars shouldn't be choosers—especially one that doesn't beg at all.

"You going to dig on Staxis or hop on another hauler?"

Iona was her name.

All I wanted to do was read and fall asleep doing so, but that wasn't going to happen. A woman who was willing to mortally wound me minutes ago was set on being pals. That's just the way it is on the loader ships.

"Not sure," I said.

There was no real point in hiding my search for Lilly, but it was a family matter and I always kept such affairs close to the vest. Most of the hobos riding on these freighters were here for two reasons, and depending who you talked to, in different proportions:

One, they were running away from the rest of the universe—after all, that's how I ended up hoboing across the galaxy in the first place. I had to leave a man who'd pulled a one-eighty on me. As soon as he was close to 'being someone' in the system, there was no room for my differing viewpoint. My story was only one flower from the same garden of motives the hoboes pulled from.

Two, the work was steady so long as your body was. Governments had encouraged exploration of the galaxy's far reaches by promising mineral wealth to those willing to seek it out. Entrepreneurs jumped on the prospect and with most of their money spent on logistics, mining robots were an unnecessary expense—hungry humans were cheap and reliable enough.

All that said, no one needed to know my next job was more than a means to a meal.

Over the years, I'd tracked my little girl through the networks, keeping a motherly eye on her whenever I could. There were times when I'd tipped back too many bottles of *Stardust*, almost convinced that I should finally meet her in person. I never gave into the temptation. Why would she want to see me? The woman who'd given up on her twelve years ago? How to explain that her father had grown tired of my dangerous ideas, had it out for me, and that the only way to make a life for myself was to strike out on my own?

It wasn't until I learned that she'd taken up hoboing that my heart broke enough to seek mending. Had she known that was the road her mother had chosen? Thought it was some romantic and poetic adventure?

I prayed that wasn't the case, but I remember being seventeen once too.

Through years of developed personal connections and searching through the hobo bulletin systems, I learned she was last seen on Staxis six months ago.

That was the final kick in my ass.

That's why I'm here.

Fighting.

Reading.

Occasionally trying to sleep.

"I killed a girl at the last gig," Iona said.

I don't know what sort of reaction she expected out of me.

"I felt bad," she continued on, apparently not expecting anything at all but a willing ear. "Didn't meant to, but I caught her trying to brute-force the passkey on my credit account two planets ago. I took a rock to the side of her head and musta' hit the sweet spot."

I didn't even look at her but I nodded, worried that Lilly would try something similarly stupid with another hobo. There were at least two or three Iona's working every gig and sometimes you couldn't tell who it was until it was too late.

Iona droned on about an ex-girlfriend who refused to share food. I closed my eyes and tried to fall asleep, hoping to dream of my little girl.

* * *

I was too late.

She'd moved on three-and-a-half weeks ago to Persephone.

When I'd last been to that dim planet, it was a place where the telorite rock was hard and the people were harder. I'd done a small stint there when I first started. It's not that it was too trying on my bones, though it was, but I left because the library was shit. People were encouraged to jack into whatever period piece drama was being broadcast on the spectrum or else spend their leisure time smoking opiates and screwing. I tried to organize them, get them reading, listening, but that's when I learned that one can't play a long game too quickly, otherwise you're sure to lose.

As soon as I got word about Lilly, I boarded the next freighter headed that way. It was only a day's travel, but having skipped work and therefore, skipped meals, it felt like a week.

At the back of the car, I sat down against any empty spot, one that least smelled of piss, and once again pulled out my pocketbook. I looked forward to picking up where I had left off, but the rumble in my stomach made it difficult to concentrate. It took only thirty or so seconds for my mind to wander toward my little girl. Would she look similar? Have the same features—the button nose, the single dimple on her left cheek that only showed up with her mischievous smile? I found no recent images tied to her name, so I could only guess and ask around when it came time to identify her.

"This is a hell of a noisy bunch."

The bearded interruption was bent over slightly at the waist. His knees popped as he slowly dropped to the floor beside me.

I tried to ignore him and continue reading. He twisted his head left and right before his bloodhound eyes finally landed on my book.

"Never saw much use in that."

I sighed. There would be no peace.

"Much use in what?"

"That. Readin'," he said. "Anything you learn from whatever's in there won't do you no good when some hunk of wires already knows it all just as soon as it's switched on."

I shoved the book back into my pocket, fully taking in the know-it-all. He was younger than his body and crusty beard let on. Behind the kinked brown hairs was a surprisingly smooth and unblemished face. He may actually have been close to Lilly's age.

"What makes you think I'm looking to challenge a machine?"

He raised his eyebrows, unsure of how to answer. "Just seems a waste of time, that's all. Wouldn't you rather have a conversation? Seems like one of the few things that can't be taken away from us."

How to explain what kind of conversation I valued? That every time I read a good book, I *was* having a conversation. It was already obvious that I wasn't going to find anything equal in him. Maybe the Matron had it all wrong. The more I got to know people, the less I got to like them.

Still, there was nowhere for me to go and even though I was a little sour on the inside, I made an effort to be a little sweeter on the outside. After all, each of us was on the same train, so to speak.

"How long have you been traveling?" I asked.

"This is my third gig. I hear Persephone pays the best."

I didn't have the heart to tell him that in his condition, he wasn't going to last three days.

"They're fair," I said. "You travel alone?" I asked though the answer was obvious.

"Yeah," he said and his head dropped down between those ramshackle knees of his. "I had some friends, at first, but most of 'em seem to be satisfied taking the same routes."

"What about you?"

He looked up and apprised the crowd surrounding him. "Nah, I have more of a sense of adventure than them."

He hadn't been able to keep up and I felt a pinch of sorrow for him.

"Just remember, life's more than credits."

The kid nodded slowly, but I recognized the look. He wasn't listening anymore. Second-guesses and regrets clouded his mind.

I took my book and handed it to him. He looked at me. "I told you—"

"In case you change your mind," I said.

* * *

Persephone station was teeming with bodies of every shape and size. Beneath the everdark skies, a mix of hoboes and vendors crowded the platform. Smells of synthetic lamb turning on spits sent my belly into a frenzy. I could spend the credits I'd won from Iona, but I'd been around the block enough to know that it was wiser to save them for when I really needed them. Though I'd hit what many would feel were desperate times, I knew better.

I knew desperate.

Just before I'd stepped out of the ship and onto the planet, I saw the young man still sitting by himself at the back of the emptied freighter, his eyes still maintaining that vacuous look, fingers gripping the pocketbook tightly.

Even if I wanted to, there was nothing I could do for him.

I checked the e-boards at the station to see if I'd received any updates to my queries.

Nothing. This was Lilly's last known spot. From here on out, I'd have to take matters into my own calloused hands.

I walked into the assignment office and stood in line with the rest of the weary souls. It took nearly two hours for me to reach the front where a tiny, fat man stood on a wooden stool that looked like it may tip over at any moment. And when I say tiny, I mean tiny—he couldn't have been more than four feet tall. Cobweb-thin strands of hair ran across his bald head and he wore a monocle over his right eye.

When I made no motion for the scanner sitting on the counter, he spoke robotically without peering up from his terminal.

"Arm."

"Manual," I replied.

That made him look. I could practically see the silvery orb focus in and out from behind the monocle. He sighed deeply.

"Number."

I rattled off my hobo code and a moment later, my photo came up. He scrutinized the screen. Then he scrutinized me.

"Ho ho!" A smile crossed his face, looking out of sorts. "A vet? A survivor?" He looked around the room as if any of the weary souls cared to listen to him. His eyes returned to mine and he leaned forward, balancing gracefully on the stool. "And you came back, *why?*"

"I'm looking for someone."

"We don't provide detective services," he replied quickly, "only work."

"Her name is Lilly."

There were grumbles behind me from hungry, impatient people. "What's the hold-up!?" someone shouted a few feet back.

"Can't help you," the fat man said, returning his eyes to the terminal. "You're assigned sector 12-B. Since you've ridden this rocket before, I don't need to tell you to dress warmly, make sure—"

I pulled out the cryptocard on which I carried my credits and slapped it down in front of him. Hoboes are typically in the system, but cryptocards are used for private transactions—they're exchangeable, but when properly configured, untraceable. He looked up again, eyebrows raised, and swiftly fingered the card. He turned it in his hand as his monocle whirred and whizzed. Finally, he jammed it into his own coat pocket.

"What's the name again?"

"Lilly," I repeated.

He raised an eyebrow. "Not much better than John Smith…" His fingers slid across the screen.

After a moment, he asked "Do you know when she signed in?"

"Three-and-a-half weeks ago."

"And you know her, how?"

"She's my daughter," I replied.

It was most definitely foolish to tell him, but I was so close to finding her.

Now, he raised his other eyebrow and looked up at me. I saw his fingers land on his coat pocket, tapping, hesitating. Finally, he reached in, pulled out the cryptocard and slid it back across the counter.

"She's in Elysium Garden."

* * *

The park was two miles away. I was shaking and panting as I ran the whole way. My legs felt detached. My head pounded. Why I was in such a hurry, I didn't know.

I finally collapsed onto my knees, ignoring the jarring pain.

She was there, all right.

I saw her name spelled out in stones. The third 'L' had shifted due to someone's careless boots, but the truth was undeniable. Someone had cared enough about her to leave the traditional trinkets—death-charms—around the grave.

I wanted to scream, but my voice was stuck in my throat. Tears refused to leave their ducts. All I had was a scorching numbness flowing over every inch of skin. I fell forward onto the mound and rubbed my nose into the dirt.

Our special little bunny kiss.

And then the tears flowed and I cried so hard that I couldn't breathe. I would have been quite the sight, had anyone actually visited this 'garden' of dust and short-lived memories.

I clawed at the dirt beneath me, feeling it run through my fingers. And then those fingers found something else. I rolled over and saw the tip of what appeared to be an old paper book sticking out from the soil. Another trinket, but one that had been buried just below the surface.

I pulled at it, ready to place it among the other deathcharms when I paused. First I wiped my eyes, and then I wiped the dust from the cover and realized why the book had been hidden.

On Suffrage and Humanity's Value.

My knuckles turned white and I started to cry again. A mix of pride and anger burned inside me.

I knew that Lilly couldn't die in vain.

I turned and looked through the gates of Elysium Garden, toward the long, straight road that led to sector 12-B.

I was in the system now.

I had work to do.

Let It Go

Segments of thought followed each other like train cars.

White van straddling the road.

Turn around?

No room.

Reverse.

Stop.

Another van.

Continue to play the game?

Continue.

* * *

"You won't come?"

"No."

The Troggs' *Love Is All Around* crackled through the coffee shop's ceiling speakers.

"I've already bought a few acres in Death Valley. We can live out of a trailer until the house is built. No one will know we're there." Howard swirled his speckled-white mug of coffee and put it to his lips. His hand shook ever so slightly while steam fogged the bottom half of his huge glasses.

The place was nearly empty. There was a pair of young men sitting in a booth on the opposite side of the restaurant. Judging by their crisp white shirts and black ties, they had to have been Mormon missionaries. At the counter sat a chubby long-hauler wearing a baseball cap. He was leaning onto the counter, exposing an ass crack just begging for someone to drop a coin.

"I can't," I said. "Not now."

Howard's expression soured. It wasn't the coffee. He set the mug down and cradled it like a baby bird that had fallen from its nest.

* * *

I put the Chevy in park, dead-smack in the middle of the two-lane highway, and turned off the engine.

To my left was a steep drop down the 1,500-foot canyon while to my right was a flat wall of dynamite-blasted limestone.

They'd chosen a good spot and my first instinct was to feel betrayed.

Facing what was coming was an easy choice. There was nowhere to run.

It was freezing outside. This big rock on which I found myself was too far from its sun. I'd been with my boyfriend, Sidney, for two months but we weren't yet at the point in our relationship for me to suggest we leave Ohio for warmer climes.

Obviously, Death Valley was knocked off any potential list.

* * *

"Alpha, you're free to do whatever you want. You're no one's prisoner."

I tipped my head to the side and raised my eyebrows at him.

"Any more," he finished.

As if seeing him for the first time in three months wasn't enough, his words all too easily triggered memories of humming fluorescent lights and cold, metallic environs.

"I'm sorry," he said. "I know this is all rather sudden. It's just….I figured we could, you know, start over."

I laughed loud enough to draw the attention of the Mormon boys.

"Start over?" I asked. "Is that why you called me out here?"

Howard took a handful of pink packets from their ceramic holder and placed them on the table, lining them up in the shape of a triangle. It was a nervous habit he'd exhibited over the five years I'd known him. It helped him think, he had said.

Thick brown hair on the back of his hands peeked out from his coat sleeves as he pushed the paper soldiers across the formica, moving them forward one-by-one, trying to maintain the pattern.

"I *helped* you." His voice was quiet and his eyes were locked on the packets as if he were addressing them. It was obvious how much he was trying to contain his emotions, but maybe only to me.

"I *cared….care….*about you."

"Howard—"

"If it wasn't for me," he said, "you wouldn't be here. You wouldn't be with him." He looked at me for the briefest of moments. Tears streamed down his face—streams of water which I was still trying to comprehend, having no faculty to produce them myself.

The tiny bells hanging on the front door rang as someone left the cafe.

"The others would have kept you locked up in a cage like some sort of zoo exhibit," he finished. I looked down and saw sweetener spilled all over. He had torn the ten packets in half.

The situation was delicate. I had to be careful, but I had to be direct. I reached out and laid my hands atop his.

"I appreciate everything you did for me. I really, really do."

It was difficult to see him this way, so I glanced out the window onto the slush-covered parking lot, watching the trucker step carefully around the building to avoid falling on his ass.

"But what did you expect to happen when you let me go?"

* * *

I should have realized he could never have truly let me go.

My feet hit the pavement and I strode around toward the passenger side. The frigid air made my insides ache.

I suppose I could have told Sidney the truth when we first met. The whole truth: that I had been living freely in the world for only a month before we laid eyes on each other. That I originally came from a place I'd never be able to see again, my only means of transportation destroyed.

And after telling him everything else that had happened since my arrival, I'd have to tell him the most unbelievable thing: that I had felt an obligation to see Dr. Howard Benevolo when he reached out to me, even though he was one of the men who aided in my captivity for five long years.

None of that mattered now, though.

The oncoming van came to a stop forty yards away.

* * *

"There's a big gap between knowing and doing," he said. "I *knew* we couldn't keep you there. It didn't make it any easier to let you go, though. At the time, I thought my infatuation was with the work itself, but I was wrong. Maybe a failing of our species."

He chuckled.

"But can you say with all honesty that you never felt something for me?" he asked. "That we didn't develop something more? I know the beginning was hard. I know."

His lips were saying one thing, but his eyes another.

I exhaled slowly. My flesh still felt the pinch of the needle, a visceral memory of when they would draw my blood at all hours. Each physical pang was associated with a crisp memory.

Its physiology is almost unremarkably similar to ours.

It took little effort for me to recall sleepless nights spent monitoring the drones in lab coats at the same time they were monitoring me. The clipboards in their hands. Their constant scribbling.

Nothing extraordinary. Its mental capacity and IQ is that of a twenty-two-year-old college graduate.

"Of course I felt something for you," I said. "My reaction was natural. You treated me like a person where others didn't. The rest of them only wanted answers to their questions, no matter how they got them."

Howard turned his palms up to meet mine and I felt their clamminess.

"That's right," he said. "I was the only one who cared. Who *really* cared and who, despite your best efforts, could see you for who you really were."

A shadow fell over the table.

"Ya'll good here?" Our waitress smacked her gum as she touched up Howard's coffee.

"We're fine," he said, wiping the remnants of his tears with a napkin.

She looked at me.

"Okay. Well, ya'll just holler if you need anything."

* * *

Five men in front of me: four in black carrying their standard M1As, the fifth as well, but still wearing his trucker hat.

From the van behind me emerged three more soldiers. A man in a crisply pressed suit and aviator glasses followed them.

Howard stepped out last.

* * *

We were silent until the waitress made her way to the other side of the cafe.

I could practically feel the sweat leaving his pores.

"You people have a saying," I said, "'If you love it, let it go,' right?"

Howard smiled, but not too broadly, and squeezed my hands.

"I'm sorry," was all he said.

* * *

I'd learned everything I needed to learn in those five years.

I was no longer constrained.

The men approached cautiously. I supposed they thought it would make a difference.

"Alpha," said the man in the suit and tie. The sun reflected off his sunglasses and he smiled a smarmy smile. "We've been concerned about you." He looked at the scientist beside him. "Howard made a mistake, for which he's partially atoned. We need you to come back home. We have more work to do."

It took all of half-a-second.

Except for Howard, each one of them collapsed onto the ground like crumpled tissue paper. I smiled at him and he waved gently before I hopped back into the Chevy.

The van in front of me was still in the way. I focused and its tires began to spin. I steered it past the guard rail and watched it dive over the edge.

I cranked up the heater and drove toward home, wondering how Sidney would take to the idea of moving into the Sahara Desert.

A Pinnacle to Heaven

And my flame made a pinnacle to heaven

As I walked once round it in possession.

–Robert Frost, *The Bonfire*

"I'm bustin' out, Sol."

Tony Pistratta shrugged his shoulders and cracked his neck like a boxer getting ready to go another round. The temperature was a nice 78 degrees. Low humidity. A slight breeze. It reminded him of the time he took a trip to San Diego, assisting his employer with a troublesome client. Back then, he thought it was the most perfect place on Earth.

Now he walked home with his only friend and a stomach full of pastrami on rye, but still feeling unsatisfied.

"You're full of it," Sol said. "Forget why you're doing it. Where you gonna go?" There was little humor in his voice.

Tony hadn't thought too hard about that. Why should he? He always was of a one-track mind. He hated overthinking things. In a former life, more former than his recently clean life, he was a dog player at the tracks. Went with his gut and felt his way out of things. Those familiar feelings returned.

"It don't matter, but I'm done. No more harps, no more people smiling for no goddamn reason, and no more of this thing following me around everywhere." Tony reached up and knocked on the glowing golden ring hovering over his head like a big brother.

"I think you need to get your noggin checked, kid."

Kid. Sol reminded Tony of his grandfather, even kind of looked like him, only he wasn't. His grandfather was somewhere else. A place that got a bad rap, but that Tony was certain was a hell of a lot more fun than where he was at. Since Tony arrived, Sol had taken on the wise old man role. Almost like how a buddy is assigned to you during your first day of school, but this buddy had a silver widow's peak sharp enough to impale a goon and puffy red bags beneath each eye that made it look like he was smuggling poker chips.

He was a good guy.

"You know what your problem is?"

Tony stood with his hands in his pockets, staring at the old man with raised eyebrows that said *educate me*.

The old man flicked the side of his head with hard finger. "You left whatever lick of sense you may have had, down there." He pointed toward the ground that supposedly lay far below the thick layer of clouds on which they stood.

"Yeah, you forget already?" Sol said. "You finally did the right thing. You confessed your sins. And I don't mean you just said what you did wrong and went on with the rest of your life. You *confessed* them, Tony. We all heard you up here."

Sol shook his head so long that Tony thought it was stuck in motion, like one of them clacking ball and magnet paperweights that sits on the desks of CEOs. "You turned your whole life around just to get on the VIP list and now you say you wanna leave?"

Shit, Tony thought. Was he being rash? His hand motioned towards the coat pocket he didn't have, searching for the pack of smokes that didn't exist.

"I didn't know it would be like this," he said. "I don't think I've been here two months and I feel like I'm gonna lose it."

"132 years."

"Huh?"

"132 years, but it probably feels like two months. Time's a little different here."

They walked among skyscrapers. All of them shined. Smooth white marble adorned with gold trim, they reached into a set of clouds even higher than those on which they stood. Like Manhattan, only without the street noise and stench. Why they gleamed, Tony never understood. There was no sun in sight. Just a radiant light bleeding out of every available space.

People of all types populated the streets, some walking just like

Tony and Sol, others riding in carriages pulled along by some sort of quiet, invisible machinery. Every face was plastered with a smile, but to Tony, their eyes seemed to be hiding something.

Sol said, "Let's say you find a way to break out. You think those cherubs are just gonna let you walk…float…jump…whatever, right out of here?"

"What's going to happen if I try?"

Sol stopped walking and grabbed Tony's arm. His grip was strong for an old man.

"Look, Tony, just think long and hard about this. You ain't a goomba eatin' clams down at Don Peppe's anymore. Don't throw this away."

The expression on Sol's face reminded Tony of a pleading bloodhound.

"You sound like you know somethin'," he said. "Level with me. What's gonna happen if I try?"

"I don't know anything. Can't say it's ever been done before, so long as I've been here."

"How long's that? You never told me."

Sol sighed. "A long time, Tony."

They continued walking in silence until they reached Sol's apartment. The two of them parted ways and Tony didn't look back.

He never looked back.

* * *

Night arrived, though it never got truly dark here. Instead, there was almost a permanent dusk, purple and orange. There were no streetlights to be found. Only a glow that surrounded the Heavens. When he left his apartment, there were still people milling about, a few sitting on stoops and outside of cafes that smelled of weak coffee. Most people were sleeping. Tony didn't understand the purpose of sleep anymore. He never felt tired. Still, many people carried it on as if it were a habit they weren't interested in breaking.

He'd been walking for awhile now, and though he hadn't found the edge yet, Tony wasn't going to turn back. There *had* to be one. He remembered how clouds looked when he was on Earth and they always ended.

Hills of white fluff beckoned him and on he went until he finally reached a point of exhaustion. To be in Heaven and still be out of breath. It was a funny thought. He fell to his ass on an undistinguished cloud, kicked off his shiny black leather shoes, and rubbed his feet. If not for the random changes in elevation, Tony may have felt like he was walking in circles. There was a small fear of getting lost, but the shining beacon of the city remained at his back. Not that he considered it an option.

"Are you lost, Tony?"

A voice emerged from above him. It was garbled. Almost like

when you talk to someone on the phone and the signal is weak. He looked around.

"Huh?"

"I said, are you lost?" The voice sounded clean now, somewhat hoarse, and it was obvious where it came from.

He looked up and saw the ring above his head. It glowed orange and red as if it had just been pulled from a fire.

"You found me," it said. The ring vibrated like it was giggling.

A corner of Tony's mouth turned up.

"Sol, you fuckin' with me?"

"No one's fuckin' with you," the voice replied. Its tone sounded so odd, Tony had to laugh.

"And this isn't, Sol," it said.

Tony's heart skipped a beat.

"What are you looking for way out here, Tony?" it asked.

Tony stood up and stared as much as he could at the ring. It was difficult because it was always on the edge of his vision. It aligned with the top of his skull and if he moved, it moved.

"I don't answer questions unless I know who I'm talkin' to," he said.

"No matter. I know why you're here."

"Then why you askin'?"

"This happens every once in awhile." The voice sounded so

impersonal. As if it could have been talking to anyone. "You should know that. You're not the first person, and you won't be the last, to think there's something better out here. Even if you could see what you're missing, you don't want to, Tony. Trust me. Go home."

His head began to hurt. He was suddenly thirsty and he couldn't remember the last time he drank anything. One of the downsides to his impulsiveness was a lack of planning. He brought no water with him. No food. Did it matter anymore? Maybe not, but the feelings in his stomach and throat told him it did.

"The cafes are always open, as you know. You like, what, cannolis? Pasta with a thick red sauce? Have you been to Salmucci's yet? They make a good martini."

Tony chuffed. "Yeah, if you like them fruity virgin drinks. Not a drop of liquor in this place."

"Alcohol brings trouble."

Tony ignored the comment. "I assume that by the fact you're talkin' to me through this…contraption…that you have some know-how. You a cherub? Without mouths, maybe, you know, this is how you guys communicate."

Silence was the only reply.

Tony's stomach churned. He swore he smelled stewed tomatoes. He shook his head like he was trying to clear a settled fog. The realization settled in that he wasn't going to get what he wanted. At least not today.

"Yeah, alright," Tony said. "I could use a bite." He knelt down and put on his shoes, suddenly feeling reinvigorated. He asked, "You want to tell me who you are or not?"

"You can call me the Don," he said. The ring vibrated again as Tony sensed another childish giggle.

The Don. The Man of Mystery living in the Grand Palace who supposedly ran the whole shebang.

"Yeah, okay, *the Don*. Thanks for the advice."

* * *

Seeing a waving set of hands, Tony skipped Salmucci's and wandered instead into a cafe named Tiki Piña. Sol was sitting on a shaded patio and waved him towards a seat. If not for the hollowed-out coconut sitting on the table, capped in tiny, colorful umbrellas, Tiki Piña wouldn't have looked much different from the hundreds of other cafes spread throughout the city. Airy piano music filled the room. Something like jazz. Completely unfitting for the name. It was also the most boring jazz Tony had ever heard.

The men exchanged small talk, ordered teriyaki chicken, and Tony told Sol what had happened.

"Just chalk it up to another lesson learned," Sol said. "You don't seem any worse for the wear."

A faceless waiter brought Tony the same decorated drink as Sol. He wondered if he could get to the straw without losing an eye.

"You think I'm going to let that stop me?"

The chicken arrived. It was sickly sweet and after the first bite, Tony pushed it towards the center of the table. Sol seemed to be enjoying his own and stabbed a fork into Tony's pieces.

"I think that your head is just as hard as it was yesterday. I could take a sledgehammer to that thing and I'd probably have to buy a new one."

Out of the corner of his eye, Tony saw two muscle-bound cherubs floating silently down the side of the street, inches off the ground. It always unnerved him, their quiet. He'd never gotten used to their lack of mouths. Instead there was only a patch of flesh. But they seemed to be made for simple purposes. They were soldiers, policemen, guardians of property. A distant memory surfaced of Tony's days working with other enforcers. He could have used some cherubs back then.

Sol seemed oblivious to their presence and he was going on about something regarding the sauce on the chicken when the cherubs stopped abruptly just outside of the cafe and entered the patio.

Tony once had a keen sense for trouble. It was still there, lurking under the surface, but now he kicked himself for letting it grow dull. The cherubs hovered over to the table and looked down at Sol. They ignored Tony. Each grabbed an arm and lifted the old man effortlessly from his seat. A forkful of chicken fell from Sol's hand and somehow clinked on the clouds beneath their feet.

Tony jumped out of his chair.

"Hey, what the—" he said, but his plea was cut off as he was pushed back down into the chair by the free hand of one of the cherubs. It felt like being crushed by a '41 Continental.

"Tony, don't start no trouble." Sol's voice was oddly calm as he hung between the arms of the cherubs like laundry drying on the line. "I'm sure they just got some questions. Routine stuff." He looked like a little old baby in their arms. The people sitting around them watched without expression. The piano man never let up with the faux-jazz.

It took all of his nerve to sit and watch as the cherubs carried Sol out of Tiki Piña and turned into tiny specks moving toward the Don's Palace.

Questions? How the hell were they gonna ask 'em, Tony wondered.

* * *

Sol was right. Time's a little different here. Though he hadn't seen his only friend for what could have been minutes or millennia, Tony made a decision as soon as they laid their hands on the old man. Now, he sat on the perfectly cut green grass of one of the many perfectly landscaped parks, pretending to soak in the sunless light. All the while, he recorded notes in his head. Patrol schedules. Routines. Fixed action patterns.

Tony smirked at the regularity of it all. Though they were big and strong, the cherubs would have never lasted two seconds on Mulberry.

He twisted the thin wire around in hands. It felt familiar. That was good. Tony doubted the piano man at Tiki Piña would notice only a clack coming from the underused high F-key.

* * *

Tony pulled until his hands bled. He wondered if the cherub was screaming inside. This guard was number four of four and he put up the hardest fight. Still, getting into the palace was easier than Tony thought it would be. This is what passed for security?

Maybe he should have been more suspicious, but for the moment, he focused with a white heat on finding Sol.

* * *

The palace looked much bigger on the outside. After running through a couple of ivory-tiled hallways and up three sets of stairs carpeted in purple velvet, he found what he was looking for. Through the powers of deduction, not to mention a bright red and white plaque that said *The Don*, Tony kicked open the only door at the pinnacle.

As it flew open, a hint of a thought told Tony he was being a little too carefree. Nothing else mattered now. He came this far and doubted any punishment handed out for the murder of four cherubs would be lenient.

Sitting on a white leather chair, aside a fire roaring in the most flamboyant fireplace, was one of the fattest, ugliest men Tony had ever seen. In one hand was a rocks glass filled with amber liquid. The other rested on the head of an ebony cane carved to look like a winding snake. It's tongue stuck out just beneath the man's palm.

He grinned with yellowed teeth.

"Not bad," he said. His voice was slightly hoarse. Tony recognized it instantly. The fat man took a sip of whatever was in his glass. Ice clinked. "Not bad at all."

Tony didn't have to be asked. He took the open chair opposite The Don. There was an untouched glass holding the same liquid and a couple of ice cubes.

The Don extended an inviting hand. "Salud," he said.

Tony took a sip. The burn was magnificent and he savored every second.

"I thought you said alcohol brings trouble."

"It certainly does." The Don took another drink.

"Alright," Tony said. "I'll admit I'm a little slow on the take these days. Where's Sol?"

The Don shifted in his seat. His movement released a horrible smell, like the decay of undisposed bodies. It was an odor Tony hadn't smelled since…before. He also noticed for the first time that there were two tall cherubs standing motionless in the shadowed corners at the rear of the room.

"Sol's no longer important. He got you here and that's all that matters."

"He matters to me."

The Don rolled his eyes and said, "Don't test my patience."

"Or what?" Tony felt oddly unafraid. He placed his glass on a table next to his chair, reached into his pocket and wound the piano wire around his fingers.

The two of them stared at each other until vertigo overtook Tony and he felt like he was going to fall into oblivion. He shut his eyes and leaned back into the chair.

"I work hard on maintaining a certain type of atmosphere here," the Don said. "We don't have a lot of trouble. I like to keep it that way."

"I wouldn't have thought there'd be any trouble in Heaven."

The Don burst into unrestrained laughter. Tony's body shook and his eyes snapped open in time to see the old man's chins quivering, one on top of the other like a stack of pancakes drenched in a syrupy sweat. Tears streamed down his loose-hanging cheeks. It seemed to be minutes before he recomposed himself. He pulled a red kerchief from a pocket and dabbed at his eyes.

"You're right, Tony. You *are* a little slow on the take today."

Tony felt his face flush. His temper, the one he had worked so hard on pushing against the very day he fell on his knees and confessed his crimes, came roaring back and he jumped from his chair.

"No more games you fat fuck."

He expected the cherubs to move on him, but they stood still. Tony rushed towards The Don, the piano wire lined up, ready to slide beneath the bottom chin.

He felt a snap and the wire turned limp.

He stopped in place and looked at his hands. A tiny snake started twisting up each arm. Tony danced like a gypsy having a seizure and threw the slimy bastards from his body. They slithered into the fireplace and disappeared into the flames.

The Don adjusted himself again and took another sip of liquor.

"You're to come under my employ."

Tony straightened up. His stomach climbed up toward his throat. There comes a time in everyone's life when the reality of a situation just hits you upside the head, sort of like Sol, and says, "You fuckin' idiot."

"I'm not in Heaven," he whispered.

The Don sighed. "It's a good thing I don't hire on intelligence." He set his glass on the table beside the chair and placed both hands on top of his cane. His eyes bore into Tony's as he lifted himself up from the seat. Tony swore it sounded like all of the air in the world had been released from a vacuum. The fat man grunted and groaned, his face turning redder than a tomato until he was finally wheezing on his feet. The top of his combed-over head came up to Tony's chest.

"But I confessed my sins," Tony said. "I did what I was supposed to do." There was a crack of pain in his voice now. "I turned my whole goddamned life around."

The Don grabbed Tony's chin, as gently as examining a flower, and directed his face down.

"There's always a scale. After decades of, if I might offer some praise, *beautiful* brutality, becoming Mother Teresa wouldn't have earned you a place in Heaven."

It took only a moment for Tony to compose himself. He had always been quick to accept a change in situation.

"Was this some sort of test? Killing your guards?" Tony asked. He shook his head. "What's the point? You're the damned Devil."

"I like a little drama." He giggled that little schoolgirl giggle. "In all seriousness, because I'm a serious man at heart, I occasionally run into a fella like you. Most folks, they come here, they're practically in a trance and they're satisfied. Yeah, it's boring as shit, but Tony…" He paused and leaned in as if revealing a great secret. "Most people *are* boring as shit."

Tony couldn't remember the last time he felt so helpless. His legs felt weak, shaky. He knew he was standing, but barely. He would have lost his bowels if he had eaten anything for lunch.

"It's been fun, but my appointment book is overflowing today. We'll talk soon." He laughed again. "Well, at least one of us will." He snapped his fingers and Tony watched him zoom by, chin by chin, until his eyes were at his feet, until he was falling into a darkness.

* * *

The player was at it again, playing the same damn riff. Tony wanted to tell him to learn a different song or else he would rip his fingers off. But he knew he couldn't—neither tell him nor rip his fingers off.

Instead, all he could do was float and watch Sol chat with a goon over sticky chicken and a coconut shell topped with too many tiny umbrellas.

The Owl His Anthem

Ernie smiled at the pinhole patterns on the drop ceiling and if he squinted just right, he could see at least six faces smiling back. A hint of bluish moonlight streaming through the tiny barred window put all of the shadows in the right places. Two of the faces were long and gregarious, one squished and wrinkled like a rotten plum. The others were just ordinary.

But they all smiled.

A tune had been running through Ernie's mind since yesterday and he hummed it as best he could. He couldn't recall where or when he'd first heard it. By repeating it aloud, he hoped to discover not just its source, but what made it so memorable. He picked it apart like a complex mathematical formula, figuring out how each variable served some purpose in a grander scheme.

A door handle twisted and clicked. Ernie stopped humming immediately and looked. Chilly air slammed into his exposed face while the rest of his body sweated beneath an itchy wool blanket.

"Ernie," a woman said in a harsh voice.

He ignored her, content to watch the faces.

"Ernie, I'm going to turn on lights," she said in that vague, Eastern European accent. Ernie tried to remember where she told him she had come from. Maybe she hadn't. He thought Yugoslavia or somewhere like that, but he was pretty sure that was no longer a place. Then again, he wasn't sure of much these days.

A flicker and then there it was—the hum of fluorescent bulbs. Ernie didn't even close his eyes. He let the brightness blind him. It was a challenge to fight the sting. He liked challenges, most of the time.

Kolinda sat a tray carrying two tiny paper cups on the bedside table. As Ernie's vision returned, he craned his neck toward her. She leaned over him and pressed a switch on the bed to incline his torso. On the way up, he caught a noseful of rosewater perfume. His eyes met the top of her breasts which were slightly exposed by the cut in her uniform.

She looked up and caught his eyes. An irritated look swept over her face, but she stood up and straightened out her top. She wasn't young and had a big nose, but Ernie was never a picky man and he wasn't going to start being picky under the current circumstances.

"Open," Kolinda said.

She placed one tablet and a large pill onto his tongue. Always bitter and Kolinda was always slow to give him the other cup of water to wash away the flavor. The one and only time he swallowed his medicine without waiting for water, the back of his throat burned for days on end. She didn't seem to be changing her attitude now, taking her sweet time to get him the water.

"Good," she said. She crushed the paper cups in her hand and her tennis shoes tapped lightly against the floor as she beelined for the exit.

"Nurse Kolinda," Ernie said. The scent of rosewater was fading and his throat felt rough.

"What?" she said, still facing the door, impatience in her voice.

"Can you please leave the lights on?"

She remained silent for a moment. "What, you afraid of boogeyman?"

Ernie said nothing, only looking at the back of her graying brunette hair tied up in a bun.

"How is it boogeyman afraid of other boogeyman?" she asked before flipping off the lights and shutting the door behind her.

The deadbolt clicked into place a second later.

* * *

The smiley faces were back, but they didn't seem to be smiling so much anymore. At least, not in the happy way they had before. In fact, their smiles seemed to grow oddly threatening as they widened like the one on that cat from the old story with the little girl.

Ernie wanted to shut his eyes. He really did, but he was afraid to let his guard down. He didn't know why. There was no active threat. Nothing tangible to fear outside another monotonous twenty-four hours of either sleeping or barely remaining awake inside this hell of an institution. So instead he kept watch, began to hum the tune again, and stayed vigilant against the nothing.

An itch crept up on his forehead. Futile as it was, he naturally tried to scratch it. He wiggled his arms around in their restraints. They'd been stuck at his side for so long, Ernie found it hard to imagine a time when they had been separated from his torso in the first place. Those doctors, he thought, they sure do a fine job of keeping things tight. He supposed they had a reason to be so thorough.

He lifted his eyebrows and shifted his head back and forth, hoping that scrunching his brow and general movement would do the trick.

No such luck. The itch kept on itching.

He stopped humming the tune and groaned.

The moon's rays cut in and out against the ceiling and wall like a hand passing over a flashlight. It had to be a bird, given that he was on the second floor. At least he was yesterday. Or maybe the day before.

What kind of bird, Ernie wondered. He'd like to see birds again.

The flashing continued several times until the moonlight disappeared altogether.

Click.

Click.

Click.

Something was tapping against the glass. Ernie craned his head as much as physics and anatomy allowed, but he couldn't see the window directly. He dug his fingers into his palms and flexed his forearms. To comfort himself, he started humming again.

Click.

Click.

Click.

"Go away!" he yelled, presuming a crow or a pigeon saw something it liked inside. The clicking stopped. Silence overtook the room once again, like a strange pressure bearing down on Ernie. "No, wait," he whispered. "Please, come back."

His eyes felt heavy and his chin bounced off his chest as he fought sleep.

Click.

Click.

Crash.

The sound of glass hitting the floor in a hundred pieces echoed across the room. Ernie's voice was caught in his throat. He wanted to scream for Kolinda, but his neck muscles tensed up. He stared at the door, waiting. Surely someone would come rushing in to assess the situation.

There was the sound of something rubbing against the iron bars, like a piece of steel wool on cast iron. It vaguely reminded Ernie of his days scrubbing his fingers raw against dirty pots and pans, all underneath canopies of hot, soapy water. The days not long after he'd gotten sick and lost his position at the University.

The rubbing continued, ending only with a heavy thump on the linoleum and the shadow bars projected on the wall once again.

The ceiling was all smiles.

* * *

"Nurse!" Ernie screamed, knowing it only escaped his mind but never his lips. His throat felt dry again. He desperately wanted another tiny paper cup of water. The smell of crisp midnight air entered his nostrils. It reminded him of recent nights he'd tried to forget but had been forced to recall in innumerable conversations with the doctors and the investigators. Smells of the countryside as his shovel catapulted worm-filled earth over his bent back.

There was a pitter-patter mixed in with the sound of something being dragged on the surrounding floor. Ernie turned his head. He thought he saw the tip of something pointed and furry in the last bit of moonlight before it entered the darkness-swept area beside his bed.

"Who's there?" he asked.

"Who's there?" came a reply, unearthly and garbled like poor radio reception.

The thing, it schlumped and schlepped up beside the bed and even though it was only inches away, Ernie's eyes perceived nothing but black mass. He swore he felt the blood pressure rising within his arteries as a heat passed through his entire body. Sweat poured down his head and streamed into his eyes, stinging them.

Yet he left them open.

"What do you want?" he asked.

"What do you want?" came the reply.

The thing's breath was like a steam kettle which boiled a mix of manure and sulfur. Ernie wanted to turn away but was more afraid to expose the back of his head and neck to this thing which he could not identify.

"Stop repeating!" Ernie tried yelling again, begging in the back of his mind for that cup of water. His throat felt so raw. Where was Nurse Kolinda?

"Do you want to scratch that itch, Ernie?" Though the voice was choppy, Ernie didn't seem to have any trouble understanding it.

"What?"

"Do you want to scuttle around? Dance like you used to with the Mrs.?"

"Leave me alone!" Ernie shouted. "Kolinda!"

"She can't hear you," the voice said. "And besides, she don't care."

He tried to scream louder and it was the pain and hiss coming from his throat that forced Ernie to realize he hadn't said a single word. Everything had been spoken only in his head. His larynx was still wound as tight as a noose. The feeling dredged up more memories that finally forced him to shut his eyes.

"You're not real," he thought. "Whatever you are, you're not real."

"What's reality, Ernie?"

"Tell me what you want," he said. "Or just kill me!"

"Kill you? Why would I want to kill you? I'm here to help, Ernie. Always have been. Seems they've sent me away for a bit." Ernie thought he heard the echoes of a crinkling paper cup being crushed. "But I found you! Oh, I'm so happy that I found you!"

A lightheadedness fell over Ernie like a thick cloud, but every time he thought he would pass out, something pulled him back.

"Stay with me, old friend. Stay with me. You know, the old docs, they used to be good. Used to be almost vicious in their work. Near orgasmic shocks to the system. Chop-chop to the brain. I could respect that. *We* could respect that. But now—" The thing spit out noise like someone was changing channels on a TV at rapid pace. "What, with the feel-good pop psychology and these pretty little pills, it almost makes one feel ashamed. Don't you feel ashamed, Ernie?"

Ernie's first impulse was to tell how he had nothing to be ashamed of, but a greater lie would never have been spoken.

"I'm getting help," he said.

"By having your limbs tied to a bed and being wheeled around in a stupor for almost every hour of your waking life? How the hell can anyone call that help?" The thing clucked its tongue. "Nope, nope. This is much worse than I thought, what they done to you so far. Maybe they did get rid of all your sense, you poor thing."

Ernie felt something stroking his arm—the arm still beneath the blanket, tensed, and still, as the thing in front of him noted, tied to the bed.

"I'll be better soon," Ernie said.

More garbling and Ernie thought he heard something wet splat against the ground. "Better. That's a landmine of a word if I ever encountered one. And soon? No, buddy, not soon enough. But I'm here to help. I can give you *soon*. I can make soon a reality. Is that real enough for you?"

Ernie's ears were alight. The warm breath that was against his face shifted to the other side of the bed. The bed's tiny motor vibrated and hummed as Ernie felt the bed began to elevate, as if Kolinda was there pressing the button to bring him to a sitting position. He was elevated to a ninety-degree angle when the motor came to a stop.

"What are—"

The thoughts were interrupted as he felt something pungent punch through his airways and jet down into his insides. Gagging, choking. It was like Ernie's guts were being clenched and yanked up into his esophagus. He leaned over and vomited all over himself, feeling chunks of gelatin exit his mouth and the bitter taste of medicine coating his gums.

After a few dry heaves, everything finally seemed to stop. The warm breath returned to his face, keeping him on the edge of nausea. Ernie's eyes were watering and he became distraught. Why could he still see nothing? Why had his eyes not adjusted to the darkness surrounding his person? He looked at the ceiling and saw the smiling faces were now crying. Smiles turned upside down.

"Shall we call for nursey?" asked the breath.

* * *

Kolinda contemplated the blinking red light on the terminal beside her desk. She had five minutes before the end of her shift. She could have left him for Sandy to take over, but she felt a certain obligation to the man. She knew she shouldn't. The things he had done, or at least what they said he had done—she tried to imagine herself in the victim's shoes or as one of her relatives. My, how they must have felt.

But Nurse Kolinda saw a pitiable old man who appeared to have every ounce of life sucked from him. She knew he would never get better. His type never did. But there were protocols and procedures to follow. The same protocols and procedures that paid her bills and let her go home every morning at five o'clock in the morning so she could nod off to reruns of *Coach*.

She unlocked the door and as soon as she entered, she thought she caught the whiff of the elm trees swaying in the wind outside—as if someone had opened a window. But the only window in this room was sealed shut and even if it wasn't, there was no easy way of opening the tiny thing as it was offset ten feet from the ground, butting up against the ceiling.

When her eyes finally caught up with her nose, her hands lost just enough feeling for the tray to slip and crash onto to the floor. A loud clang echoed through the room and into the hallway. Cool water splashed on her right ankle and her hands flew up to her mouth as if to keep her soul from escaping.

Crouched on the bed like an alley cat ready to pounce a rat, Ernie sat looking at the nurse, humming the tune she'd caught him humming for the past two days.

Protocols and procedures, she thought.

But drills were drills and Kolinda remained slack-jawed and frozen in the face of reality. While Kolinda was debating whether or not to hit the emergency page button attached to her uniform or run for the door, the decision was taken from her hands.

Ernie leaped from the bed and slammed into Kolinda, knocking her to the ground. The wind was knocked out of her, and the second be-fore she regained it, the second before the scream began to leave her lips, Ernie's hand clasped over her mouth. His face was inches from hers and she could feel his balmy, putrid breath penetrating every pore in her flesh. It smelled like feces and mud.

Ernie pulled his face back and his expression shifted between bliss and sadness, like quickly-turned pages in an animation flip book. His red eyes shifted left-to-right as he looked into Kolinda's own pupils. Yellow crystals of dried phlegm hung around his sockets like algae on a stone. All the while, he kept humming the tune.

As her breath was leaving her, she recognized the song, falling asleep once again to the theme of *Coach*.

ᛋHIPLAP PLAGUE

Sara's bloody nose.

As Devin lay against the worn polyester couch in the hospital waiting room, immobile, vision blurred, the connection jolted him as if someone had hooked his spinal cord up to a car battery. Not that first signs mattered at this point, other than to appease Devin's insatiable need to know. He tried to focus on his wife's face, but the lenses of his eyes refused to cooperate. He could only see the faint outline of her body collapsed over that of a patient she had been checking on—what, maybe ten or fifteen minutes ago?

She always put others before herself. It's why she wanted to become a doctor in the first place. It's why they both became doctors.

And now they were the patients without anyone left to tend to them.

Thinking back to the morning, Devin realized his watering eyes were probably the second sign that something was very wrong in the town of East Warhaven.

Of course, they brushed the symptoms off as hay fever, all too easily attributed to the unusually dry air and wind they'd been experiencing. Spring pollen was in full effect this year.

The notion that something bigger was at play didn't take long to come to him, though. At 9AM that morning, they had dragged themselves into short-staffed St. Margaret's Hospital after a reserved, yet obviously urgent, call from the head of ER who informed them that an unusual number of patients were flowing into the hospital and they needed all hands on deck.

First, it was the elderly and young children. Bloody noses, teary eyes, and trouble breathing. By 5PM, there were more patients than beds and the town's population had been slashed in half. The CDC was supposedly on their way, but Devin couldn't recall who had said that and if it was even true.

Since he couldn't dial in on Sara's face or even generate enough force to move his body close enough to hold her hand, he closed his eyes and tried to remember happy moments of their life and the new life they had begun to build.

It was the kind of small-town life Sara would have dismissed a couple of years ago, but the nightly shootings, stabbings, and recurring drug-addicted patients had taken their toll and he had been able to convince her that a change would be good for them. On a visit last month to see family in Virginia, they came to the decision. It took them only one day to decide on purchasing a white plantation-style home with a wraparound porch and a beautiful view of the Blue Ridge Mountains, marred only by an old shiplap shed—the shiplap shed which they had reduced to rubble the evening before everything went to hell.

* * *

"You hide, we'll find you," Nate Henderson said. Robbie Silva's head bounced up and down in agreement.

Katelin thought the boys were rowdy, but she didn't have any brothers or sisters of her own to play with and the two of them were the only kids within walking distance. She thought it was odd that they'd want to play with her, given that she was ten and they were thirteen or fourteen. They'd also ignored her for as long as she could remember. But, a playmate was a playmate, so any qualms she had flitted away just as fast as they'd come.

Counting down from twenty, they hid behind a willow tree in the half-mile-long copse between her house and Nate's. Katelin's heels reached into the air and her baby blue dress caught the wind as she rushed into her backyard. She thought about hiding in her house and watching the boys through the kitchen window, but she worried that if they found out she was hiding somewhere off-limits, they wouldn't want to play with her again. Looking over to the corner of the yard, sheathed in foot-tall bluegrass was her father's workshed. It was empty. Papa had taken Katelin's brother and Mama to town for groceries and to pick up some hardware needed for a new project. This was the second time Katelin had ever stayed home alone.

"You don't leave the house. You don't answer the door for strangers. Any trouble," Papa had said, "you know where the rifle is." Katelin didn't know if her father expected a band of robbers to swoop down on the house as soon he left, but she only said, "Yes, Papa."

Of course, ten minutes in, she was bored out of her mind with only three television channels, so when Nate and Robbie came knocking at her door, she jumped at the opportunity to play hide and seek. It wasn't as if they were real strangers. They went to the same church, had gone to the same school before they went on to junior high, and their parents had known each other for even longer.

"Wheeeerreee areeee yoooou?"

Nate's voice echoed across the landscape as Katelin quietly closed the shed's wooden door. She stifled a giggle and looked for a good hiding place. It was dim inside. The only light came from a small window of frosted glass just above her father's workbench. She climbed up onto Papa's stool and saw the outline of the two boys creeping onto the property line. Quickly, she remembered the storage cabinet standing tall in the corner of the room. She was small enough to fit on the bottom shelf, so she ran over, opened the cabinet door and crawled inside. She closed the door behind her, tucked her legs up to her chin and wrapped her arms around her knees. Heavy scents of wood shavings, turpentine, and grease filled the air in the cramped space. She hoped the boys wouldn't force her to hide there too long as the fumes were already starting to give her a headache.

It was only seconds later when the shed door squealed open on its hinges.

"Weeeee're gonna fiiiind ya!" Nate said again.

* * *

The tiny excavator dug into the shed with its faded black claw. Dust flew into the air as one corner of the dilapidated shack came crashing into the ground.

Sweat ran down Devin's cheeks. His lips were sealed shut in a grimace and Sara could see every vein in his taut arms peeking out from a worn, sleeveless gray t-shirt. A pair of translucent goggles covered the top half of his face and he had orange earplugs stuffed into each ear. He looked back at Sara who was standing on the porch, hands on her hips. As if he had been pulled out of deep thought, his expression changed quickly into a plastic smile.

Sara was surprised he wasn't having more fun. In her experience, something in the male blood couldn't help but get men excited when it came to knocking things down and breaking them into hundreds of pieces.

An hour later, the two of them stood at the kitchen sink. Sara wrapped her hands around Devin's bicep and leaned into his shoulder as the majestic Blue Ridge Mountains rose in the distance, flooded in orange twilight and completely unobstructed. Despite some obvious adjustment time, Sara had to admit she'd fallen in love with the house and the whole notion of country living. She'd trusted Devin to find them a place, knowing that he'd grown up somewhere in the area. Given how quickly they'd come upon their new home, he'd obviously done his research.

"I know we'll be happy here," Devin said, gently stroking his wife's head. "There's not a single doubt in my mind that we made the right move."

She looked down at the ugly pile of wood at the end of their property line. The junk guy would be by the next day to haul away the debris.

"I know," she replied.

Feeling her nose beginning to run, she grabbed a paper towel from next to the sink and wiped. Devin looked down at her.

"Honey, you're bleeding," he said.

* * *

"Kaaaatelin."

Through a crack in the cabinet door, she saw the two boys skulking around inside the shed. The floorboards creaked beneath their mud-covered boots while the two of them whispered to each other.

Nate's auburn hair fell into his eyes and shaded the freckles on his face. Robbie had a nose like a pig's snout and a gap in his two front teeth that created a little whistle whenever he said certain words starting with *s*.

Robbie looked at the cabinet and Katelin shrank back. Her head hit the bottom of the shelf above her and she bit her lip. She could still see them through the thin crack when Nate raised his eyebrows and they both flashed grins.

"What do you think, Robbie? She hidin' in the cabinet?" Nate's voice sounded exaggerated.

"I don't know...Maybe we ought to check," Robbie replied.

They crept over and stood in front of the cabinet. Katelin held her breath.

The cabinet door came flying open and Robbie ducked down to meet Katelin's face.

"Boo!"

She shrieked and hit her head again.

The boys laughed while Katelin crawled out of the cabinet and dusted herself off.

"No fair!" she said. "You followed me."

"Fair and square," said Nate.

She rubbed the top of her slightly tender head. "Your turn, I guess," said Katelin.

Nate looked at Robbie and Robbie looked at Nate.

"Okay, but let's rest a minute first," Nate said.

Katelin stepped towards the door, but Nate pulled out in front of her and leaned his back against it nonchalantly.

For some reason, Katelin didn't feel right. She wasn't sure if it was the vapors from the chemicals in the shed or something else. She tried to hold back a sense of panic. "I can't stay out late," she said. "My folks are gonna be home soon and I'm not supposed to be outside."

"Hold up," Nate replied, dipping his head toward his friend. "Robbie wanted to ask you something."

With that ugly smile still stuck to his face, Robbie stared at Katelin. He inched toward her and put a hand on her shoulder. Katelin shrank back on instinct. The hair on the back of her neck rose up like a cat's and she started looking around for a nail or something to throw at the boys.

"I gotta go," she said, her voice quivering slightly.

"Go ahead," Nate said to Robbie, ignoring her plea. "Ask her."

Robbie didn't say anything, just stared down at her with dumb eyes.

"You chicken, I'll say it for you," Nate said. He looked at Katelin. "Robbie wants to kiss you. He says if you don't let him kiss you, he ain't gonna play with us no more. And if he don't play with us no more, than I ain't gonna play no more either."

Katelin wanted to puke at the thought of the gross boy's lips coming anywhere near her. "No way!" she said. She wished her dad kept a rifle here too like he did at the house, if just to scare the two of them. "If you don't let me out, Papa's gonna get angry and come after you both with his gun."

Nate laughed so loud, it hurt her ears. "Hear that, Robbie? We gonna' get plugged by the old man. Well, if that's the case, we're definitely gonna need a kiss before we kick the bucket."

Katelin heard the low whistle through Robbie's teeth as he let out a soft, hissing laugh. Before she knew what was happening, Robbie's sweaty hands squeezed her arms and pull her into him. His phlegmy breath cut through the other smells of the shed as he pressed his lips all over her face, struggling to make contact with her own lips as she flipped her head back and forth.

Robbie giggled like a lunatic.

She screamed her first scream, which was also her last because as soon as she started, Nate came barreling over and rapped a palm across her face, shocking her into silence. Her face grew hot from the pain. Had Robbie not still held onto her, she would have fallen onto the ground like a sack of potatoes.

"You shut your mouth and let Robbie kiss you," he said. "And if you scream one more time, we're gonna hurt you bad."

Katelin started to whimper and tears dripped down her face. She tasted something metallic and realized that blood was streaming from her nose and into her mouth.

"Please," she cried. "I won't say nothin', just let me—"

Her voice was cut off as Robbie pushed her down. The back of her head slammed onto the floorboards and her vision went blurry. Robbie felt so heavy on top of her and his breath was even more pungent then before, now that he was breathing hard. He lost his grip on Katelin's right arm which she quickly brought up, grabbing ahold of Robbie's ear and twisting it.

He screamed like a cat whose paw got caught in a mousetrap.

She thought she heard Nate yelling at him to shut up, but the only thing she truly noticed was Robbie's elbow coming down on her throat like a blunt stick. She tried to scream again, but only a gurgling whistle came out. Katelin panicked as she found it hard to breathe. Robbie let go of her other arm and sat back on his knees, gripping his ear and wincing. Katelin grabbed her neck as if it would help open her airway.

Nate ran over, stared down at her and then looked at Robbie. "What the hell did you do?"

Robbie looked stunned, hand still on his ear, and said, "Nothin'! I was just...."

The taste of blood Katelin had noticed earlier was pooling into the back of her throat, making it even more difficult to breathe.

Nate's head flipped back and forth, his eyes darting between her and the window.

"Let's go," he said. He grabbed Robbie by the shirt sleeve and yanked him onto his feet. Though her head swam and her everything sounded muffled, Katelin heard the fabric tear across Robbie's t-shirt.

"It was an accident—"

"I said let's go!" Nate said, throwing open the shed door, causing it to slam against the wall. His footsteps vibrated across the wood floor-ing, followed swiftly by Robbie's.

Katelin was trying to cry but she couldn't take in enough air which made her panic even more. She dug her fingernails into the floor-boards, trying to overcome her sudden lightheadedness. Trying anything to get more air. For a few seconds, she hoped and prayed that her folks would be back soon but she knew deep down that it would be too late.

Finches chattered outside. Katelin stared at the outline of raf-ters overhead. Only bits of air worked their way in and out of her lungs. Blackouts came and went and somehow she knew that she was dying.

Emotions grew confused within her as she thought about being left alone out here. Surprisingly, she wasn't sad. She was going to miss her family, but mainly, she focused her thoughts on the sickening smiles of Nate Henderson and Robbie Silva.

As she stared at the shed's shiplap ceiling, Katelin felt only a red-hot anger at what the boys had done to her.

* * *

Devin fell in an out of consciousness. He was sure Sara was dead now. Visions of his life played randomly in his head like film clips.

His wedding on a beach in San Diego.

Turning his tassel at graduation from St. John's Medical School.

His sister's vacant eyes.

Replayed with vivid color and sound, it seemed like only yesterday when he found Katelin laying face-up in the shed. Barely dried tears ran down her blue cheeks. Blood streamed from her left nostril onto her upper lip. Images of his father rushing past him to pick up her limp body. His mother's unearthly howl as she collapsed outside of the shed's door.

He thought he could come back and make things better. A culprit was never found. The family moved away a year later, trying to pretend as if nothing had ever happened.

But Devin remembered. His dreams never let him forget.

Coming back to knock down the shed was something he had to do. Now he drifted into black and realized just how wrong he was.

Katelin had her own idea of closure.

The Sun Stone: An M. G. Towne Adventure

Jump!

The singular thought snapped into existence, zipped down the spinal cord and raced through every nerve ending of one M. G. Towne—professional archaeologist, amateur conspiracist, and world-class imbiber of spirits.

That lone notion wasn't lone for long. As M. G. leaped carelessly down the yellowed limestone steps with his pocket-sized flashlight bouncing off the inner tomb walls and a heavy backpack slapping into his kidneys, an image of a mouth-watering Tom Collins entered his mind. It was enough motivation to get out and get out quickly. Given the gallon of sweat pouring down his head, he feared he wouldn't make it back to the bus let alone back to the hotel bar in time to enjoy a fine cocktail. At the age of sixty-five, he was reluctant to admit he was half the man he used to be, but somehow twice the size. If security found him unconscious on the ground, they'd surely search his backpack. Nearly a year of planning to snatch the artifact would have been all for naught.

M. G. could see beams of sunlight as he neared the entrance. The unwanted cell phone in his pocket buzzed over and over again. He cursed himself for even bringing the damnable thing, but his assistant, Carla, made him promise to take it when he was traveling and he never knew when it may actually come in handy.

Get with it, old man, she had admonished, *I even made sure it was an ancient flip phone—just your style.*

It had taken him a half-hour just to figure out how to turn the ringer off and though the soundtrack may have been appropriate, he didn't need to broadcast a beeping rendition of *Flight of the Bumblebees* in the middle of a heist.

At last, he was outside.

Twenty or so of M.G.'s fellow tourists were lined up beneath the steady sun, only half of them with white sunblocked noses, but each and every one of them entranced by their guide's ability to blabber on about basic Egyptian Middle Kingdom stuff. M.G. attempted to casually insert himself behind a stocky, overweight woman wearing a flowery sundress and floppy hat. He nodded and smiled as the guide spoke. Even if he'd forgotten twenty times in historical knowledge than what that chump knew, M.G. still would have had a hard time paying attention. He was too focused on catching his breath, trying not to stand out. Obviously failing, the woman turned and gave him a disgusted look, then stepped to the other side of the group.

If his peers saw him now, an inch of white belly peeking out from the bottom of his khaki shirt, they would joke that "he was too old for this shit." A part of him wondered if maybe they weren't wrong, but M. G. ignored the possibility. This discovery was too important.

As if connected to his thoughts, the artifact pressed into his back like a hot poker and he thought he heard a low hum emitting from within. Every remaining minute of the tour was almost unendurable, but by some miracle, he eventually found himself sitting on a lumpy bus seat carrying them back to the *Al Bustan* in Cairo. Upon entering his room, he pulled out the cell phone and counted twelve missed calls from Carla.

* * *

"What!?" he exclaimed. He wanted to put off the call for at least another thirty minutes so he could head downstairs and suck down that Tom Collins, but he knew she'd continue hounding him.

"Where are you?"

"Prague, remember?."

"Oh, that's right. Well since I know *that's* a lie, maybe you can tell me the truth about why you shut down the Komesh Painted Cave for maintenance."

M. G. grumbled. The two of them led the excavation and preservation of sacred Komesh Indian land and artifacts along California's central coast, so he had taken a risk to do so without telling her.

"Hold on, hold on," Carla continued. "Let me see if I can answer that for you. I'm just going to take a wild stab here and say that you've been surfing the alien conspiracy forums again, came to the conclusion that the Lisht Sun Stone has some sort of intergalactic connection to the cave, and decided to play Indiana Jones."

M. G. hated his assistant director and potential successor for the same reasons he loved her. She was the smartest archaeologist he knew— besides himself, of course. "Since you know such much about my whereabouts and plans," he said, "you should also know the artifact was just sitting there in a minor tomb, barely remembered."

"Probably for a reason," she said.

M. G. refused to answer.

"Well," she said, "even if you're going to play the derring-do antiquity thief who sloppily leaves behind a travel itinerary sitting on his desk, I'd appreciate the courtesy of having at least one of my phone calls answered. I might have something important to say, you know."

"Yeah, sure." M.G.'s thoughts drifted to the bar downstairs. He could almost smell the squeezed lemons sitting beside the bottle of *Tanqueray*.

"Shut up, please, and listen," she said. "So, while I was out checking on the cave, trying to figure out just what maintenance was needed, I noticed something odd."

He remained silent, but she had his attention now.

"Aren't you going to ask me what I noticed?"

"What?" he said, failing to sound nonchalant.

He knew she was pausing for effect. She loved to tease him.

"There was an odd...humming...coming from the rock behind the painting."

Questions piled up in M. G.'s mind like a car accident on the I-5 freeway. "Do you think someone's going to hear it?" he asked as calmly as possible through his state of inner frenzy.

"Doubt it. I only noticed because I was so close inside."

A deep exhale made his whole body shiver in release. "Good."

"And just to iterate, you're really bad with the details. My memory extends beyond that of a goldfish, you know. Did you really think I'd buy that excuse of you going to a conference in Prague? Not only do you hate small talk, but they banned you from returning three years ago. They still haven't forgotten the raining frog incident."

"I was just trying to prove a point," M. G. said.

"You certainly did that."

He said nothing more, worried she was getting too involved in his extracurricular affairs. It wasn't that he didn't trust her, but there were some things a man had to keep to himself, no matter how poor a job he made of it.

"Anyway," she said. "I don't know why you think the cave and stone are connected. Granted, the humming is a little weird and I'm sure you have one of your crackpot theories involving alien technology, but my guess is it has something to do with ferromagnetism and atmospheric conditions. There could be a deposit of iron in those cave walls."

She was the Scully to his Mulder, always dousing any flame burning inside.

"Well it's a hell of a coincidence that the Sun Stone is doing the same thing, then."

Now there was silence on the other end.

Sometimes it was just better to believe their separate beliefs.

"Look," Carla said, picking the conversation up again. "I'm crazy for even talking to, let alone aiding and abetting, a known antiquities thief, so just tell me when you're coming home."

He was relieved to change the subject.

"I'm flying out tonight," he replied.

"I'll pick you up at LAX tomorrow, assuming you make it. And if your little rock is indeed humming like the cave, good luck getting it past airport inspection. I'm not flying out to Egypt to bail you out on attempted terrorism charges."

"Yes, yes," he said dismissively. "I'll be fine. Look, I need to take care of one final thing, then I'm off the airport."

M.G. hung up the phone, changed his shirt and headed downstairs. Omar, the lobby bartender, smiled as M. G. approached and began pulling out all of the ingredients for a top-notch Tom Collins.

* * *

Getting past airport security had never really been a concern for M. G.. He'd smuggled so many treasures through corrupt checkpoints over the years, the ways were uncountable in which he could convince customs officers that a prized artifact was really a cheap memento he'd purchased at a gift shop—something by which he'd remember the beautiful people and lands which he visited. As a last resort, he was always willing to pay in cash for whatever 'fines' were required for whatever 'laws' he had violated. That was always part of the travel budget.

No, security wasn't the issue. The more pressing concern was the short man M.G. first noticed outside the terminal.

The pulled-down vanilla fedora, the pitch-black aviators, and the tan coat which ran from chin to boot seemed strangulating in the heat, but M. G. initially thought nothing of it. Even the surgical face mask concealing most of his face wasn't *that* unusual. Perhaps the man had an embarrassing disease. Such was common in third-world countries.

It wasn't until M. G. checked in and sat down on a stiff metal bench that the alarm bells began to sound off in his head. He tried to be clever with his newspaper, peeking over and around the edges, avoiding any signal that he was aware of the man's constant hovering presence.

And then his nervousness grew when the shadowy man stepped in line a few people behind him to board the eighteen-hour flight with a layover in London.

Finally, he had taken his seat and the man brushed by him, smelling of must and mildew. M.G. tried to make out identifying features, but all he caught was his own pale reflection in the dark sunglasses. His feet clasped tightly on the backpack. He definitely sensed that the artifact's drone was much louder now, but luckily difficult to hear over the bustle of recycled air and boarding activity.

Now that he was aboard, his muscles stiffened and he ground his teeth. Sure, the stranger could just be flying back home or off to conduct business, M. G. thought, but the true conspiracist was never one to carelessly toss aside a gut feeling.

The man *might* be connected to the artifact.

He *might* be here to take it for himself.

Knowing he had to relax enough to think rationally, M. G. ordered a miniature bottle of *Teacher's* scotch. Occasionally, he turned and looked at the seats behind him, but the man was nowhere in sight. As M. G. sipped his medicine, he knew that he would have to get up to relieve himself at some point. He'd try to get a closer look then.

Three more bottles down and a pleasant warmth running through his body, M. G. pulled himself to his feet, secured the backpack to his person, and stumbled to the bathroom. His eyes bounced from face to face, not once seeing the man, but certainly made more difficult by the dimmed cabin lights. It was only when he'd slid the bolt along the toilet door that M. G. wondered if the stranger had also removed his layered outerwear, which would make it nearly impossible to figure out where he was.

M. G. closed his eyes and breathed a loud sigh of relief as his urine splashed into the bowl.

And then the familiar scent of mold entered his nostrils. A cold breeze hit the back of his neck.

His eyelids popped open and his whole body froze in fear. In the mirror, he saw the man squeezed between himself and the door.

M. G. shrieked and on instinct, jammed his arm back into the man's gut. M. G. cursed and winced as his elbow crunched against the rattling door. He turned, ready for a confrontation.

There was nobody there.

Then came a knock. "Is everything alright in there, sir?"

M. G.'s breathing grew shallow. He searched every corner of the tiny commode. He felt around for hidden doors and false walls. Zip. Zilch. The tell-tale smell had been replaced with the overly-sterile odor of an airplane bathroom. Finally, he unlocked the door and rushed out, nearly colliding with a short, chubby flight attendant.

"Can I help you with something, sir?" he asked.

M. G. frantically searched the aisles and the galley behind the bathrooms.

Nothing. Everyone was seated.

He straightened up as much as he could. "I'm fine," he replied. He squeezed by the snifter of a man and grabbed every headrest along the way, holding himself up while his legs wanted to give out. He sat down once more and held the backpack tightly in his lap, relieved to feel the outline of the Sun Stone. His seatmates were fast asleep. There was the radiant hum again, and though he was on full alert, the sound seemed to woo him, bringing him back to a more relaxed state. He closed his eyes, promising himself that he was only doing so for a moment. M. G. was startled when the plane touched down in Heathrow. He quickly relaxed again, hearing the low-frequency still coming from the backpack tucked safely in his arms.

* * *

The layover was entirely uneventful. M. G. was on full alert, avoiding all restrooms, but he never saw the man. By the time he landed at Los Angeles International airport, his bladder was full again and he couldn't hold back any longer. He urinated with paranoia. Thankfully, the airport bathroom was populated with only the smells of hand soap and urinal cakes.

At baggage claim, M. G. spotted Carla. With a youthful glow on her mahogany cheeks and sympathetic brown eyes, she looked as relieved to see him as he was to see her.

M. G. assumed she caught on to his cautious demeanor because the two of them said nothing until they were in her sedan.

"You seem extra nervous," she said. "Interpol on your tail?"

M. G. wasn't ready to tell her about the incident on the plane. He wasn't sure he was ready to accept it himself.

"No," he said. "Everything's fine."

"I figured this would be old hat for you by now. I'm curious, do you keep records of how many of these treasures you've collected throughout your lifetime?"

"Some things are better left uncounted," he said, remembering snippets of thievery—like the time he was almost spit-roasted by Shining Path guerrillas in Peru after a run through an Inca temple, or when he nearly lost his toes to frostbite after recovering the world's finest jade Buddha in a remote corner of the Himalayas.

"Interesting," she said.

"Not really," he replied.

"No. I mean I can hear the hum."

"Oh," M. G. said and inclined an ear towards the backpack. "You still think I'm crazy?"

"Of course," she said. "Sometimes, M. G., you can be annoyingly unscientific with your flights of fancy."

"I'm telling you, there's some connection here."

"A connection between an American Indian tribe in California and ancient Egypt?" Her incredulity practically dripped with each word.

M. G. didn't have the patience at the moment to get into all of the research he'd done. He was exhausted and just wanted Carla to drop him off at home so that he could sneak over the cave after she'd left.

So, he changed the subject.

"It's good to see you," he said. "I really do appreciate your help keeping things quiet." He meant it.

She flashed him her best *you owe me* look. "So are you going to fill me in on your plans?"

She wasn't going to let him off easy. Fine, M. G. thought, peering out at the sea of red tail lights in front of them. He turned to face her.

"First off," he said with a bit of sarcasm in his voice, "I don't think little green men are involved. I've never been one of *those* people. But I do believe in two things: One, there are powers and realities outside of our senses that we're unaware of day to day. Other dimensions, as some scientists have theorized. Two, ancient peoples are not given enough credit for their ingenuity and capabilities. There's plenty of evidence for a shared culture between the Komesh peoples and the Egyptians. That is if you're willing to see it."

Carla was focused on the road, but her eyebrows were in a perpetual state of up. "Okay, let's assume all of that is true—which is a *huge* stretch. Why did you feel the need to 'borrow' the stone and bring it here?"

"If I say why, you're just going to hassle me."

"Of course I am. I consider it a part of my job description."

M. G. shrugged. It was all or nothing. "I think the cave is a doorway to one of those alternate dimensions and the stone is the key." He braced for impact.

Instead of a biting response, Carla was simply silent. Perhaps she was quietly debating whether or not to drop M. G. off at the nearest mental institution. M. G. thought maybe he'd finally gone too far for even her to put up with, but he was a man of risks.

"Actually, it's sort of your fault," he said. "The idea began to stir based on those Egyptian astrology and astronomy books you lent me. I found the patterns painted on the cave to be tightly coupled with the stone. After rereading Komesh mythology and confirming some theories on one of my regular Internet forums, I felt that I was on to something. I needed to get the pieces together in order to figure out how they work in tandem."

More silence in response. M. G. knew he was pushing it.

"Before we get back to the lab and begin the real work, can we make a pit stop?" he asked. "I'm parched."

She reached behind her seat and pulled out a bottle of water.

"I was hoping for something with flavor," he said. "You know, there's a little place on the corner of Venice and Washington called Mahoney's——"

"Damn it, M. G., do you really need to have a drink right now? You know I'm not going to support your nasty habit."

"Fine, fine." He waved her off and took a swig of the tepid water while he watched the passing Los Angeles highrises. He didn't dare mention the frightening experience on the plane now, not after Carla's chilly reception. She *definitely* would have thought the whole thing was an alcohol-induced hallucination enhanced by a brain which had finally cracked. She must have been feeling overly sympathetic to help him this much. Perhaps she was jockeying for a raise, he mused. He opened up his backpack and pulled out his hat, taking a final look at the Sun Stone. From the corner of his eye, he noticed Carla couldn't help taking a peek as well.

He zipped up the pack and reclined his seatback. "Who thought sitting on your ass for a whole day would be so exhausting," he said before placing the hat over his face. "Wake me when we get to my house."

* * *

M. G. woke up feeling groggy, stiff, and as cold as ice. His breath was sour and he had to unstick his tongue from the roof of his mouth.

He shivered, smelling something lingering on the breeze.

Saltwater.

And then his ears registered waves crashing against stone as grains of sand blew onto his face.

Wherever he was, it wasn't home.

He reached up to remove his hat, only to discover two problems: first, the hat wasn't there and, second, his arms were bound tightly across his stomach.

"Carla?" he tried to say, but it came out more like a frog's croak.

He was lying down on his back and with a simple turn of his head, he knew exactly where he was.

The Komesh Painted Cave.

The gate securing the entrance was open and he saw a pair of shadows emerge.

"Carla?" he shouted, this time more clearly. "What in the devil is going on here?"

Carla stepped into the moonlight with a flashlight in her hand.

"G'morning, sunshine," she said without emotion.

He tried to peer around her and look at the second shadow.

"Who's with you? Why am I tied up?"

Carla grabbed his arms and helped him onto his feet. He'd never noticed just how strong she was.

M. G. was at a loss for words, grasping for meaning as to why they were here. Just as he opened his mouth to ask more questions, the familiar stench of mold entered his nostrils. From behind Carla, out stepped what could be described as a monster to be found only in the old zombie movies. Its flesh was a greenish-gray, shriveled and flaking, while the eyes were milky and translucent. Clumps of stringy gray hair fell from its head and across its face. Only a tattered cloth covered its torso down to its thighs and clasped in its left hand was the Sun Stone.

"This is Eneq," Carla said, stretching her hand out as if introducing the beast at a cocktail party. "I believe you two have met."

"The Sun Stone does not belong to you," the foul creature gasped. The sound made M. G.'s case of dry mouth seem minuscule in comparison. He suddenly remembered the pain in his sore elbow and his legs felt weak.

M. G. managed to steer his eyes back toward Carla, the sweet, smart-as-a-whip 27-year-old who'd quickly worked her way from intern to assistant director in a brief six years.

"I don't get it," he said. "You know about him?"

"Her. She's Komesh." She looked with sympathy at the shriveled thing. "Or at least she was. She's been slowly decaying for over 3,000 years, but being stuck between dimensions will do that to a person."

If M. G. could have reached up to scratch his head, he would have. He felt as if his brain could cook an egg.

"Come on, M. G., don't tell me you're suddenly a true believer in rationality."

"I don't know what to believe, right now," he replied. His eyes narrowed at her. "What do *you* have to do with all of this?"

"Really?" Carla said with indignance. "Did you forget I'm Komesh?"

He knew she had American Indian in her blood but had never bothered to ask her lineage. Had she mentioned it? Probably. He'd likely been his usual arrogant self, thinking it unimportant enough to ignore.

Carla continued without waiting for his answer. "My people have known of the gate for millennia, known of the power that exists behind it, but we've been unable to retrieve the key ourselves."

"So you needed someone with my skills and mindset to bring it to you."

Carla was grinning now. "You're not a *completely* useless drunk."

Like Pavlov's dog, just hearing the word *drunk* made his mouth water for the sting of gin. He could certainly use a stiff drink.

"I still don't understand how the key ended up in Egypt," M. G. said.

His curiosity required satisfaction, but he was also buying time trying to figure out a way to extricate himself. The coastal highway wasn't far from here, but it was a considerable jog up a series of steep trails. He didn't doubt Carla would have any trouble catching him in a fair race. Still, he realized she wasn't very schooled in tying knots as he began to slyly loosen his bonds.

Eneq's scratchy voice chimed in. "Because of me."

"What do you mean?" he asked.

The decrepit Eneq laid it all out for him: "I was the priestess who opened the gate. Many paid the price, not least of all me. The Komesh were once a great civilization until my mistake. I unleashed pestilence and creatures beyond that which you can imagine. After much hardship and death, I was able to close the door, but was cursed in many ways." She looked up at Carla and now her eyes had a sense of sadness. "A part of me had become anchored in the other place. I found that I could travel between our world and that place at will. In fact, I was forced to as I found myself rapidly decomposing if I spent too much time on any one side."

Carla added, "What was left of our people determined that such a thing should never happen again, so a group of them set sail on the ocean with the Sun Stone in hand. They were committed to making sure it was deposited somewhere far away."

M. G. interrupted her there. "If this thing is so terrible, why wasn't it just destroyed?"

"You think they didn't try?" Carla asked. "It's indestructible. The best that could be done was to take it far away from here."

"Okay," M. G. said, "So here I am bringing Pandora's Box back when your people worked so hard to be rid of it." He looked down at the rope wrapped around his wrists. "Maybe now you can tell me why I'm standing here with my hands tied, freezing my ass off to see you two bringing the pieces back together again."

Eneq's and Carla's eyes met simultaneously.

"For a clever thief, he seems very dull," Eneq gurgled.

"Do you think it was a coincidence that you happened to steal this particular artifact?" Carla said. "For a man who sees conspiracies on cereal boxes, you missed the conspiracy happening right in front of you. Who do you think led you on by loaning you books and posting a trail of half-clues in those alien abduction and flat-earther forums you subscribe to?"

It was another one of those magical moments in M. G.'s life where all of his far-out theories and assignations came together to form a perfect picture.

Carla continued, "We *want* to open Pandora's Box."

"By spending time in the other world," Eneq cut in, "I have learned some things. I've come to understand the monsters that live within. I've learned how to harness the powers within. We just didn't know how to do so when we first opened the gate."

"I see." Now for the question that he wasn't sure he wanted to be answered. "Well, since you could have just taken the stone while I was sleeping and left me in the car, why bring me here and tie me up?"

"Retrieving the stone was only one-half of the problem," Carla said.

Eneq said, "You are also here because those with Komesh blood are unable to open the gate. It was one of the curses I was forced to place on the stone after the gate was sealed."

Carla put on a devious smile. "Think about it, M. G. You can take solace in the fact that you'll be aiding a culture that you've spent so much time helping already. The Komesh can become a great power again, even more so than ever before."

With that, Carla picked up the Sun Stone from the ground and put it in M. G.'s hands. He balled his hands into a fist.

"And if I refuse?"

Carla looked out at the ocean. "How good are you at swimming with your hands tied together?"

A plan had rapidly come into place during their conversation. He would do what she asked.

"Fine," he said. "But I expect you to buy me a drink after this."

She simply sneered at him as he took hold of the Sun Stone. She pointed at a notch on the ground beneath the painted symbols. He walked over and dropped the Sun Stone into the slot where it slid in like a perfectly cut puzzle piece.

The hum was incessant now and the low frequency began to make M. G. dizzy. And then he saw the miraculous. It wasn't showy. There were no flashes of light—no strange zip or zaps to indicate to any-one but those standing in front of it that an interdimensional portal was spreading across the back of the rocky cave wall. Its dimensions reached that of about six feet high and four feet across.

The moldy stench of Eneq was amplified as a harsh wind broke through from the other side. It was a noisome and peculiar world. The zombie-woman seemed to blink out of existence and appear on the other side. "I will alert the otherworld forces that we are ready," she said, walk-ing to the left and out of the scene.

Carla stepped in front of M. G., entranced as she watched the bizarre dimension come to life. M. G. was saddened that he had only a few moments to take in its purple sky flecked with tiny blue clouds and endless maroon-tinted sand dunes before he would have to carry out his plan.

"You're forgetting something very important," he said. "You think you have this all figured out, but you're wrong."

She barely cocked her head. "Oh really? What haven't we figured out, M. G.? What haven't the very people who discovered this millennia ago learned?"

"I'm not the only one that misses the little details," he said.

He slipped his hands from the bonds that he had been slowly working himself out of and yanked the stone up from the floor. The hum began to soften and the portal began to slowly close.

Carla turned toward him and shouted furiously, "What are you—
"

Before Carla knew what was happening, he lobbed it into her arms. As she instinctively reached out and took hold of it, M. G. lifted a leg and kicked her with all of his might. She tumbled through the rapidly shrinking window with the Sun Stone in hand and collapsed onto the red sand.

"You didn't realize that the key only works in one direction."

"No!" she screamed and scrambled up on to her feet. But it was too late. The portal was nearly sealed.

He dusted the remaining sand off of his pants and spoke through the softball-sized gap. "I bid you a wonderful day, Carla, but I have to run. I hear Mahoney's calling my name."

M. G. took one final look at the cave before departing. The wall and its paintings were completely restored, as if they had never been touched.

It's a shame to lose such a good assistant, he thought. He reached into his pocket, pulled out the flip-phone, and threw it into the ocean.

Closure

He was afraid to leave her alone.

As Anita lay on what had once been their bed, Dominic sat in an uncomfortable folding chair beside her, slightly disturbed by the lack of things he used to take for granted—the expected rise and fall of her stomach that accompanied inhalation and exhalation, the fluttering beneath her closed eyelids when she used to dream, and a million other tiny indications that even though she was asleep, she would eventually wake up.

She was posed in almost the exact fashion as she had been the previous Saturday. Streams of reddish-brown hair flowed from her head, down alongside her shoulders and onto the comforter. Her arms were placed across her chest, one hand overlapping the other. Though the undertakers had tried their best, they were unable to adjust the restless look on her face. Anita appeared in death almost every way as she had for the twenty-six years of her life.

Dominic leaned over and pressed his cheek to hers. There wasn't much of a scent, but traces of something sulfurous lingered. The questions came rapid-fire to his mind, but he was afraid to ponder any of them too long.

Am I dreaming?

Will you ever talk to me?

Will you leave again?

It had only been a week-and-a-half since she had come to lay down in this very bedroom for what Dominic believed would be the very last time. He had come home from work to an empty pill bottle tilted over on the nightstand and a newly-formed crack running through his core. It felt like an entire year had passed since then, both emotionally and physically. Dominic had avoided mirrors since, but he was sure that if he looked into one, he wouldn't recognize himself. Unshaven black whiskers made his neck itch. His nose had adjusted, yet he knew he stank to high heaven. It didn't matter. The newly returned Anita hadn't seemed to mind, either.

How she came to stand at his front door earlier in the afternoon, Dominic wasn't sure. He also wasn't sure he cared. The drapes had been drawn on all the windows since Saturday. Several visitors had knocked on his door over the past few days. Dominic normally waited ten min-utes before opening it, just enough time for them to have gone away and leave behind a plastic-wrapped plate of cookies or a flavorless casserole. Always, there was an accompanying condolence card.

But today, it was her. As soon as he'd opened the door, she had stepped forward and he let her by as if it were the most natural thing in the world.

Now here they were in their bedroom again.

Dominic slumped into his chair and tilted his head back to work the kinks out of his neck. A swirling pattern of rainbow lights danced across the ceiling—red, green, and blue stars shot out of a cheap plug-in light machine that he had chivalrously won for Anita at the Hilton County fair two years ago. She hadn't wanted to go, but he'd somehow convinced her. It had only taken him a couple of years and she had a mostly miserable time, but she seemed to take a liking to the machine afterwards.

Mudvayne's *All That You Are* played quietly on a tiny CD player. It was her favorite song. Dominic often found her musical tastes a little depressing, but it was *hers*, and therefore it lost some of its glumness.

He wasn't sure what he'd gain from any of the lights or music. He supposed, hoped, really, that it would generate a memory or a reaction. Get her talking to him. But Anita seemed as introspective now as she had always been. She hadn't said a word since coming home.

The night gave way to sun at some point. The only indication was a small stream of light poking through a centimeter-sized gap in the curtains. Dominic sat and silently pondered what his wife's return meant for the rest of own life.

* * *

"I can't come in today."

"I understand, sir. Yes, I know the policy."

"Yes, but—"

"You do what you have to do, sir."

Dominic hung up the phone and turned to see Anita standing in front of the dining room table, staring out into the living room. He tried to figure out what she was looking at. He grabbed her hand and when she didn't seem to resist, led her in gently.

"What is it, Nita?"

Saying her name out loud didn't feel as strange as he thought it should.

Her eyes were unfocused, directed at an empty white wall, but she came to a stop in front of their loveseat. It was covered in an illustrated pattern of a country ranch, replete with chickens and horses and wood-post fencing. Dominic's parents had given it to them as a wedding present and though Anita hated it as she'd hated most of his things, Dominic had somehow convinced her to keep it in the living room. It wasn't as if they ever had much company over anyway.

"Do you want to sit?"

There was no response. Not even the slightest twitch. Her hair was slightly kinked from where she had been laying on it.

He tried to get her to sit, but her body was impossibly stiff.

Dominic whispered, "Nita, please, I don't know what—"

There was a knock at the front door. Dominic held his breath, triple-checking that the curtains were still closed and that there was no way for someone to peek inside. At the top of the door was a thick, yellow stained glass cutout in the shape of a half-circle through which he saw the profile of a woman's hair.

Anita slowly turned around and walked towards the hall. Dominic's pulse quickened.

There was another series of knocks and he thought he heard a muffled 'Hello.'

Dominic started to follow Anita, urging her on mentally. *Come on, come on.*

The two of them were almost in the hallway when he suddenly heard a click. He looked back and saw the deadbolt turn to the left.

Dominic made a decision and was forced to watch Anita continue her slow march to the bedroom. A draft of cool air swept in, fresh and not altogether unwelcome, as the door cracked open and sunlight pushed against the dark shadows of the entryway tiles.

* * *

"Dom?"

He was frozen between the hallway and the front room. The visitor's head appeared slowly through the opening of the door. Her blond hair was tied up in a bun and she wore a thin heather-gray sweater.

"Oh!" she said, narrowing her eyes in the dimness. "You're home." Even though Dominic sensed an effort, she didn't sound entirely surprised. The smile on her face seemed genuine enough, though.

"Uh. Yeah. Hi, Barbara." He tried not to appear nervous, flitting his vision back and forth toward the bedroom's threshold that Anita had almost entered.

Barbara was their neighbor of three years and single mom to a seven-year-old boy named Jacob. Though they'd lived next to each other for only a short period of time, Dominic and Anita had known Barbara since junior high. Barbara ran with a more popular crowd than Anita, though that was an understatement. Anita's crowd consisted of Dominic and herself. She'd never been one to make friends easily and Dominic had taken it upon himself to ensure she always had someone to talk to, even though Dominic found it easy to fit in with nearly every clique in their small town.

Anita was a different story. Most people stayed away from her. Dominic had been questioned more times than he could count as to what he saw in her, but he could never explain it to anyone's satisfaction. Maybe not even to himself, other than to say that he felt it his life's mission to make her happy since he had first seen her sitting alone, sullen-faced and scooping dirt into her palms in their kindergarten sandbox, watching it run back through her fingers again.

The door swung open slowly. Bundled in her hands was a foil-covered pyrex tray. "I was going to leave this on the porch, but….I didn't want any animals getting to it….and I had a key…."

Dom's face remained blank.

"Remember?" she continued. "You gave it to me for emergen-cies….um….I saw your car outside, but I wasn't sure….I'm sorry if this is a bad time."

She stepped in to extend the tray to Dominic. He moved quickly to meet her.

"Thanks," he said, taking the tray.

"I didn't mean to barge in," Barbara said. "It's just….your car hasn't moved for a couple of days." She tilted her head towards the covered windows. "The curtains have been closed…."

He felt moisture began to form under his arms as he tried to form a barrier between the front room and the hallway. He stared at her dumbly, capable of recruiting only a minuscule amount of brain power to process what she was saying.

"Chicken enchiladas," she said suddenly.

"Huh?"

She nodded at the dish in his hands. "My mom's recipe." He began to really see her now that she was closer—light-green eyeshadow, a thin layer of foundation on her cheeks, and pale pink lipstick. She smelled like a field of flowers. Dominic was quickly reminded that both he and the whole house must be giving off a terrible odor and he backed up slightly, but Barbara gave no indication that it bothered her.

"Pretty sure she got it off a can, but they're good."

"Oh."

"I'll go ahead and put it on the dining room table." She made a move to grab the dish.

"No!" he exclaimed, pulling away and feeling like a fool. She shrank back.

"No, please," he continued more quietly. "Thank you. You're too kind. I'll take care of it." Dominic rushed to the dining room table. The glass bottom clacked against the wood as he practically threw down the dish and almost skipped back to Barbara. He breathed a little easier seeing the hallway empty.

Just stay in the bedroom, Nita.

He bounced nervously on his heels. Now, Dominic and Barbara stood facing each other in silence.

"It's really dark in here," Barbara said. "Are you coming down with something? I haven't seen you since Saturday."

"I'm….I'm fine," Dominic stuttered. "I'm just….taking some time off from work."

Barbara nodded gently. "Look, I know you've been dealing with a lot. I appreciate that you invited me to the funeral."

Dominic wanted her to leave so badly, but he was a victim of his nature—always wanting to be the nice guy, even if he was uncomfortable. She was only trying to be cordial and he didn't want to be rude.

She suddenly straightened up and walked into the living room. "I'm going to turn on some lights. Don't want to fall. Then I'd have to sue you for all your worth."

Dominic wasn't sure how to respond to her unexpected movement and statement.

"A joke," she said.

"Oh," Dominic replied. "Huh."

With the flick of a switch, two lamps sprang to life and Dominic realized just how long he'd been cooped up in gloom. He squinted to see Barbara pick up one of the tiny pillows from the loveseat, sit down, and place it in her lap. She analyzed the country-life pattern like it had been hanging in the Louvre.

"Have I ever mentioned how cute this is?" she asked. "Reminds me of my grandparents."

She looked up at Dominic and patted the open seat.

His eyes darted back to the open bedroom door. Still nothing. Every second he acted like he was building bombs in his bedroom would be another second that increased the chance of Barbara learning that the impossible had happened. He was unsure of what to do now. Everything had happened so quickly and he needed time to figure things out, so he rubbed the murk from his eyes, and put on his best smile as he took a seat.

She fiddled with the pillow, flipping it around in her hands. "Jacob has been asking about you," she said. "He misses his play buddy."

"Yeah?" Dominic lit up momentarily, and just as quickly, felt bad about the whole situation. The week had been a blur and some of those knocks on the door had probably been Jacob. He was a nice kid, but a bit of loner like Anita had been. He didn't have many friends, so Dom would throw around a football or skate with him a couple times a week.

"Tell him I'm sorry. I promise I'll hang out with him soon. I just...."

Barbara looked at him with calm, but expectant eyes.

Dominic cleared his throat. "So how have you been?"

"Fine," Barbara replied. "I've been fine. Work is work." She looked down at her watch. "I have to head to the cafe in an hour."

"Oh, I don't want to keep you. I'm sure—"

"But I've got time to catch up," she said. She looked around the room. Her eyes settled on a pair of unframed photos propped on the bookshelves surrounding the TV. She stood without warning and walked up to them. "Wow, I don't remember those. Granted, I don't remember the last time I was in your living room." Their eyes met briefly. "Around the 4th of July, I think? You had a couple of us neighbors over."

Dominic remembered the 4th very well. It was one of the few times of year that he begged and pleaded with Anita to take a chance and socialize a little. She might even have fun, he had told her. Of course, she didn't. While he was entertaining, she always found something to do—cleaning dishes, putting away laundry, or trimming the trees outside that were nearly stubs already.

Dominic said nothing, only watching Barbara as she stood with her back to him. She was wearing a tight pair of blue jeans. They revealed that she was still as slim as she'd been in high school and his eyes fell to the curve of her hips as she leaned forward to observe the pictures. Dominic felt suddenly flush. He jumped to his feet and walked toward her, afraid to look toward the bedroom.

"They're new," Dominic said. "I just put them up the other day." Barbara grabbed a photo of a grinning Dominic, his arm wrapped around a slouching Anita. They were standing outside of The Dark House, a small venue in Lincoln where they watched Anita's favorite bands play several times a year. Her arms were hanging down and she appeared to be looking at something unseen beyond the camera. "She loves live music."

"Loves?" Barbara looked up at him and asked.

Dominic's throat grew constricted. "Er, loved."

Barbara leaned in and put a hand on his shoulder. He shook involuntarily at her touch. Sweat began to form again on his brow. He put the photo back in its place.

"I don't have many photos of her. She wasn't a big fan of cameras," he said with a half-smile.

"You two always seemed the odd couple to me," Barbara said. "I wished I had gotten to know her better. She was always….introverted, wasn't she? The tortured artist type?" Her teeth dug into her lips after she spoke.

Dominic wasn't sure how to respond. Anita was just down the hall. Surely she could hear every word they were saying.

"Oh my God. I'm sorry. I didn't mean…."

"No, no, it's okay. She wasn't exactly a social butterfly." Dominic didn't feel bad saying that. Anita would have been the first to admit it.

Barbara inhaled deeply. Her hand slid from Dominic's shoulder to his arm. Her touch was sending shockwaves through his bare skin.

"I'm just going to be blunt, Dom. What did you see in her?"

That question. He may have heard it as many times in his life as he had 'good morning.' His answer now wasn't any different than it had been the myriad times he'd been asked.

"No one knows her like I do," he said. His voice rose. "No one ever gave her a chance but me. Yeah, she was in her own head a lot, but that didn't mean she didn't deserve love like anyone else."

"Did you feel sorry for her?"

Dominic had come to expect people to leave it alone after he'd spoken his piece, but Barbara wasn't letting it go. Fine. If she wanted blunt, he would be blunt.

"It's complicated," he said. He sat back down on the couch and stared at the open bedroom door. He felt the couch shift as Barbara sat beside him.

"Did you ever feel like you had a mission in life? Like a direction you had to head toward and if you tried to go the other way, it just felt wrong?"

"Sure," she replied. "But sometimes we can run right into a ditch. What about you? Were you *happy*?"

"Of course!" he said.

Barbara remained silent. Her eyes felt like a vacuum sucking hidden truths out of him along with thin layers of resentment that had built up over the years. "Being happy doesn't mean everything is always great a hundred percent of the time. Besides, if it's always about you, isn't that just being selfish?"

"Yeah," she said, "but you've never been one to make it all about you. You deserve some happiness too."

It was a lot for Dominic to dwell on. Warm breath flowed in and out of his mouth as he gaped at Barbara.

"I don't doubt that you loved her, Dom. But were you *in* love with her?"

Nuance. Dominic tried to avoid it because it just made things worse. Who could really say what love was or should be?

Anita was sad, Dominic tried to make her happy. That was their pattern. Their balance. That was who they were. If he were to act differently now, to believe that his sacrifices for Anita had maybe been in excess, it would be too much to take. Too large of a change, too quickly.

"I can't," Dominic said. He could feel his eyes beginning to well up with tears. He cleared his throat and straightened his back.

Barbara put a hand on his leg. "Can't what?"

His whole head was shaking trying to contain the emotions churning through him like a maelstrom.

"Everything." He turned toward the bedroom without thinking. Standing in the doorway was Anita's silhouette. Dominic suddenly didn't seem to care if she was seen or what she may be thinking. His eyes penetrated her looming figure. "She needs me," he almost whispered.

"She's *gone*, Dom." Barbara's hand squeezed his thigh and she leaned in closer. The floral scent of her perfume struck him again.

"I failed her," he said.

"No," Barbara said with a sternness that shook him. With her other hand, she directed his chin back toward her. "You did *not* fail her. You did more than anyone could possibly have done for her. You are *not* obligated, do you understand?"

He fought to turn back to the hallway. He could feel Anita's presence growing closer.

"Do you understand?" Barbara repeated.

Dominic blinked hard. Again, he tried to look into the hall. With a surprising amount of force, Barbara grabbed his face with both hands and planted her lips on his.

Her fingernails dug into Dominic's face. He felt too tired, too weak to resist. And then he didn't want to. The feeling of her moist lips was such a novel feeling. He found himself fighting back thoughts of Anita. Memories of nights where she had been more depressed than normal and rejected his overtures, saying that she didn't deserve his love. He had told her that wasn't true, but they had never been able to bridge that gap.

He felt awkward, yet his hands found their way around Barbara's back as he hugged her tightly. Tears transferred from his cheeks to hers.

She pulled back and rested her forehead on his. Dominic closed his eyes, sensing Anita standing behind him. He didn't want to look. He wished now that she would just go away, but he still felt he owed her something. He turned, looked up and opened his eyes.

Dominic's heart nearly stopped pumping. Anita was indeed standing before them both, looking directly at him, but there was something wrong with her face.

"Dom?"

Barbara's voice sounded so far away. Dominic stood and came face-to-face with his dead wife. Her eyes were no longer lifeless and unfocused, but instead met his. Wrinkles formed at their edges. As soon as Dominic comprehended the strange vision of a smiling Anita, she turned away from him and ambled to the front door.

He felt a pair of arms reach across his chest, holding him securely from behind. Barbara's head fell across the back of his right shoulder.

"Are you okay?"

Dominic's hands fell over hers.

"I'm okay."

THE HUFFALLUM

The Huffallum stretched and groaned as he woke up from a long night of sleep. He rubbed his tiny, little eyes and wondered why the house was so quiet.

Still, he went about his morning routine. He got out of the warm bed and brushed his teeth which were as sharp as nails. Then he polished his nails which were as sharp as teeth. He washed under his hairy arms and around his back until he smelled like flowers.

When he was done, the Huffallum left the bathroom and entered the living room, only to find it empty. Mom was not reading a book in her chair and Dad was not at his desk, doing what he called *tinkering*.

"Mom?" the Huffallum asked.

There was no reply.

"Dad?" he asked.

Again, no reply.

The Huffallum began to feel scared. This was all so unusual. Every morning, he would wash up and then come out to the living room to see Mom reading a book and Dad tinkering. A warm bowl of pookanut soup would be waiting for him on the table.

Where could they have gone?

The Huffallum searched every room in the house, which did not take long since there were only three rooms and they were all very small. He looked under the couch, he searched under the bed, and he even crawled under the kitchen table.

Mom and Dad were still nowhere to be found.

The Huffallum went to the window next to the front door and looked outside. Could they have gone somewhere without me, he wondered. They have never done that before. He squinted at the green grass, the tall brown trees, and the white mountains in the far distance. The Huffallum wondered if they had decided to climb one of those mountains. The Huffallum had never been allowed to go out alone, so he had no way of looking for them outside.

As he was thinking, the Huffallum heard a growl. At first he was startled, but then he realized that it was his own tummy. He really wished he had some pookanut soup right now. He walked into the kitchen and saw a bowl sitting on the sink. Next to it was a brown bag filled with

pookanuts along with an empty pot. The Huffallum had seen Mom make

the soup many times. He even helped her once or twice. He tried to

remember how it was done and while he was thinking, his belly growled

once more. The Huffallum decided that he would try to make his own

pookanut soup.

He remembered that Dad would make the fire and Mom would

hang a pot of water filled with pookanuts above it. Dad taught him how

to very carefully stack the wood and throw bobobumpum powder on the

wood which would cause it catch fire. The Huffallum decided he could

do that too. He placed logs in the fireplace and carefully tossed a pinch

of bobobumpum powder onto the wood.

He cheered when the fire began to roar!

He then filled the pot with water and pookanuts, and with all of

his strength, picked up the pot and hung it over the fire. After a few minutes, the Huffallum could smell the soup cooking. His tummy growled again. He took a spoon and tested the soup several times before deciding it was just right.

He carefully spooned some soup into his bowl and sat down to eat. The Huffallum thought about how only a few moments ago, he was scared that he would be hungry forever. Now he had a warm bowl of pookanut soup and he was proud that he made it all by himself.

With his belly full, the Huffallum cleaned up and sat by the fire. Perhaps Mom and Dad will be back soon, he thought. He couldn't wait to tell them how he had lit the fire and cooked his own pookanut soup!

And so he waited and waited and waited and waited some more, but Mom and Dad had not returned. He spent the time singing songs and spinning in circles.

Soon, it grew dark outside and the fire cast scary shadows on the walls. The Huffallum did not like being in the house alone, but he did not know what to do. He grew scared again and began to cry.

"Mom!" he shouted.

There was no reply.

"Dad!" he screamed.

Again, no reply.

The Huffallum continued crying, but after several minutes he knew that crying would not help him find his parents. He worried that Mom and Dad may have left the house for some reason and gotten hurt before they could return.

What if they need my help, he thought.

The Huffallum walked to the window and looked out once more. Now it was dark outside. The moon and the stars barely provided any light.

I must go, the Huffallum thought.

Even though I'm scared, I must, I must, I must.

If the Huffallum could make his own pookanut soup, then surely he could go outside for just a little bit and see.

Though he was frightened, the Huffallum pretended to be brave. He opened the door and stepped out into the night.

The front yard was filled with scary sounds.

An owl hooting in one of the nearby trees.

Crickets chirping in the bushes.

The wind blowing through the leaves.

Just as the Huffallum was ready to run back inside, something caught his attention.

A tiny moth flew up to the Huffallum and landed on his shoulder.

The moth flew from his shoulder and landed on a bush. The Huffallum followed it. Then the moth flew onto the grass. The Huffallum followed it again. It was like they were playing a game of chase!

The Huffallum was soon out of breath from chasing the moth, so he sat on the ground to rest. He realized that he had forgotten all about the hooting owls and the chirping crickets. The noisy wind and the dark night did not bother him anymore.

Just then, there was a rustling in the bushes. The Huffallum became nervous again. He even thought about running back into the house, but he was not scared. He grew curious and waited to see what was hiding in the bush.

Maybe it was more moths?

Two large creatures came out and the Huffallum jumped up from the ground.

"Mom!" he shouted.

"Dad!" he shouted as well.

The Huffallum was filled with excitement. He ran up and hugged his parents and asked, "Where have you been?"

"Did you forget?" Dad said. "It's Thursday. Every Thursday, we visit your Aunt Doodleflukes."

The Huffalum thought about it and then he remembered.

"Oh," he said, "that's right!" He had forgotten it was Thursday.

But then he asked, "Why didn't you take me?"

"Whenever a Huffallum is old enough, his parents leave him alone for one day. They do that to teach him how to overcome his fears and learn how to help himself. Do you think you did that?"

The Huffallum thought about it.

"Yes!" he shouted. "At first, I was scared. But then I got hungry and I made my own pookanut soup! And then I was scared again because I was worried you may have gotten hurt and I knew I had to find you. So even though I was scared of the dark, I came out on my own. But then I got scared once more by all of the sounds. And then a moth came and we played chase. After a while, I wasn't scared of being outside anymore either!"

"We are very proud of you, son," Mom and Dad said at the same time. "Why don't we go back inside? I'm sure you're hungry for more soup."

Just then, the Huffallum's tummy growled.

"Yes," he said. "I sure am!"

Captain Coffee

Captain Coffee preferred a French roast. Lighter brews would seem more the Captain's speed, but they lacked the complex, chocolatey undertones that made life worth living. Undertones that gave him purpose. The light-reflecting puddles of oil floating on the coffee's surface represented islands of refuge from the surrounding darkness. Islands the Captain felt an obligation to protect. He would consume the surrounding midnight murk of evil so the rest of the population didn't have to.

"Sir?"

"Hm?" Through the slits of his eye mask, he appraised the young girl behind the counter. She had rosy plump cheeks and her dirty blond hair was tied up into a bun. Wrapped tightly around her person was a forest-green apron with *Kenzie* stitched in white cursive on the top right. She was new.

"I said that I'm sorry, but it will take us about five minutes to brew another pot of the dark roast."

"I see." There were four people in line behind the Captain. He was watching them all. They didn't know it, but he was. A little black-haired girl and her mother stood directly behind him. The little girl was rubbing a piece of the Captain's silk cape between her fingers. He smiled down at her and she smiled back. Her mother pulled her back and chastised her.

"If you're in a hurry," Kenzie said, "I can pour you a cup of our medium-bodied house blend and add a shot."

"No!" the Captain replied.

Kenzie raised her eyebrows and looked at the other customers.

Mixing roasts was a definite no-no. Captain Coffee couldn't put a finger on it, but it always seemed to dampen his abilities. But Kenzie didn't know any better.

"No, thank you, young lady. I will wait."

She rang up the total of two dollars and nineteen cents.

"Can I get a name?"

He preferred to use an alias when he wasn't in uniform, but he hadn't bothered to wait today. He had woken up that morning with a strange feeling in his gut, so he came in dressed for action, prepared for anything.

"Captain Coffee," he replied.

Chuckles broke out in the line. He heard the little girl gasp. Kenzie picked up a thin black marker and wrote *CC* on the side of an empty paper cup.

"We'll call you when its ready, Captain," she said nonchalantly.

The Captain's scuffed boots tapped across the brown tile. He carefully took a seat, draping his cape over the back of the wooden chair, and clasped his hands together over the tiny round table. The whine and burr of roasted beans being ground into fine powder accented the low acoustic guitar and airy female vocals drifting out of the store's ceiling speakers. The mother who was behind him was leaning over the counter now, placing her order while gripping her purse strap tightly. Her little girl danced back and forth behind her, occasionally peeking at the Captain. Last in line was a pair of blue-collar guys in gray t-shirts and baggy blue jeans. One of them had a smirk on his face and pointed with his chin at the Captain while he said something to his buddy.

The Captain sat back and admired the low bohemian bookshelves lining the wall opposite the coffee bar. They held a smattering of sleeveless hardcovers and tattered paperbacks. In front of the shelves were two comfortable-looking armchairs, one of them occupied by a young woman resting her temple on a fingertip while she was engrossed in a magazine. The other engulfed a young man with a thin, white notebook computer cracked open on his lap and a large pair of designer headphones covering his ears.

The microcosm of society gathered here every morning reminded the Captain of what he was sworn to protect.

After his name was called and he brought the aromatic cup of joe back to his table, a little pair of bells rang as the front glass door swung open. A familiar feeling rose up from his stomach as his eyes landed on the entrant. Captain Coffee realized immediately why he had hopped straight into uniform that morning.

There would be trouble.

* * *

"Except those behind the counter, everyone down on the ground, now!"

He wore a black balaclava and dark sunglasses. Only his pink lips were exposed. The tip of his black handgun swang around the room, moving from person to person as if it were scanning their minds for thoughts of escape.

The front of the smirking blue-collar guy's jeans grew moist around the crotch. The mother shrieked, grabbed her little girl and turned around, exposing her back while hiding her child. Folk music continued floating through the speakers, but the grinders and hissing milk steamers fell silent.

"I said NOW!" As if they were disconnected dominoes, customers started falling to the floor, but the Captain remained seated, as still as a stone.

The little girl began to whimper.

Her mother started, "Please, she's scared—", but she stopped talking and bearhugged her daughter to the floor when the bad guy pointed his gun at her and thumbed back the trigger.

The man then ran over to the student with the laptop and yanked off his headphones.

"Hey!" the kid responded instinctively.

"Down," the bad guy said. "Now."

The boy looked up and his jaw dropped. The laptop slipped off his lap and cracked against the tile as he scrambled to kiss the ground alongside the magazine-reading woman.

The gun floated the Captain's way. "Hey, Mr. Halloween. You think you're special?"

Now was not the time. With his eyes locked on the bad guy, the Captain slowly pushed his chair back and dropped to his knees. He then pressed his hands onto the floor and lowered himself into a position from which he could observe.

The man was alone unless one of his cohorts was working an inside job. Kenzie? She didn't seem the type and her face was a pale as the other two baristas working the machines.

"Everyone behind the counter, come out front and join your friends," he said, rushing toward the far edge of the counter where it opened up to the lobby. After he waved the workers past, he peeked in what looked to be a storeroom, followed by a quick check of the bathrooms.

"I'll be walking around now, collecting donations. Purses, wallets, and shiny accessories are acceptable forms of currency. Be good and you can go home to your loved ones. Do something stupid, everyone pays."

* * *

"I ain't gonna reach into your tights, but you paid for that coffee somehow. Move slow."

Captain Coffee would be polite, but he would not be pushed around. He kept his face to the ground, staring at the man's dirty sneakers. "You do not have to do this," he said. "If you put down your weapon and allow me to take you into custody, I promise that you will not be harmed."

The thief crouched and yanked on the back of the Captain's hair, painfully forcing his head up. "I picked you first, because you're a goddamn freak and I don't trust freaks. I don't have time for this." His breath reeked of alcohol. "Now, stand up slowly, reach into your panties, and give me all your money."

Captain Coffee pushed himself up with the tip of the barrel digging into the side of his nose. Once on his feet, he reached into the side of his underwear where he kept a small amount of cash inside a billfold

"There is still time to do the right thing."

"You think this is a joke? You say one more thing and—"

The man cut himself off abruptly and stared at the Captain, his eyes squinting slightly.

"Wait a second. Take off your mask."

It was the one thing any superhero was reluctant to do in public.

"Please," the Captain said. "I cannot reveal my identity."

The thief pointed his gun now at the mother who whimpered and curled over her daughter more tightly.

"I said take it off."

The Captain was left with no choice. He reached behind his head and undid the twine holding his mask in place, letting it fall to the floor.

"Holy shit," the thief said, removing his sunglasses for a seemingly better view. His familiar steel-blue eyes struck the Captain. "Brian. Brian fucking Mulrooney."

Captain Coffee could feel his face turning red. Ashamed and vulnerable, he stood before a ghost.

The thief relaxed his body as he laughed. His gun-hand fell to his side. "I should have known you'd stay a freak after high school. Didn't you get your ass kicked enough then—"

All bad guys make mistakes. It's just a matter of time and opportunity, two things of which a superhero like Captain Coffee is aware of at a subconscious level.

Ronnie King, bully and apparently perpetual dreg of society, let his guard down long enough for Captain Coffee to descend on him like the plunger of a French Press. The Captain seized the steaming cup of dark roast from his table and splashed it across the thief's face. It spattered into his eyes and scalded his lips. The gun clattered on to the floor as his hands raced up toward his face.

The Captain lifted his knee to meet the bad guy's crotch, sending him crumpling to the floor, howling in pain. With one of his boots, Captain Coffee kicked the man's gun across the tile, flipped him over and sat on his back, holding his wrists together as he pulled his arms up toward his upper back.

"Kenzie, contact the authorities," the Captain said, calm and collected.

* * *

After the police interviewed the witnesses and the captain posed, mask on, for a final photo, the mother with the little girl came up and hugged him tightly.

"Thank you, Captain Coffee," she said.

"Just doing my job," he replied.

"I want to be like you when I'm older!" the daughter said from below.

The Captain dropped to a knee and met her at eye level. "You can be like me now," he said. "Get good grades in school and help those in need."

"Do I have to drink coffee?" she asked, her face slightly twisted as she scrunched her nose.

"That is not required."

"Whew," she said. "Good."

Devilleaf

Beneath the king's oak table, Lurian rolled the smooth glass vial filled with powdered *devilleaf* in his palm. He thumbed its cork stopper, nervously confirming that it hadn't fallen out, and with it, any chance of saving his own neck from the king's chopping block. In truth, if he did not proceed with the girl's demand, the chopping block would be a charity compared to what he'd likely face.

He focused on the empty cup at the far end of the table. Between Lurian and the jeweled goblet sat silver platters overflowing with the king's favorites — sweetmeats from the game warden's private stock, piles of salted almonds, and Marsinian grapes. He recalled a time many years ago when the two of them were nearly caught behind enemy lines at Marsinia, all because the then-prince insisted on stealing barrels of a finer vintage then their regiment had in stock.

A cough made Lurian nearly leap out of his skin, but he was well practiced in hiding surprise. Stanislo, the silent, crooked-nose cupbearer, hovered above, giving Lurian one of his rude looks while holding two brass pitchers of wine in his hands. In the hierarchy of things, Stanislo's official status was below that of Lurian, but he'd been in service to the king at least a decade longer. Admittedly, the servant took impudence to a talented level—one couldn't outright accuse him of being excessively bold. He had a slippery way about him, like that of a sidewinding snake. Lurian would have been within rights to be jealous of the lackey's talents, but he had his own by which to make up for them.

"The king is very tired this evening," Stanislo said, touching up Lurian's goblet with the weaker crimson wine. "It would be well not to keep him late."

Maybe he shouldn't be late, himself, Lurian wanted to say, but if he was going to potentially lose his head, it wouldn't be due to a trivial, spiteful statement.

Instead, he smiled. "Of course." Killing a man he had come to view almost as a brother was not something Lurian wanted to do, but to be rid of Stanislo? That might actually be a pleasure. He watched the cupbearer glide to the other side of the table and pour from the king's personal stock into the empty cup. Their eyes never left each other, as if the servant was trying to pry into Lurian's soul.

Stanislo walked through the wooden double doors and closed them gently behind him, disappearing into the hall. Lurian was alone now in the imposing dining room, leaving him to do the thing which he did not wish to do. He slept little the previous night, searching for a way out. One night was not enough time, but that was all the king's daughter had given him.

Slip this into his cup tomorrow evening. I'll take care of the rest.

Her speech still echoed in his ear. The moment he heard those words, Lurian felt as if his heart had stopped beating and never started again.

He pushed his chair back. The skidding sound was absurdly loud. He stood and waited for the doors to swing open, but there was no indication of the king's arrival. Sweat beaded on his forehead. The vial nearly fell from his wet palms.

A part of him was still unbelieving of the words which had left the princess's lips, but he had no way to prove the truth. Her word against his? She had insisted he drink with her. What drugs were slipped into his own cup, he had no idea, but he found himself out of sorts, unable to focus and resist as she took advantage of him. The very idea that she would claim that *he* raped *her* outraged him, and alone would be enough to seal his fate, but that she would also claim to be carrying his child? That ensured an unpleasant exit from this world.

She promised him a position if he cooperated, but who was to say that she would not accuse him of committing the treachery alone after the king fell into the long sleep? That was a very real threat, but in Lurian's position, there seemed to be no good option.

He longed for the days when he had been a minor noble; before he had impressed the king with his performance in battle; before he had become very close to him and eventually made an advisor. He wished he had been as much of a student of domestic history as he was of war-making and trade. Maybe then he would have foreseen the lengths that those in the royal family would go to seize power.

"Damn it, man, just go," he whispered, realizing he'd been standing still for some time.

But his legs wouldn't carry him forward. The king's cup of wine sat, both compelling and repulsing him. Heavy winds outside of the castle rushed through tiny cracks in the stone walls, creating a low whistle in one corner of the room.

Lurian was unsure how much time passed between his standing and waiting, but it was clearly too long. He was still on his feet, undecided, when there was a brief bustle of noise outside of the doors. Lurian pocketed the vial as the pair of heavy oak planks swung open and an obviously exhausted King Jorn entered the room.

* * *

The king was slouched in his chair, popping almonds into his mouth, one by one.

"No, tonight is fine," he replied.

Lurian had politely suggested postponing their meeting for the following night. The king's tired state provided a potential out. It was a gamble. Lurian would beg the princess for patience. It was only one more night, after all.

But, alas, the king would not hear of it.

Now Lurian was finding his ability to poison the king severely hampered. How could he do it while he was in the room? He cursed himself for letting the opportunity slip.

"Give me the latest," the king said as his lips smacked.

"Do you want to hear about the markets first or reports from the ambassadors?"

"The important things."

Lurian knew that, but he was stalling for time, trying to think of potential distractions. Maybe he could get the king drunk enough to not notice a subtle slip of the poison. Lurian picked up his goblet and raised it in a toast. "To the important things," he said. The king smiled and followed suit.

"Get on with it," he said.

Even though Lurian had assassination on his mind for the past twenty-four hours, he'd still managed to prepare talking points for the king.

"Travian sends word that the marauders from the Bexton Hills have been taken care of. They'll no longer be pillaging our primary wheat supply."

The king released a gaping yawn. "And how has this been confirmed?"

"The band's head, Sibea the Bold, has been taken care of. His various body parts rest on pikes outside the town—covered in thorns to keep the carrion off, of course. The rest of his tribe are working under the lash and sun to maintain the very fields in which they plundered, of course."

The king released a low chuckle and popped an almond into the air, leaning back, hoping to catch it in his mouth, but instead missing by several inches where it bounced and clacked onto the cold stone floor below. He grunted and took another pull of wine.

"Tell me, Lurian, what are we going to do with all of these up-starts?"

Lurian scrunched his eyebrows. "The Bexton clans were only a nuisance, your Lord—"

"I'm not talking about them," the king interrupted. "I'm talking about the enemies *within*."

Lurian tried his best to keep the blood from rushing to his face.

King Jorn continued, "A king is always aware that the world is filled with plotters and schemers and they're rarely far away."

Had word gotten to the king? Was he trying to get Lurian to confess?

"Your Highness, I'm your man for foreign affairs and the mer-chant trades. Internal affairs, spycraft—these are a bit outside of my areas of expertise."

The king slammed his goblet on the table. "Damn it, man, but you have ears. Tell me, what do you hear?"

The room was heavy with silence. Lurian felt a lump caught in his throat.

"I've heard nothing, my Lord," he managed to squeak out. "Your kingdom is secure."

"Hmph," the king said, taking another swig of wine to wash down the almonds. He sank further back into his chair, his ruddy face looking pleased. "Good. I assume you'll keep me informed should the slightest hint come your way."

Lurian felt a bead of sweat slip down the front of his left ear. He was grateful the king was so far away.

"Of course," he said.

The king closed his eyes. "What else do you have to tell me?"

As Lurian went on about the affairs of state—the swiftly snuffed-out uprising in Southern Drakoria, the rising cost of wool imported from the Pahnus Isles—he noticed an odd sound reverberating within the dining room.

Lurian fell silent, and for thirty untenable seconds, he simply watched as the king's chest rose and fell in rhythm with his snoring. Lurian lurched slowly toward him. His eyes shifted between King Jorn and the doors until he was close enough to see the crumbs of almond nestled in the old man's gray beard.

He wouldn't get another chance. It was now or never.

Lurian reached into his pocket and pulled out the vial. He popped the cork, all the while keeping his eyes on the king. Was he ready to do this? Ready to kill the man who had seen his potential beyond being that of a mere knight, taken him under his wing and elevated him to his current station?

What type of kingdom would exist under the princess? She was a stubborn and emotional woman. To try and steer her would be like trying to quiet the Northern Blizzards. Then there was the question of whether or not Lurian would live long enough to see her reign through the year's end.

He realized his hand was shaking to the point that he might drop the vial. In an instant, he knew what he had to do.

Quickly, he rushed back to his side of the table and emptied the powder into his own cup. He collapsed into his chair and stared at the vessel, cognizant only of the king's snoring and the whistling wind. This was the best option, he thought. The only reasonable option. Still, he could not bring himself to drink. It's not easy to dispense with one's life at a moment's notice.

There was a commotion outside of the doors which woke the king from his catnap. He stretched his arms and flexed the crick out of his neck.

"I must have drifted off," the king said. He reached for his goblet and drank as if he had just spent a week marching through the deserts of Samar.

He wiped his mouth with a silk sleeve and looked to Lurian. "You know I never like to drink alone, friend."

It was the final push he needed. He couldn't convince himself to partake but having someone else make the decision for him somehow made things easier.

He picked up the goblet and raised it toward the large wooden chandelier hanging overhead.

"To my king."

His hand began to shake violently and splashes of wine spilled over the lip before he grabbed it with both hands and gulped it down. Though Lurian had been told that the poison would be unnoticeable, there was a slight bitterness to the drink.

Devilleaf worked within a matter of minutes, suddenly seizing the heart. He decided to spend the rest of his time admiring the glorious man who sat at the other end of the table and think about his next statements.

The disturbance that had awoken the king raised in pitch and there was an argument outside of the door. King Jorn seemed not to take notice, instead popping more almonds into his mouth and staring back at Lurian.

"Your Highness," Lurian spoke, "may I just say that it has been an honor being both your companion in arms as well as your humble servant. I hope that you have also considered me a friend as much as I have considered you such."

The king was silent for a moment. Finally, he said, "They say a king should have no friends, especially among his advisers. But tell me—what's a life without friends?"

"Indeed," Lurian replied. He found himself oddly at ease, now. The tremors had exited his body and there was a sudden clarity running through his mind. "There's something important that I need to tell you, my lord."

"Oh?" The king grinned and leaned forward as if awaiting something lurid. "Been holding out on me, have you?"

"It's about your daughter, the princess—"

Before Lurian could complete the sentence, the doors through which the king had earlier entered came bursting open. Stanislo stood, feigning indignation and looking like a whelp between the king's two burly guards whose obsidian skin and light blue eyes spoke of their Dursinian lineage.

He pointed a shaking finger at Lurian.

"Seize this traitor! He has poisoned the king!"

Lurian leaped to his feet. On impulse, he pulled the empty vial from his pocket and threw it onto the table where it clunked on the hardwood and came to rest beside his own cup. "I have done no such thing," he said, "as you will soon discover." He looked at the king with sorrow, trying to determine how he should explain himself in the little time granted.

The king raised a hand toward his guards who stood like marble statues. He then slowly pushed himself up from his chair and leaned down to palm some more almonds before gliding towards Lurian. The room was filled with a deathly quiet. The two men's eyes never left each other until the king finally towered above Lurian's sweaty skull. King Jorn's free hand came to rest on Lurian's shoulder as he peered down into his advisor's empty cup. Then Lurian felt the king's grip squeeze down lightly, followed by a friendly smile.

"Your Highness," Stanislo impressed, "we must get you to the priests so that they may prepare to drain—"

"Silence," the king interrupted his cupbearer. King Jorn ignored Stanislo's pleas and turned his attention back to his advisor. Lurian's pulse quickened. It seemed the poison was beginning to take effect. There wasn't much time and he had to confess—to warn the man who had put his faith in him until the end.

"Explain this," the king said, looking toward the empty vial.

"My lord, nearly two months ago, I was drugged by your daughter and she took advantage of me. She recently revealed to me that she was with child. I know not the truth of this, but she plotted against me. Unless I poured this poison into your cup tonight, she would accuse me of rape and impregnating her."

Lurian took a deep breath before continuing. "I wish that I could say that my first response was to come to you with the truth and face the consequences, but I feared I would not be heard above your only daughter. And I would be lying if I did not once think, selfishly, that carrying out her wishes might not be the worst course of action, given my potential punishment. But in the end, I could not do it. Instead, I chose to tell you everything before taking my own life."

He finished his speech with a quiet tone, staring at the few drops of wine left in his cup in an effort to avoid both the king's glare and Stanislo's triumphant eyes. "My king, I am sorry that I could not be a better friend and servant."

The unendurable silence returned. He felt King Jorn's hand squeeze his shoulder once more.

"You *are* a worthy servant and indeed my friend."

At that moment the king looked at his guards. "T'was not the sparrow, but the lark."

While Lurian tried to decipher the message, there may have been an imperceptible nod by the hulking Dursinians, but it was Stanislo's yelp that grabbed his attention. Within the span of five seconds, one of the strongmen had taken hold of cupbearer's arms while the other slapped on a pair of iron shackles.

Stanislo protested. "What— is the meaning of this?!" His cheeks were red, jiggling fiercely under restraint.

The king shoved the handful of almonds into his mouth and

wiped the salt from his hand on his royal robe. He walked back to his own cup of wine which he gulped down until it was empty, releasing a satisfied gasp.

"When possible, I prefer to bag two birds with a single stone," he said to Stanislo. King Jorn did not look rattled in the slightest. There was further commotion coming from down the hall. A woman was screaming bloody murder until the moment she was dragged through the doorway between another pair of Dursinians.

The princess grunted as she nearly fell onto the cold floor. Tears streamed down her pale cheeks. She looked up at the king.

"Father! I don't know what you've been told, but there's been a mistake!"

King Jorn stepped in front of his daughter and shook his head slowly. "There certainly has been."

He gazed up at Lurian.

"You see, my daughter decided to hedge her bets. She took advantage of both you and Stanislo. Each of you was an insurance policy against the other. After my first sip of wine, I knew that I had been betrayed by him. Stanislo, no doubt, intended to hold you responsible for my death though he had slipped what he thought was *devilleaf* into my personal stock."

The princess protested. "No! That is not true!"

Again, the king looked at her with true sorrow in his eyes.

"What my daughter believed was pure *devilleaf* was something which my chemist concocted and placed where one would normally find such an ingredient stored for foreign espionage. There were two samples, each with a flavor profile of its own."

The bitter flavor Lurian had tasted upon drinking the wine had suddenly come back to him.

"Granted," King Jorn said, "there was an element of *devilleaf* in each to give it a genuine appearance, but not enough to cause true harm."

Lurian only now started to feel the blood flowing back to his extremities. He had not been fatally poisoned after all. Any notions of dying were in his head. A whirlpool of relief swirled within his core.

The king continued, "As soon as I drank my wine, I knew Stanislo had done his part. I simply gave you the opportunity to carry out yours as well. I don't blame you for your indecision. Had I been in your place, I imagine I would have behaved the same. In the end, you confirmed my faith."

"Take them to the dungeon where I won't be disturbed by the screams tonight," the king commanded his guards. The princess cried an unearthly howl, protesting as she was pulled from the floor and dragged away. Stanislo fainted as the other Dursinians removed him from the room and shut the door behind them.

King Jorn walked toward Lurian and embraced him. "My friend," he whispered into his advisor's ear. "Go. Sleep. Drink. Do whatever may bring you relief from tonight's events, but I recommend you eat some of those almonds or you will be on the privy for at least a week."

With that, the king released Lurian, grabbed another handful of nuts, and exited the dining room.

Apollo's Revenge

This wasn't the Italy of passionate opera, nor the Italy of Da Vinci and Michelangelo.

Maybe it was the Italy of the Romans.

Not that Private Hubert Bausman had half a clue about those guys. All he remembered were primary school tales of men in togas who turned Christians into lion chow. And not that it was the Romans he had to worry about, anyway. It was their Teutonic brethren from the North, members of that overall not-so-nice-guy organization popularly known as the Nazis.

Only weeks ago, they had been here at Monte Cassino, about eighty miles south of Rome. Axis and Allies faced off against the elements as much as each other. Even though it was well into Spring, Bausman felt New England weather had nothing on this place. Maybe it just seemed that way.

"You're up, Chief."

A puff of steaming air wandered out from Private Munson's mouth, curling beneath the three-quarters moon.

Munson extended his hand and pulled Bausman up onto his feet.

Bausman's muscles ached. He cursed himself for not standing and moving around, but he acknowledged that three to four hours of sleep would, without fail, eventually have its way.

In a daze, he popped on his helmet, slung the strap of his Browning A-5 over his shoulder, and marched towards the designated lookout point.

"Where do you think you're goin'?" Munson asked.

Halfway through the question, Bausman realized he'd forgotten something. He reached into his shirt pocket, pulled out a nearly-empty pack of Lucky Strikes, and tossed it into Munson's receptive hands.

"Sarge seems to be agitated," Bausman said. "Command's probably itching to send us to another slaughterhouse. Best hide yourself well."

Munson fell on his ass and flicked the flint wheel of his Zippo as if he hadn't heard a word. The amber glow of his cigarette could probably be seen from a mile away.

* * *

Bausman and Munson were two grunts tasked with keeping watch over a hundred-yard section of winding road leading past a Polish Army operating base and up to a bombed-out monastery. Four months ago, the two of them along with the rest of the US 36th Infantry Division had initiated a trade in flesh for these seven acres.

The price was steep.

The two privates were survivors, though. Two from a regiment of originally one hundred and eighty-four soldiers, all who had been delivered into the earth's snowy maw by chattering *maschinengewehr* and camouflaged Panzers.

Of course, other armies came and made their sacrifices: the Brits, the Aussies, along with more nations than Bausman had ever bothered to learn about, with the Poles finally wrapping things up.

For some undefinable, yet likely bureaucratic reason, Bausman and Munson's commanding officer decided it would be good for morale to bring the surviving Americans back so they could participate in the final assault: to see, Bausman supposed, what all the fuss was about. It had been several weeks since the landmark monastery was captured. War raged further north while their small contingent was left behind.

And that's how Bausman and Munson came to shiver in the middle of the snowmelt, handpicked for the privilege of scanning the night's forest for the ghosts of partisans who were long gone.

* * *

Knowing he would be undisturbed during his six-hour shift, Bausman deviated from his assigned route as he had the past few nights and walked to the ruined abbey.

He hoped that Francesca would be in the cellar.

Last night, he had drunk wine and conversed with the monk, Benedict, instead. God's man was good company, admittedly, but the woman was better looking. Her raven hair and oceanic eyes reminded

Bausman of Hedy Lamarr. So what if she berated him over his "barbarian" manners. He liked a woman with a little fire in her veins.

Maneuvering among the crumbling structure was an exercise in extreme caution. Bausman had already sprained his ankle a week ago, and it was finally feeling good again. His flashlight lit the way, only beginning to flicker near the middle of the abbey. He turned it off to preserve the batteries for the walk back. Besides, there was an oil lamp hanging off the wall near the bottom of the basement staircase which gave off enough light by which to navigate to his destination.

As he rounded the corner of the dusty library archives, he couldn't help but smile.

She sat at a thick wooden table, intently reading a book.

"*Buonasera.*" It was one of three Italian phrases Bausman knew.

"What took you so long?" she asked drily. Though her English was heavily accented, Bausman was happy that he didn't *have* to learn more than three phrases. He pulled up a chair opposite Francesca and a poured a cup of wine from a clay pitcher. Being the gentleman that he was, he topped her's off first.

He swirled the cup under his nose and sniffed.

"I got here as quick as I could. It's a real war zone out there." He snorted at his own joke but quickly stopped. Francesca was not amused.

Her nose was still buried in the book. Script was handwritten on one page and there was a drawing on the other which the private couldn't quite make out.

The air in the library was thick with silence. Bausman sat back in his creaking chair and surveyed the crooked shelves lining the walls. By modern standards, the place was tiny, but he pictured the monks reading the same few books over and over again. It must have been utterly mind-numbing, but he guessed that was the point of being a monk. He was just amazed that the room survived the heap of bombs that had been dropped on it.

"Benny sleeping?"

She may have nodded.

Alright. If she wasn't going to be much company, he could sit here in silence too. It didn't bother him much. So long as he could drink and look at her, he'd be fine. Bausman took another sip of the wine. It was nothing like the rotgut he was used to drinking back home—at least when he drank wine, which wasn't often. This vintage wasn't nearly as sweet as what he was used to and he spent time swishing it over his tongue, trying to discover the nuances that rich folk seemed to find all the time.

He swallowed.

And burped.

Francesca looked up.

He smiled.

"Why are you here?" she asked.

"I like good company," he said.

"No. Why are you *here*?"

He threw his hands up. "What, in Italy? On Earth? You gotta help me out, little lady."

She breathed in deeply and closed the book. Dust puffed out into a small cloud as the pages slapped shut.

"I think the *real* question," he said, leaning forward, "is 'Why are *you* here?' Did you lose your home? Husband grow tired of your charm?"

Francesca laughed and it startled Bausman, but he was happy to see some cracks in her facade.

"Yes, *Hyooo-bert*. Yes. I've lost my home. Just like you."

The way she said his name made the hairs on his arm stand straight up, but in a good way. He took another drink, this time slugging the wine straight down his gullet. He poured himself some more.

"I know exactly where my home is." He looked at the bookshelves as if reading a particular binding. "374 Peck Street, Charlestown, New Hampshire."

Her fingers traced the embossed pattern on the cover of her book. "So when do you plan on heading home?"

"As soon as the fuckin' Army—pardon my French—lets me go. My tour's up in a couple of weeks."

"You must really be looking forward to it."

Bausman had to really think about his response. He assumed he'd be shipped back to Texas, and from there, he'd had the vague notion that he'd get a ride back to New Hampshire. But then what? He'd see his parents and they'd be happy to see him. His old man would likely bring him back on as an insurance agent.

So instead of answering, he simply took another drink and changed the subject.

"You know, Franny, if you opened up a little more, these conversations would probably be a lot more pleasant."

Her eyes narrowed, turning their blues into a darker ocean.

"Fine," Francesca said. "Let's discuss all of the *pleasant* things going on around us, okay? Have you been to the cinema lately? Read the papers? I hear there is a bit of drama happening in Russia. Things are heating up further east in Japan. Oh!"

Her voice quickened and her eyes widened again.

"Then every once in awhile, I hear a child in the forest crying out for his parents. It's been happening for months. And that wonderful odor? Can you still smell it? I can. Your men may have removed the corpses of German soldiers, but some things tend to linger."

She clapped her hands and it made Bausman flinch.

"So many pleasantries, my soldier, so many. Which would you like to talk about first?"

"Enough," Bausman said. He felt his blood rushing through his veins, heating his face. "For someone hiding out in rubble, you sure know a lot about the world."

She sat back down and stared off into space. "I know enough."

As Bausman imagined the horrors through which she had suffered, which she *continues* to suffer, his demeanor softened. He imagined that feeling of powerlessness, the case of being a mere civilian at the mercy of a deranged government. And as much as he supposed standing around in the middle of the night in a foreign land was next to helpless, at least he was doing *something*.

"Seriously," he said. "Don't you have any family that can take you in? Who brings you food? Benny?"

"I'm not very hungry these days. The wine sustains me."

He reached across the table and grasped her hands. She didn't pull back. For Bausman, to feel her soft skin was like grasping his own little slice of heaven.

"I'm sorry. I know it's really none of my business. I just..."

She shrugged and smiled gently. It may have actually been genuine.

"No matter, she said. I am here. You are here. Let's drink some wine while we can, no?" She lifted her cup. Bausman met it. The clacking echoed lightly in the tiny room and they both took a gulp.

The young private licked his lips and held his cup up to the light, examining it like a tiny idol. "I don't know how this has remained undiscovered, but I'm as happy as a pig in shit. You don't want to know what those Poles out there would do for a sip of this, let alone barrels full of it."

* * *

The previous few hours were a blur. The memory no more than a wine-induced vision. Bausman found Munson sitting in the same position, smoking a cigarette as if he had been frozen in time since the moment they parted company.

"Welcome back," Munson said, nearly expressionless. "You catch any bad guys?"

"Of course," Bausman replied. "Hitler and Mussolini both. Found them holding each other in their arms and smooching down at the inn. In fact, I'm booked on a transport out of here tomorrow and FDR is scheduled to wrap the Medal of Honor around my neck." He winked, though he doubted Munson could see the gesture.

Munson took a long drag of his cigarette. "Careful you don't choke." He snubbed it out just in time for the morning shift to arrive.

The two of them walked back to the base in silence.

* * *

"Before all this," Benny said, waving his hand around, "a temple to Apollo stood here. People made sacrifices, you know. Human sacrifices."

He poured himself what had to have been his fifth cup.

"The altar was smashed. His sculptures were destroyed and a tiny chapel was built in its place."

By Bausman's count, they had been engaged in conversation for barely an hour. He'd always assumed most monks were in it for the drink, but could he blame them? After all he had been through, he was ready to throw away his rifle and sign up himself.

"You really know your history," Bausman said. "Must be all the time you have to read these dusty, old books."

Benny laughed uproariously. It was the kind of gregarious laugh that could carry for miles on a light breeze. "Must be," he said. "Someone has to read them."

In fact, as soon as Bausman stepped into the cellar this evening, he realized that the monk had the same book open as Francesca had the previous night.

"I have a wrinkled copy of *Hamlet* in my footlocker," the private said, "a gift from a long lost friend, but haven't touched it since February." Bausman felt his thoughts beginning to sink, so he took a large drink. "What's that one about?"

"Just what we've been discussing," Benny replied, opening his hands. "History. The present. The future." He paused for a moment. "Time, really."

"Time?"

"Sure." The monk smiled. His teeth were stained a rose red. "You know, we're all prisoners."

Bausman's look demanded an explanation.

"Of time," Benny said. "There's no escaping it."

The conversation was growing a little too philosophical for Bausman's tastes. He had a sudden urge to see Francesca, but he didn't want to be rude. Instead, he did what he usually did in this sort of situation. He made a joke: "Well, I'm pretty sure if you put a bullet through my head, I'll be free of it."

Benny sank back into his chair and just stared at Bausman. The muscles on his face were taut. Clearly, the joke did not sit well.

"You're wrong," he said.

At this point, Bausman had enough wine in his system and was feeling slightly punchy. "Oh, really? How do you know? How are you ever going to prove it?" With only a slight hesitation, he pulled his Colt .45 from its holster and laid it on the table. "Let's make a deal. Why don't you shoot me and I'll come back to haunt you. I'll let you know how things are."

The monk said nothing. His glassy eyes stared at the gun while his head bobbed slightly in every direction. Images of the bookshelves reflected off this corneas through the low light of the oil lamp. Bausman was about to check his pulse when Benny slammed a fist on the table. His cup of wine fell over. Red liquid spilled out onto the wood and the sound of it pouring over the edge seemed much louder than it really was.

"Do you think this is funny?"

Bausman sobered up a little. He raised his hands in surrender. "Look, Benny. Just a joke. Come on." The monk had never been so serious before, especially after a bottle. He expected that sort of indignation from Francesca. "I don't know what's gotten into you and Franny lately, but it seems the wine is making you so serious lately. Maybe we ought to open a different barrel."

Benny leaned across the table. The elbows of his robe dipped into the spilled wine as he took hold of Bausman's hands. The monk's palms were freezing. Bausman shivered at the contact and tried to pull away, but Benny's grip was too tight.

"You. Me. Francesca. We're all prisoners of time, even after death. Why won't you admit it?"

For some reason, Bausman grew furious and he ripped his hands away from Benny's, nearly pulling the monk over the table. The private was on his feet now, his chair tipped to its side on the ground. He felt his breath quicken. There was drunk, and then there was *madness*. He wondered if God's man had finally slipped too far to the other side.

"You don't believe me?" The monk slid back into his chair, picked up the book and launched it at Bausman's chest. Dust puffed into the soldier's face as he quickly caught it.

The book felt as if it weighed fifty pounds. Its binding was thick, the pages within nearly the same. How Benny launched it with such force, Bausman didn't know. Didn't *want* to know.

"Read," Benny said.

Bausman dropped it onto the table and looked at the cover for the first time.

Monte Cassino: A History

Astonishingly, the words were written in English. He imagined these monks would be reading Italian. Bausman flipped it open and looked at Benny. He could humor the guy if it would put him in a better mood. "Any place in particular I should be starting?"

The monk crossed his arms, tossed his head to the side and stared off into space. "It doesn't matter."

For the first time since they'd met, Benny looked utterly exhausted. A rush of cold air came down through the cellar entrance and Bausman shivered.

The first page was titled *The Dedication of Apollo's Temple - 312 B.C.*

An illustration of the mountaintop depicted those toga-endowed Romans that were shades of Bausman's childhood memory. They wrapped around a humongous, stiffly-posed statue of Apollo sitting on a stone. A harp lay on his lap while in his hands was a bow with an arrow drawn, pointing north. Someone was being carried overhead to the altar, their hands and feet bound by golden rope.

Bausman thumbed to the next sheet of paper: *The Destruction of Apollo's Temple - 529 A.D.*

Smoke reached into the dark sky and over the decapitated and cracked statue of Apollo, hundreds of tiny arrows fell from the clouds onto the monks below.

Private Bausman had never been what one would call a scholar, but he found himself being pulled into the story of this tiny piece of the world. There was a kinship to it that he couldn't describe. The breeze that had come from above ground seemed to kick into a wild howl now and he buttoned his coat as he flipped the pages to a new chapter titled *The Lombard Invasion - 581 A.D.*

Dark-Age soldiers with pointed helmets rushed toward the flaming abbey of Monte Cassino. One of them depicted a warrior holding the decapitated head of a monk who had been dressed just like Benny. Another showed a bearded man with a vicious smile on his face, looking up at a baby propped high on the end of his spear. Bausman skimmed the vivid descriptions of death and destruction.

He turned through the pages again.

The Saracens - 884 A.D.

Turbaned soldiers in chainmail rode horses along the steep roads of the mountain. The monastery sat quietly atop, waiting, while hundreds of bloodied bodies lay behind the riders.

Bausman's breath left him momentarily as the wind kicked up. It was strong enough to rattle the table and spill his wine onto the page. The red libation stained the page, drying instantly.

He looked up at Benny who nodded at the book. The seriousness was gone, but his face was grave nonetheless.

Bausman did not remember turning the page, but he looked down and read:

The Americans - 1944 A.D.

Depictions of giant planes flew over Monte Cassino. An uncountable number of bombs screamed toward its peak.

The wind stopped as quickly as it had started. An eerie stillness remained. Bausman frantically flipped through the rest of the book.

Blank pages.

He backed away from the table and grabbed the nearest bookshelf to keep himself from tipping over. His stomach lurched. He thought he was going to be sick.

"What—"

"Rest, soldier" Benny said gently. "Time is going nowhere."

Private Hubert Bausman caught his breath, though a dull pulse punched his brain at regular intervals, matching the rhythm of his heartbeat.

"I've...been here before," he said as if he already knew the answer.

Benny nodded.

Bausman looked down at the book. Images of murder and rape sprung into his head. Images he didn't remember seeing in the book itself. Images that held back nothing and finally drove Bausman towards a half-filled barrel in the corner of the room where he evacuated the jug of wine he'd just consumed.

When he was sure he could speak again, he talked with his face held down.

"You're saying I'm one of these people? That I'm one of these *monsters?*" His voice grew indignant. "We came here to *save* you!"

"Yes and no."

He flung his head up. A bad idea as the throbbing punches turned into needle-like stabs.

Sitting in the same chair where Benny had been was Francesca. Bausman hadn't heard the monk leave. Hadn't heard Franny arrive.

"At least, you're not an intentional monster," she said. "Not this round. It's complicated. You fought to liberate this place from the monsters this time, but you've still destroyed the abbey. Still killed those inside seeking refuge."

Bausman indignance allowed him to ignore Benny's vanishing act for a moment. "We didn't know. We thought the Germans were here."

Francesca dismissed the notion with a wave of her hand. "It doesn't matter."

"What do you mean it doesn't matter? Of course it—"

Bausman took a deep breath and wiped sweat from his eyes. "Please, Franny..."

"No matter. Things are looking up, no?"

Hubert blinked. Francesca, gone once again. Benedict was back.

"We all come out of darkness and toward the light," he said. "Only, the light always seems just out of reach."

Bausman felt disoriented again. He leaned over the barrel, unsure of what he had left to give.

He stared at the unholy mix of puke and wine. At his reflection. At someone else's reflection. A glint of light reflected from the steel helmet that was not on his head. He reached for the mangy beard and long, matted hair that was not his own. Finally, he saw a whiskered GI who wanted nothing more than to go home.

He pushed himself off the barrel with what little strength he could conjure. "Why?" he asked weakly.

"You're tied to this place," Francesca said. "*We're* tied to this place. A curse of Apollo, maybe. There's something sacred about this ground. Something tied to time and space."

"We'll all be leaving soon, but we'll meet here again," Benny chimed in. "They rebuild, we come back, they destroy. *Ad infinitum.*" He chuckled. "Or in your case, *ad nauseam.*" Bausman heard Francesca laugh as well.

The world was collapsing in on the young private. He had to get out of the stifling cellar. He ran up the stairs, foregoing one last look at the company he had been keeping for nearly a week. His legs carried him over the rubble as he navigated only by a thin strip of moon.

Bausman's irregular breathing made him cramp up, so he stopped and leaned on the trunk of a nearby tree. He was beaten down, so weary. He turned his back to the tree and slumped to the ground.

None of this made sense. Too much wine, he thought. That was it. Who knows what sort of contamination those barrels may have gotten after all of the destruction. He was so tired now, he just wanted to sleep. Despite the spinning earth, Bausman closed his eyes and dug his fingers into the damp soil beside him.

"So who told you? Him or the looker?"

Bausman looked up and saw Private Munson standing a few yards away, a lit cigarette bouncing from the side of his lips.

Bausman said nothing.

"Must've been God's man," Munson said and laughed. He walked over and extended his hand. "Come on, soldier. Let's go drink some wine."

Killing Dixie

The Colonel's blue eyes shifted ever so slightly. His crow's feet appeared rugged and deep in the low light of the lantern hanging from the entryway trellis.

"Now, son, let's be reasonable gentlemen and take a walk." His voice was measured. "Talk about whatever it is aggrieves you."

John Cunningham, Jr., son of the recently deceased Corporal John Cunningham, Sr., left the tip of his father's .31 caliber "Baby Dragoon" revolver pointed at the Colonel's heart.

"You have no right to talk reasonable with that thing hanging over your home," John said, nodding toward the flag fluttering proudly in the moist São Paulo breeze. He fought back a retching feeling rising from his belly. A light rain swept across the pristine rectangle of woven wool hanging above the entryway of the ramshackle cabin: Thirteen white stars swam in crisscrossed rivers of blue, surrounded by triangles of blood-red sand.

"Look, I don't know you from Adam, son, and—

"I am not your son, so you had best stop calling me that." John cocked the hammer. "Now are you going to welcome a weary traveler into your house or not?"

The Colonel turned his head slightly, but his eyes never left John's. John could see a crack of light emanating from one side of the door.

"I don't know why you're raising old ghosts, but I am most certain we can hash this out without resorting to—"

"Whoever's in there, you had better not be itchin' to be clever," John shouted over the Colonel's shoulder. The cylinder was fully loaded, five rounds, and he had a couple of spares in his coat pocket as well.

"Sarah," The Colonel said with a raised voice which, somehow, still sounded genteel. "Tell your mama to put on a pot. We have a guest."

"Don't nobody do nothin'," John said right after.

He spoke in a quieter tone to the Colonel. "Walk."

Though he was glad to escape the sticky, Brazilian drizzle and the strange animal sounds emanating from the surrounding ferns, John felt a low reticence. Old ghosts was right. He was stepping into shadows of something from which he knew there was no return.

* * *

So long as there were only four folks in total, everything would be fine, especially given that one was a pretty woman maybe a few years older than John, and another who appeared to be her little girl, not much older than six or seven. That must have been Sarah. She had the woman's curly brown hair and her grandfather's narrow eyes.

The other remaining stranger was a wildcard: an elderly negro, standing a head taller than all of them, and wily looking too. He kept his head up and his yellowed eyes occasionally shifted between the Colonel and John.

The cabin wasn't large, but seemed spacious enough: a few straw beds lining the back wall bookended by a pair of ornate armoires, a wood stove in one corner, and a small, round table surrounded by several sturdy-looking chairs near the center of the room.

"Where's her daddy?" John asked the Colonel, indicating toward Sarah.

"No longer with us. Yellow fever got him two years ago."

John didn't trust the Colonel as far as he could throw him. Thanks to his father's vivid and colorful recollections of the man he blamed for everything that had happened, John knew Colonel Nathaniel Dandridge as much as anyone. As sure as the sun is hot, the former commander of the Confederate 33rd Virginia Cavalry was a sneaky one. But, John figured as long as he could keep everyone inside the house, it would prevent any chance of fetching help. He'd just have to keep his ears open and one eye on the door in case someone dropped by.

"Everyone on that side of the room." John waved his gun towards the beds. The little girl whimpered a little and grabbed hold of the big negro's hand.

"C'mon girl," the man said in a low voice. "It'll be alright."

John avoided looking at her face. He really wished the Colonel had been here alone, but circumstances were what they were.

They all sat down on the bed except for the Colonel. Sarah sat on the negro's lap.

"I don't have no beef with any of you but for one man," John said. "Colonel Nathaniel Dandridge."

The Colonel raised his eyebrows.

"Do you claim to be him?" John finished. He needed an admission.

There was no hesitation. "I am Nathaniel Dandridge, but I am no longer a Colonel. Granted, you're a youngin, but old enough to know that the country for whom I served no longer exists."

"And yet you fly the flag."

There was a heavy pause. Rainwater tapped against the clay tile roof.

"And yet I fly the flag," the Colonel said with his chin held high and a sickening pride in his voice.

Before John could get a word out, the Colonel spoke up. "If you wanted to come here and just shoot me for hanging a piece of cloth, you would have done so already. So what is it that you want, Yankee? To scare women and children too?"

It was a transparent attempt to bring John to shame. He wasn't about to fall for it.

"Two things. I *will* make you pay for your crime, but first I want an apology."

The Colonel looked at him incredulously. "For what, exactly?"

"In good time. First, I'm guessing that a man who has such pride in a dead country still has his uniform."

Silence.

"Well then," John said, "I'll take that as an affirmative. I think it's fitting that you reacquaint yourself with it. You say you're no longer a Colonel, but it's the Colonel for whom I'm bringing justice. Where is it?"

Again, no response. John pointed his gun at the wall just over the old rebel's shoulder, and after a moment of his own hesitation, he pulled the trigger. The percussion clapped his ears and set them to ringing lightly. Bits of wood splintered just above the negro, far from where he intended to fire. John caught himself looking at a bewildered Sarah, her mouth caught open in a scream, but he turned away quickly and forced himself to lock eyes with the Colonel. His hand was shaking and he thought the Colonel noticed, so he grabbed the gun with both hands under the guise of cocking the hammer.

"Lucius," the Colonel said with a raised voice, though his demeanor remained irritatingly calm, "fetch me the uniform."

As if on instinct, the old black man was almost on his feet upon hearing his name. He lifted the crying little girl from his lap and handed her to her mama. John moved the gun towards him and Lucius froze.

"I don't know why you followed this man down here," John said. "Probably threatened you otherwise, but you don't have to do a damn thing. Just tell me where it is." John's motives weren't entirely charitable. He figured that if Lucius showed this level of loyalty to the Colonel, he might go far enough to pull out a rifle or pistol.

The negro looked at his master who nodded almost imperceptibly.

"He keeps it over there," Lucius said, pointing at one of the wardrobes that must have accompanied the family on their long journey from America. "There's a box sitting on the bottom, at the back."

John wondered briefly how he'd be able to keep an eye on the family, yet get the uniform. The answer was obvious, though.

"Sarah," he said, ducking his face and glancing to the side. "Be a good girl and bring out your grandfather's box, please. And set it on the table."

John didn't want to, even felt like he'd damn near faint, but he pointed the gun in her direction. Beads of sweat gathered on his brow. He had told himself that he wouldn't rush this, that this was a scene that should be savored and stamped in his memory for all time. But now, he wanted nothing more than for it to be all over. With each passing second, John felt less enthusiastic and more obligated to his father.

"Sarah," her mother said, speaking for the first time, "honey, it'll be fine. Please, do as he says." Her voice was much harsher than the

Colonel's.

Sarah's eyes were like that of a reprimanded beagle. She bounced off her mother, ran toward the wardrobe and opened the door quickly. John was nervous about the speed at which she moved, but he accepted the risk. With her small hands, she tossed aside several blankets and pulled out a brown leather box a foot deep and two feet wide. She began to lift the lid.

"I said put it on the table," John snapped. He cringed as she started to cry. He didn't want to scare the girl, but his nerves were overwhelming him.

"Sarah," her mother said snapping as much as John, "do as the man says and get back here!" John's eyes briefly met the Colonel's and he knew that with every stressful moment, the Colonel was sizing up an opportunity to make a move.

"It's too heavy," she sobbed.

Flustered, John said, "N-nevermind. Go back to your mama." Her feet clapped against the floorboards as she flew into her mother's arms. The look on the mother's face told John that if he dropped his guard for one blink of an eye, she would make him regret it even more than the Colonel.

John walked up to the box. "Don't nobody move an inch," he said to them all, keeping both eyes peered in their direction. He'd hoped he could pull the .31 quickly enough should they make a move, but he knew that if they chose now to do so, he would be at a disadvantage. He cupped his pistol with his palm and quickly slid his fingers beneath the box. It was indeed heavier than he expected, but he lugged it to the table where it fell from his hands without any solemnity.

The family was still lined against the wall, motionless, overflowing with expectation. John readied his pistol again and with his free hand, lifted the lid and tossed it onto the floor.

His vision was greeted with the damned Confederate gray and yellow trim, delicately laid out. There was the woolen kepi—a cap with a dark bill and buckled band across the front. Below that lay a golden sash and white riding gloves. John removed all of them from the box and placed them on the table.

He rifled through the rest of the contents. The Colonel's shell jacket had been folded neatly with its three golden stars still pinned onto each side of the collar, and two columns of gold buttons lining the front. Beneath were gray trousers and the officer's sabre secured in its scabbard. The bulk of the box's weight was a stack of old newspapers and other hokum.

"Where your boots?" John asked.

"Sold 'em to help pay for transport," the Colonel said.

So much for pride, John thought.

He pulled out each piece of clothing and tossed them at the Colonel.

"Get dressed."

* * *

John was not disappointed as his hackles rose at seeing the Colonel in full uniform. He had to admit the old man wore it well. He was almost everything John had imagined, one of the "devils in gray" his father had rambled on about through whiskey-induced tirades.

"They don't need to see this, young man," the Colonel said, nodding at his family and slave. "I don't know who you are or what I've done to you, but they don't need to see this."

If John let them go now, he'd probably be wrapped up by the time they were able to get very far, but they may have a rifle or two stashed away nearby. It wasn't uncommon.

"They stay, so that they know about your crimes and understand that I'm not here to murder you—I'm here to enact justice on a fugitive."

The Colonel's face took on a shade of ruby red. "I am no fugitive."

John laughed, surprising himself. "That so? Then why did you turn tail and run down to Brazil?"

The Colonel took a step forward and straightened up. John moved his pistol up, but the old man maintained his defiance.

"You say I turned tail, but what do you know? You couldn't have been ten when I lost my country. My means of subsistence. Half of my family slaughtered by men in blue. What do you know, son? What do *you* know?"

John thought he knew enough.

"Ten years ago, my father, Corporal John Cunningham, Sr., came back from the war a broken man. Unable to see because he had been shot once in the head and lost his vision. Unable to walk because another minie ball had made him lame. And because of that, my mama left us shortly after his return, making him an even more broken man. But for the charity of the few friends my father had, we would have starved each year. We barely held on as it was." He looked at Sarah, "I lost my little sister because we couldn't afford no medicine."

The Colonel seemed to deflate a little bit, or so it seemed to John.

"I'm sorry to hear the circumstances, but that is the hell of war, son. Your daddy was a soldier just like the rest of us. He—"

"No!" John shouted with an unexpected fury. Sarah sank into her mother's arms and the negro recoiled. "No! Not just like the rest of you." John fought back tears. He felt an odd mix of fire increasing in his belly, but also a slightly dwindling resolve. He'd spent months tracking the Colonel's whereabouts, coming all this way with barely a moment's rest and it was all catching up with him. He'd heard that he was among many of the Southern soldiers had left for Brazil, a land still friendly to those invested in the machinations of slavery. Apprising the Colonel in his uniform, standing here in a small cabin in the middle of a foreign land, made the entire scene seem uncomfortably ridiculous.

Still, John continued. Deep down, he knew he was doing something right, yet still felt a need to confess and justify it all. "I buried my father six months ago, and that night I had a dream. I was walking through the scrub oak of Albany and there was a flash of light, just like the preacher used to go on about Paul on the road to Damascus. The voice cried out for vengeance. I knew that it was my father. Day in and day out, he drank from his jug and related to me the truth of you, Colonel Dandridge, and your damned 33rd Cavalry."

The Colonel's gave John a penetrating stare. Something changed in the way he appeared. John couldn't place a finger on it, and before he could ruminate on it anymore, the Colonel asked with the gentleness of a rabbit, "With what regiment did you say your father served?"

"I didn't," John replied. "It don't matter anyhow."

"Oh, but it does, son. It does."

John had confessed enough, but he supposed he didn't see any harm in explaining more to a dead man. "The New York 195th."

Silence. Behind his eyes, the Colonel seemed to be seeking something.

"And where was it that your father honorably took these Southern bullets that I so directed?"

The words were fresh in John's mind as if it were John Sr. himself speaking through him. "Bakerstown, just inside the northern tip of Shenandoah."

"I see," the Colonel said. The coolness of his voice grated on John. He felt anxious to get it over with.

"Do you deny you were there?" John said. This new line of conversation was irritating him and he was happy that it was building back up his resolve.

"No, son. I don't deny it at all. I was there alright." He slowly removed the hat from his head and held it in his hands. "Thing is, I don't think events took place exactly as your father told you."

As if his legs carried him on their own volition, John walked directly to the Colonel and dug the tip of the pistol into the soldier's chest. "Are you calling my father a liar?" Out of the corner of his eyes, he saw the daughter shift closer to the negro.

The Colonel never looked away from John.

"I got some papers in that box," he said. "There's one you ought to read. Seems you wouldn't believe me if I told you myself."

"You're delaying," John said. "I don't need to read no papers."

Those cold blue eyes challenged him. "Son, I don't want you to do something you'd regret. You might have never known that you were about to make a mistake, but now a part of you can't help but wonder if I'm telling you something you may have already been thinking for a long time."

The Colonel placed the hat back on his head and straightened it out. "Please, not for my sake, but for yours, read that paper."

A sound of creaking wood pulled John's attention. Lucius was on his feet again and walking toward the box. John couldn't fully understand why he let him do so, but he did. The black man stooped over and rummaged through the small stack of newspapers until he seemed to find what he was looking for.

He marched over to John and handed him a piece of yellowed paper.

John only stared back at him, unsure of what to do. His pistol was still pressed against the Colonel's chest.

"Lucius, if you would, please," the Colonel said.

The old slave pulled the paper back, unfolded it and cleared his throat. "Though Johnny Reb puts up a worthy scrap in the various corners of this dear country, some of our boys in blue have become their own worst enemy. While awaiting orders in the Shenandoah Valley, the New York 195th Infantry regiment found themselves with an excess of time and liquor. Reports have come in of six killed and eighteen wounded from an explosion at the munitions depot, all due to a drunken exchange. With dispatches indicating the Confederate's 33rd Cavalry making a move to the North, the 195th is being disbanded with the remaining soldiers being reassigned to other regiments."

Lucius stopped there.

"Lies," John said quietly, trying to convince himself that the cracks which had appeared in his father's stories had never been there.

He used to think it was just the liquor which had confused him some-times. Whenever he'd asked to see John Sr.'s bullet wounds, his father flat out refused. After being reprimanded and chased away with his father's swinging cane, John had stopped asking for details.

"That there's a Union paper, son," the Colonel said.

John's notions were being hit from all sides. He eyed the Colonel with suspicion.

"You taught your slave how to read?"

Before he could answer, Lucius interrupted. "Freed man, Mr. Cunningham. I'm a freed man. I come down with Mr. Dandridge because ain't nothin' waitin' for me up there. The Colonel had always been good to me, and at least down here, I got work and get to learn from Ms. Dandridge, alongside Sarah."

John realized at this point that his gun was no longer raised at the Colonel's chest, but directed towards the ground.

"I've made my mistakes," the Colonel said. "I came down here with my ways set, but I've learned much over the past ten years. I freed all my slaves. Any that chose to stay with me, I've given an education and a fair wage to work my crops."

John felt a light grip on his arm.

"Look, if there's one thing a Southern man can abide by, son, it's honor. You came here because you felt it was the honorable thing to do. I don't blame your daddy. Any man in his condition would have spoke the same."

The Colonel looked to his daughter, "Why don't you put on that pot I mentioned earlier," and then he turned back to John. "Please, join us for supper. We can have us a conversation about all our wrongs and our inadequate attempts to make up for them."

Swag

As the convention's low-level hum of conversation and clatter carried through the black polyester curtains, Gerry flipped the strange device around in her hands. It wasn't heavy and appeared to be made of cheap tin. Glossy orange paint flaked in spots and cracks formed a pattern of uneven tiles, reminding her of a gaudy bathroom floor in an upscale restaurant. It had a short handle in the back, presumably so that you could hold onto it with one hand, and for whatever reason, spin the gear around with the other. She noticed that a smaller gear was attached to the middle of the larger one. They didn't appear to interlock in any way. She squeezed the toothed edge of the larger one and gave it a spin. The other gear twisted and clicked in the opposite direction. Tiny sparks of light began to ignite and pop and Gerry felt a warmth run through her hands.

Rose quickly clamped down on the apparatus, bringing it to an immediate stop.

"Not here," she said. Her voice was emphatic and she peered over Gerry's shoulder with suspicion even though they were the only two inside the makeshift room—one of several twelve-by-twelve curtain-lined squares that were set up by the convention staff so that vendors and customers could meet with some level of privacy.

"Oh," Gerry said, looking at Rose with some surprise. "Sorry."

"It's okay," Rose replied. "It's just that you really should wait to try it until you get home."

Gerry continued to inspect it. "Well, thank you."

"You have lots of questions, I'm sure. It's a prototype of a new product," Rose said. Her voice dropped to a whisper. "It's going to change everything."

Rose acted as if she had just handed Gerry the week's winning lottery numbers. For a software company, this seemed like something outside of their purview.

"What is it?"

"It's something better experienced than explained," Rose said. "Just trust me."

"Why are you giving it to me?" Gerry grew a little suspicious.

Rose looked at her as if she had asked why rain falls from the sky. "You've always been there for us, Gerry," she said. "But for you, Cortega Systems wouldn't be here—wouldn't be *anywhere*. We almost went out of business, you know? But it's been three years now since you helped us climb out of that hole and we're market leader. I can hardly believe it. You went to bat for us when everyone thought you were crazy to do so."

"It's what I do." Gerry smiled, reflecting appreciation.

She was good with the smile. It came easily to her. And while she was genuinely happy for Rose and Cortega, the seeds for their success weren't planted due to a simple case of charity or friendship. Gerry never threw good money at bad product and she never got too close to anyone, let alone business partners. Her knack for picking winners had taken her from Baldwin Capital's dim and mold-infested mailroom to a large corner office on the 13th floor with Chief Technology Officer imprinted on her nameplate. She remembered how proud her father had been every time she had received a promotion. Even on his deathbed, when she would try to awkwardly connect with him beyond work talk, he'd always redirect the conversation to her accomplishments and how it reminded him of the time he had made a big sale or gotten a one-up on someone jockeying for power in the office. He never cared about anything else she might have to say until she determined it needed to be the other way around—she had to care about what he wanted to hear.

In the case of Cortega, Gerry had seen their eventual success coming. She was an avid reader of trade journals and college alumni newsletters. It was something she'd learned by watching her father the few times he was around the house. Cortega had been snapping up sharp kids out of MIT and Stanford over the past seven years: kids who'd focused heavily on machine learning, artificial intelligence, and even quantum mechanics. The company obviously wasn't focused on building the same old business analytics software as their competitors. Gerry wasn't one to dig too deep into any one subject, but upon further investigation, she'd gotten that familiar feeling in her gut and that was enough to convince her Cortega was on a path to a breakthrough. Their software would lead Baldwin towards greater sales opportunities, and therefore, greater profits. Most of Gerry's competitors had initially passed Cortega by because their proposed technology was unproven and the price tag was considerably high. For a time, Gerry had them all to herself, but now others saw their potential impact on the industry.

Rose gently pried the device from Gerry's hands and placed it in a reusable swag bag along with a folded piece of paper. She handed the bag to Gerry, then her eyes narrowed.

"I don't need to tell you this, of course, but *do not* lose this."

Gerry flashed another congenial smile.

* * *

As she stepped into her hotel room, Gerry checked the calendar on her phone. It was just before seven o'clock and she was scheduled to attend a dinner in thirty minutes with the sales reps at Perseus, a cloud-based inventory systems company. She considered texting her assistant, telling him that she was feeling ill, but it wasn't worth it. Gerry would only have to make it up at another time and things wouldn't go any easier. Perseus was looking to secure a multi-year contract. They'd arranged a dog and pony show dinner for her and other Baldwin officers. It would be business as usual—they would order ten bottles of the most ridiculously expensive Burgundy wines and fawn over her, trying to get her to make regretful snap commitments.

So, Gerry, I saw that piece about you in Forbes. Top Forty in their Forties? Nice! Have you seen what Perseus has to offer? Let me just tell you….

As she threw her collection of swag onto the ground beside the minibar, a rank aroma wound its way into her nostrils. Walking the convention floor all day in a three-button pantsuit had left her desperate for a shower, but she had to make a choice—a quick shower and deal with reapplying makeup or unwind with her little ritual and just touch things up. Option number two sounded best.

She turned the deadbolt on the hotel door and drew the curtains closed. It wasn't as if anyone would burst in or peep through the 27th-story window, but her self-consciousness defied all reason. With the down pillow folded and propped beneath her head, Gerry kicked off her shoes and took a deep breath. She put on a pair of headphones, hit play on her phone and began to sing along at the top of her lungs to Taylor Swift's *You Belong With Me*. A familiar image formed in her mind. She was on stage, a contestant on *The Voice*, posed before the bright lights, enraptured by the accompanying music. The song crescendoed as it approached the chorus, yet something wasn't right. The longer she sang, the more embarrassed she grew which tightened the muscles around her larynx. She sensed harsh judgments from the hundreds of imaginary eyes peering out from the audience. As her confidence cracked, so did her voice.

Negative assessments hit her from all angles. How ridiculous I would look, she thought. She knew the crowd was seeing right through her—a woman in her mid-forties trying to live out silly, youthful fantasies.

Halfway through the first song, she paused the music and sat up. Her mind's eye settled on an image of her father sitting uncomfortably in a chair during her first and only singing recital. His demanding eyes were those she had seen in the audience just now, but they had been multiplied there.

After several moments of holding court with her father's phantasmic image, she fell back onto the bed and gazed at the ceiling. An orange-tinged imitation of a Michelangelo fresco covered it from end to end, reminding her of the strange device Rose had given her.

Gerry pushed herself off the bed and walked toward the bag of swag. She tipped it over, emptying its contents onto the floor. Buried beneath oversized t-shirts, hundreds of stickers and a dozen reusable water bottles was Cortega's apparatus along with the folded note. She picked up the piece of paper, unfolded it, and read.

> *Gerry,*
> *I know you're probably reading this from your hotel room.*
> *It's okay. I didn't expect you to wait until you got home.*
> *Let me just advise a couple of things:*
> *1. Lay down when turning the gears. You don't want to*
> *fall and hurt yourself.*
> *2. It only works once, so enjoy the moment.*
> *Happy travels.*

Rose

What this had to do with Cortega's analytic systems, Gerry had

no clue. Maybe they were looking to expand into a new field? Introduce

some sort of virtual or augmented-reality aspect? That could be a boon

to website hits; bring in more traffic from the millennial segment.

Maybe it was even more benign than that, though. Maybe it

was just some sort of viral marketing scheme concocted by a group of

college-aged interns. Who's to say that these funny looking toys wouldn't

start showing up as stickers slapped onto the backs of street signs or

wind their way into Internet memes.

Suddenly, the room felt entirely too quiet, so she turned on the

television. A *Married with Children* rerun was playing—Al Bundy was

berating his wife while his kids were sneaking cash from his wallet. She

wasn't really a fan of the dysfunctional family sitcom, but it served its

purpose.

She picked up the device and took it back to the bed. She laid

down again and held it over her head, examining it a little more closely

under the dim table lamp lighting. It didn't look any different than before.

It still appeared to be made of cheap, thin metal and was shabbily paint-

ed. There were no wires or batteries. As she had in the convention hall,

Gerry gripped the handle and with her other hand, spun the large gear.

Al's voice carried on in the background.

You know, Peg, it would be nice if you could make us a hot meal every once

in awhile.

Tiny sparks jumped again between the gaps in the cogs. What a family, Gerry thought as she stared at the device, captivated by the pattern beginning to form. As the wheels spun, they seemed to be picking up speed on their own volition. A vague notion formed in her head—a vision of those old hypnosis wheels that were popular in the early 20th century. The kind that you could order out of the back of *MAD* magazine. She giggled at the thought, and then Al's daughter, Kelly, chimed in.

Dad, I'm going out with my new boyfriend, Spider. I'll be back in a week.

The sparks turned into thin strands of electrical current. Bright light flashed in an indiscernible pattern. Gerry felt as if she were standing before a window, watching a violent lightning storm dancing in the distance. She tried to latch her attention onto the sounds of the sitcom, but her attention was being rapidly sucked into that swirling spiral pattern forming in front of her. As the flashes grew more intense, a wave of vertigo swept over her. She tried to let go of the handle, but the muscles in her hands squeezed down. She could *feel* her knuckles turning white. She wanted to shut out the world, look away, but even her own eyes seemed to align against her. Her mind twisted like one of the gears and a nauseating, low-frequency whir thrummed against her inner ear.

I coulda' been something, Peg. Four touchdowns in a single game. Then I met you. Now I sell womens' shoes.

Finally, Gerry's hand released the device, but instead of dropping onto her, it floated in the air just above her chest. As she squeezed the comforter between her fingers, the TV's canned laugh track was going off in the background like a machine gun.

She thought she might be able to roll off the blankets and onto the ground, but there was a dread weight across every inch of her body. Unable to fight the pressure any longer, Gerry released her grip and allowed herself to fall into the abyss.

* * *

The familiar vanilla scent of coneflowers entered Gerry's nostrils. The sky above her head was almost the same shade as their pink petals.

She sat up and listened to the rapid-fire snaps of what sounded like audience applause morphing into the rhythm of cicadas. Her first thought wasn't a concern with where she was or how she had arrived, but a single, focused memory. The one most tied to the smell of those coneflowers and the music of those tiny creatures with transparent wings.

Terre Haute, Indiana.

1978? 1979?

She had been hiding in a field.

Why?

She couldn't quite pull the answer to that from her mind's tight grip, but the feeling was undeniably the same as she had felt that very day—a blend of fear and giddiness. The kind of nervous elation that brings an otherwise unreproducible smile to a child's face.

She remembered now.

Her and Father were playing hide-and-seek. Gerry couldn't remember if he even knew that he was supposed to be looking for her. That happened a lot. She thought her instructions had always been clear. He seemed to acknowledge her from behind a newspaper or by giving her a thumbs up while he was talking on the phone, but often she would lay in the dirt as the sun slowly fell, waiting, poking at roly-polies with thin sticks and drawing patterns in the soil. Then she would sing her heart out in the middle of that field—every song she could remember, whether they be church hymns like *Go Tell It On The Mountain* or the Bee Gees.

But her throat felt parched at the moment. She didn't feel much like singing.

She stood up and dusted herself off, appraising her clothing as she did so. On her impossibly small feet were a dusty pair of once-white, but now yellowed Nike Cortez tennis shoes with a red elongated checkmark running along the outsides. She was wearing Jordache jeans and a rainbow-striped tank-top.

Gerry tried to look across the field, but her head barely reached above the edge of the bloomed perennials. She stood on her tippy-toes to gain her bearings. Her old house was not only exactly where she'd expected it to be, but also looked exactly as it had in at that time. That was a little jarring since she had last seen it ten years ago, just two years after Father's funeral. It had fallen into great disrepair: splintered wooden siding, the outer fieldstone wall having come down in parts, and almost all of the trees dead and gone due to a lack of water. Her mother had entered a period of rapid mental decline after Father's death, so Gerry had sold the place quickly and cheaply, then moved her mother into an assisted living facility.

She turned slightly toward the tiny river which ran along the rear of their home. On the far end of the dock, she could see the top of her father's Greek fisherman cap that he had picked up during one of his business travels. He was sitting with his back to her, facing the water.

Gerry broke into a run and was breathing hard by the time her shoes slapped against the wood planks. The rickety dock swayed gently beneath her feet just as she had expected it to.

"Dad!" she exclaimed. "You're supposed to be looking for me!"

Her voice was youthful again, but she had an awareness that this wasn't completely her. In fact, it seemed to her as if she was composed of two different identities, like those mythological creatures with multiple faces on each side of their head. She was both Gerry, accomplished businesswoman, and Gerry, the little girl who desperately wanted her father to pay attention.

What did they call this, she wondered. A lucid dream? Maybe that's what Rose's device was. A tool guaranteed to induce such things.

Her father remained motionless but for a tiny breeze whipping around the hairs sticking out of the back of his hat. Gerry saw that he was holding a fishing rod in one hand, its string pulled taut to the right, disappearing into the running currents.

Gerry frowned and her eyes narrowed. As long as they had lived on this beautiful stretch of land beside the river, she had never seen her father fish. It was always a little amusing to her that for a family who lived in such picturesque environs, Father and Mother were never 'outdoorsy' people. Mother rarely went outside unless required and when Father was home a few days out of the month, he spent much of the time working in his upstairs office, the door shut tight to the distractions of the outside world.

"Dad!" she shouted again. She crept up and laid a hand on his shoulder.

He turned and simply smiled as if he had heard her all along. She expected him to look as he had during those early years, and he sort of did, but there was an understated tiredness that revealed itself through sallow bags beneath his eyes and sticky, gummy lips. "Hi, honey. The fish are biting."

"You don't even fish," she said.

He shook his head at her as if that were the silliest notion in the world.

"Nonsense. We all fish," he said. "Sometimes, if we sit still long enough and pay attention, we even catch a few." He leaned over and whispered. "Hey, do you think mom would be happy if I brought some home for dinner?"

Gerry thought about it for a second. "Probably not. She hates fish."

That set her father to howling. He gripped his gut and teetered back and forth, nearly losing his fishing rod to the river before he quickly recovered it. He gave Gerry a funny look—a mix of relief and sudden fear as if he was going to lose everything he'd ever known in an instant. He must have realized he was scaring her a little because he straightened up and smiled at her again. It seemed like a shadow of a smile this time, though, like the crumbling wall and chipped house-paint. Still, his eyes had a strange sparkle in them that she'd never noticed before. A chaotic pattern of tiny stars flickering on and off in a manner that was sitting on the edge of her comprehension.

"Yeah. You're right," he said. He looked at the empty space next to him. "Come on, have a seat anyway," he said. "We can always catch and release."

If Gerry felt any reluctance, it quickly dissipated. A familiar smell of his Old Spice aftershave hovered like a cloud as she sat down beside him. His eyes never left her.

She kicked her feet back and forth. They dangled at least a foot above the waterline. "What are we doing here?" she asked.

Gerry inspected every ounce of his being, from the sunspots on the outside of his forearms to the gold wedding ring that seemed to have been grown over by his own flesh.

"You tell me," he said, the grin still on his face.

Tell him? As if she had planned this dream?

"Why didn't you come looking for me?" she asked. The question seemed to impose itself on her.

The sparkle in his eyes was mesmerizing. It wanted to hypnotize her, pull her away from such lines of questioning, but she refused to let it. Her father took a deep breath and looked to the tiny whitecaps forming on the river.

"I got busy," he said.

"With what?" Gerry demanded. Before she realized, she was on her feet, her fists clenched. Her torso was tipped toward him as if she wanted to prevent him from packing up his gear and leaving.

"With absolutely nothing, honey. Absolutely nothing." The clicking of cicadas picked up in the background. He grew animated again. "Hey! Come on, fish with your old man," he said. He indicated toward a second pole sitting on the dock beside him, already baited with a slimy worm dancing and curling under the blood orange sun.

What was the harm, Gerry pondered. But something tugged at her from the inside. She turned back toward the fields from whence she came and saw the top of a little girl's head moving, spinning in a circular pattern as her long pigtails flailed back and forth. Though the air was filled only with the song of insects, she sensed that little girl was a part of their music.

Gerry leaned in and hugged her father tightly as if he might float away. "No," she whispered into his ear.

He pried her arms loose and craned his neck to face her. The sparkles in his eyes were still there, but now Gerry ignored them as if they were inconsequential specks of dust.

"No?" Her father laughed again with all of his might. Laughed until his eyes were flowing with tears, but then the laughter turned into something not so funny and he was sniveling at her feet now, bawling and choking on his own sobs. It scared Gerry and she found herself backing up. Her father had been the strongest person she'd ever known. Even behind his smile lay a steely, invulnerable resolve.

The moment she considered bolting back to the field, his outburst came to a complete stop. He reached out to her with a pleading hand. "No. Please," he said. "You don't have to fish, Gerry. I'm sorry you ever thought you had to fish."

Those words sent a shockwave through her system. Her belly felt as if it might flutter away.

I don't know, Al. Marcy isn't going to like it if she finds out I was hanging out all night at The Jiggly Room.

Where the atmosphere had once felt thick and constraining, Gerry felt as if she were breathing freely again.

Ohhhhh Aaaalll….

Yes, Peg?

Al, come rub my feet.

Gerry opened her eyes. Michelangelo's fresco sharpened into focus. Her head was pounding. She rubbed her temples, but her fingers felt gritty. She looked at them and there was a sort of glitter stuck to their tips.

She sat up and saw a small pile of the same sparkly powder fall from her blouse and onto the bed. Gerry looked over at the alarm clock: 7:45 PM.

"Shit!" she yelled. She grabbed her phone lying beside the clock. There were several missed calls and text messages from her assistant.

Where r u?

They're waiting!

Gerry stared at the television screen. A shampoo commercial played. Though her eyes were directed that way, her thoughts were focused only on what she had just experienced. There was an unexplainable weight lifted from her chest. She turned to see her earphones laying tangled on the floral-print comforter. She grabbed them and walked toward her phone just as another text message made it vibrate.

Malcolm seems a little pissed ur not here.

Gerry popped her headphones into the jack, turned up Katy Perry's *Roar*, and sang loud enough to drown out every dinging notification.

Fantastic Shorts - Volume One

Be Kind

Be kind.

Tenet number one in the Book of Stanton.

For ten years, it had been etched into the pathways running between Ernie Bowen's amygdala and hippocampus. He'd spent the better part of two decades bouncing at bars and nightclubs all over the Western Confederation, finding success and salvation in the commandments set forth by the most revered bouncer of the before-times—Jerry Stanton.

But something went wrong tonight.

Tenet number two says: *Be kind until it's time to not be kind.*

That's where the rub is for most Stantonites and why so many of them never make it to the Cooler priesthood. It's one of those invisible lines that takes a patient, learned mind to feel—almost like a single strand from a spider web brushing against your cheek. Ernie thought he was there. He had the title. Had the vestments. Had the respect of his congregation.

How would he explain what went down?

The music had stopped, all the bright white overhead lights were on, and Ernie's mind was a jumble as he looked down at the four men splayed across the sticky floor inside of Luna Loca, the most popular club in New Las Vegas.

Three of them were big. Bigger than Ernie on a good day and without an ounce of fat. They were all on the ground, still breathing, but in various states of incapacitation.

It was the fourth body which was a cause for concern. That man's neck had been snapped so thoroughly, his head hinged until his nose touched his shoulder. Gelled black hair fell across his open eyes like feathers.

Then there was a woman, but she was gone.

To Ernie, it all went down in a blur and now he was faced with two problems: This wasn't just anyone lying dead on the floor. And assuming he could deal with that little issue successfully, there were still the Stantonites from whom Ernie would have to beg absolution.

* * *

"Bless me, Cooler, for I have sinned."

There was an uncomfortable moment of silence. Cooler Schoen must have been expecting him but was probably still shocked to hear Ernie through the thin barrier of the sweatbox confessional.

Ernie filled in the gap. "It has been 3,651 days since my last confession."

"That's an awful long time, son," Schoen said. His inflection was fatherly, filled with his signature gravel tone. Ernie pictured the old man sitting on the other side with his arms crossed and his legs extended in his signature pose. He saw the faded green tattoos on the forearms almost forming new patterns as Schoen's loose, leathery skin pressed into and overlapped itself. "Have you lived such a clean life?"

A tiny voice in Ernie's head wanted to toss out a bevy of excuses, but Ernie rubbed the sentiment out like a boot on a glowing cigarette.

"I've lived according to the Book."

"That's not an answer."

More silence.

"But what matters is that you're here now," Schoen continued. "Please, go on."

The Cooler had to have known the story. The incident only occurred last night, but by the looks and whispers Ernie observed on his walk to the church this morning, it had traveled through the ears and mouths of all of Downtown. That was really something in a place where dead bodies popped up like desert primrose. Still, Ernie would do what he came here to do.

"I murdered a man last night."

"Murdered?"

"Pretty sure."

"Only pretty sure?"

"Well…" Ernie paused to think how much his future with the Church hinged on the story he was about to tell. If he were to be excommunicated, he didn't know what he would do. Before bouncing, there was nothing. After? He hadn't thought there would be an after. Still didn't think so.

"...I can't remember everything. I know what happened before and after—when he was lying on the ground, limp as a codfish. I only know what the witnesses said."

"I see. And what is that you think called you to commit this murder, son?"

"Nothing." The answer was instinctual.

A gritty laugh. "Nothing? Just felt like a good night for murder?"

Events had been replaying themselves in Ernie's mind since last night.

"Cooler, I've had my head stomped into the ground until it looked like my face was covered with strawberry jam. I'm sporting six scars across my belly where I've been shanked. I got a goddamn glass eye after the original got punctured by a spiked heel."

At the time that they occurred, each event seemed to be a big deal. Now they were simply as much a part of his being as the slab of ham steak sitting in his stomach from breakfast.

"Not once," he continued. "Not once have I lost control."

"I believe you. Take a deep breath. Concentrate. Walk me through what you *believe* happened."

Ernie had been a walking bundle of nerves since the incident. He closed his only eye and focused until he could almost feel the wall-rattling bass just outside of the club.

* * *

He'd just started working the door on that warm evening when Dorney came rushing out from inside and whispered into Ernie's ear.

"We have a situation."

"What's going on?"

"A guy won't leave, no matter how much we've asked him to. He's starting to get riled up and piss people off."

Ernie wondered why he was being bothered for a rudimentary task. "Grab a partner and kindly walk him outside."

"He won't budge." Dorney stepped back slightly. Sweat was pouring from his curly hair, down onto his brow. "And there's something else we learned."

Ernie waited stone-faced.

"It's Sammy Verillo's nephew, Mel."

* * *

At this point in the story, Ernie stopped to see if Cooler Schoen would react. Sammy Verillo had a stranglehold on almost half of Downtown. Many casinos, bars, and clubs within the four-square-mile area had Sammy's signature touch on them and a lot of people were happy to work for him. But, you so much as sneezed in his direction, you did so at your own peril.

"Continue," was all Schoen said.

* * *

Ernie recounted stepping inside with Dorney who needlessly pointed at the middle of the bar. Mel Verillo was throwing cocktail glasses around like they were baseballs, trying to hit targets across the room. A couple of the guests were too slow to duck and took some hits to the chest and shoulders. The rest of them were breaking for the exit. Never a good sign.

Be kind.

Ernie's eye started with the troublemaker and the three muscled goons surrounding him, then ended on the laughing girl beside him. She was sitting on a stool next to Mel, one leg crossed over the other. Her creamy thighs were illuminated by the strobing red and green lights while her wavy brown locks brought back memories of how it smelled of vanilla and spices.

"Oh look," she said, staring at Ernie as he and Dorney approached along with two other bouncers. "They brought in the talent." Her words were slurred and her eyes narrowed like a predator focusing on its prey.

Mel had been making a name for himself lately, and not in a good way. Word among the congregation was that he'd been going on benders lately with his new girl. This was the first time he'd made any scene at Luna Loca, though.

Ernie ignored him and bent toward the girl's left ear.

"What are you doing hanging around with this guy?"

She pushed him away. "I'm fucking him, Ernie. You have a problem with that?"

Be kind.

"I have a problem with you two sending paying customers away. I don't give a damn who you let play in your sandbox." A lie as hard to think as it was to say, but now was not the time to let things get personal.

* * *

"So you knew her?" Schoen asked.

Ernie supposed only in a sense. He came to understand that, as desperately as he wished to, he had never been able to truly know Bea. She used to dance at some of the same clubs he worked. He made it a point to never see the people you work with, but that point had only come into existence after his experience with Bea. They had been together off and on for the past three years, each sudden ending of the relationship as explosive as each rekindling. The last blowout had been epic. She cursed him down to his bones for suggesting she quit dancing. He hadn't seen her for several months until last night and there was no denying his desire to build something again.

"Yeah, I knew her."

Ernie took Cooler Schoen's silence as a request to continue.

* * *

"She's got a great sandbox," Mel chimed in. "But you probably know that, huh?"

A smarmy smile stretched across his face. He was leaning back against the bar, arms spread out with his elbows on the counter, bouncing another cocktail glass in his right hand. His entourage was visibly itchy but doing a decent job of acting cool.

Be kind.

"I'm going to have to ask you all to leave," Ernie said. His good eye took note of Mel's wrist flicking up and down.

"Well, Ernie, I kinda don't want to leave. I'm just having such a good time at my uncle's club. Look, how about I buy you a drink."

Ernie was ready as the glass came hurtling through the space where his head had been. His fist caught hold of it in mid-air.

Be kind.

"Ha!" Mel looked at Bea. "You didn't tell me the monkey knew tricks!"

"He knows a few," she said as if egging on her new boyfriend.

This was the first time Ernie had ever needed to deal with a situation like this.

"Does your uncle know you're here?" he asked.

"He ain't my parole officer. I don't need to check in with him on a regular basis." Mel hopped to his feet and wobbled around a little bit. He fumbled with the zipper on his black slacks, proceeded to whip out his penis and started pissing on Ernie's shoes.

Dorney and the two other guards looked to Ernie who stood in place and shook his head slightly. Mel hummed a tune, interspersed with giggling.

Be kind.

At this point, Bea seemed to find room for a little embarrassment as she turned back toward the bar. After a long fifteen seconds, Mel's stream dried up and he released a loud sigh.

"Much better."

It was time to make a move.

"Good, now you can go," Ernie said. He edged toward Mel and grabbed his arm. The goon tried to shake himself free, but it was no use.

"Get your hands off me, monkey!"

Ernie signaled to Dorney to grab the other arm and motioned for the two other bouncers to watch their backs.

That was when Ernie saw one of Mel's goons reach into his coat.

That was when time stopped.

* * *

"Things kind of went south from there," Ernie said. "At least that's what they tell me. I only remember standing above the muscle and a dead man, feeling absolutely exhausted."

Through the screen, in the candlelight, Ernie could see the slight silhouette of Cooler Schoen's experienced face.

"Do you believe you were in control of your emotions up to that point? Acted how Stanton would act? Did what Stanton would do?"

Ernie hadn't actively reflected on those last two questions in a while. Every move he'd made had been pure instinct for a long time. He trusted his gut these days. Trusted that he'd digested the teachings from the Book.

"Yes."

"You're concerned you lost control. You believe that jealousy got the best of you."

Even though it was a statement, Ernie replied, "Yes."

Schoen took a deep breath and then continued, "Dorney and his brothers came to us. Told us what they saw. We all agreed. It seems to me that you were not in control of your faculties."

Ernie's heart skipped a beat. Here it came. The banishment. The shame.

"This has been known to happen to a blessed few," Schoen said.

Ernie stopped breathing. He wasn't sure he heard correctly.

"The Spirit of Stanton can inhabit one's body for a few moments of time so that He can exert His divine will. A miracle of sorts to remind us that he walks among us. Watching. Protecting."

Sweat ran into Ernie's eye as he leaned against the side of the confessional.

"I'm going to read you a passage from chapter nine, verses seven through eight." Cooler Schoen cleared his throat. "*[7] Sure, I thought of a hundred different ways in which I could gut him. But what would that accomplish? [8] There are many methods by which one can inflict harm and disable a troublemaker, all valuable at the appropriate time, but there is only one way to steer the atmosphere in a productive manner and influence the long-term—kindness.*"

The verse wasn't new to Ernie. Every first-year Stanton Seminary student needed to recite the entire chapter from memory. But his mind went suddenly to more earthly matters.

"I'm grateful to Stanton for choosing me as a vessel, but I don't know that Sammy Verillo cares who was in my body at the time."

Cooler Schoen's voice was soothing. "The Church has spoken with him. Above all else, Sammy is a businessman. He can't allow for a drop in foot traffic, no matter who's involved. He related to us a palpable sense of relief that his little problem seems to have resolved itself."

Ernie felt the weight of the whole damned world lifted from his shoulders. "I don't know what to say, Cooler."

"Rejoice," Schoen said. "Go, give thanks to Stanton, for He is Kind."

Slab Lords

Her skin was as black as freshly poured asphalt and her tall, thin legs resembled those of a roadrunner. Then there were her lips. They had a natural pucker that would make a goldfish cry. A pair of over-sized sunglasses covered her eyes with thick aqua-blue frames and lenses resembling the peepers of a giant fly. In other words, she was the most beautiful girl Webster Mitchell had come across during his six-month stay in this dry, dusty land and he had nary a clue of how he was going to tell her he couldn't pay up.

"Can't you just tell Stephen that I wasn't home?"

The guy next to her chimed in after shoving the corner of a crustless peanut butter and jelly sandwich into his maw. "Do you know how many people ask us to tell Stephen that?"

The sandwich looked like a cracker between his fingers, which wasn't to say it was small but that the man's hands were huge, as was every other visible part of his body. Not an inch of fat, either.

"I mean, do you honestly know how many people ask us to tell him that?" His speech was peppered with the sound of his lips smacking together and visible strings of saliva and moist white bread stretching from the tip of his tongue to the roof of his mouth.

Webster stood in silence.

Yeah, he had a good idea how many people came up with that particular notion. He wasn't proud of the excuse and if he was smarter, he would have been more prepared. But that's just the thing. Stephen never gave anyone time to prepare. Webster certainly wasn't prepared for the goddess and the oversized lapdog standing before him.

The woman looked down at the open spiral notepad in her hands and ran her index finger along a handwritten list. Tiny pieces of dried skin hung off the sides of her chipped fingernail.

"Mr. Mitchell," she said and then looked up.

Her voice sounded as sweet as he imagined it would, like the songbirds that sometimes fly over his slab looking for a better place to land. Webster grinned with both the upper and lower teeth he had left, which always made it look like he was squinting into the sun even though it was morning and he was facing west.

She removed her glasses and Webster thought he was going to faint. Those big brown eyes surrounded by a sea of white almost put him in a state of delirium.

"Mr. Mitchell," she said, "you've already been given two extensions and you already owe an extra twenty percent. Do you know what happens when a third extension is requested?"

So many questions, Webster thought. And these were the types of questions he hated. Questions with answers that the other party knew the answer to but still insisted on baiting you with. He turned his head back toward the inside of his tent as if the answers were somehow there. All he saw was a tiny ten-foot by ten-foot canvas square with a low ceiling that added to an already growing hunch. He couldn't spot an inch of ground because it was covered in dirty clothes, plastic bottles, and flimsy, discarded cereal boxes. The only two things visible above the debris was a cot topped with a brown, cotton-bleeding bunny for a pillow and matted faux-fur coat for a blanket. And then, of course, there was the bucket for when he couldn't stand to get up and piss in those ass-freezing winds of the desert nights.

"Yes," he said, "I know what happens."

If only he could have come across this vision a year ago when things weren't so bad. If she's working for Stephen, Webster was sure she had her own sob story.

"I have twenty more appointments today, Mr. Mitchell. I have to come back this way. I expect payment when I return." She spun around on her sandals and started walking down the dirt trail towards the next tent-covered slab a quarter-mile down. Webster took a moment to imagine the full aspect of her svelte body only hinted at beneath the floaty yellow dress decorated with a print of white flowers.

He was pulled out of his brief reverie when muscleman shoved the rest of his sandwich into his mouth and wiped his hands clean across

Webster's chest, leaving the sweet mix of sticky strawberry jam and sugar-laden peanut butter spread across his t-shirt and its scent floating up into his nostrils. It made him salivate. The man winked at Webster and followed the woman.

"Wait," Webster yelled, "I didn't catch your name!"

The woman kept on walking and muscleman floated two middle fingers over his back.

* * *

Options were limited, but at least they existed. Webster had that to be thankful for that, he supposed. After a half-hour of sitting in front of his tent with his knees pulled up to his chin, feeling sorry for himself beneath the warming sun, he reviewed those options.

He could head down to the limestone quarry and request more hours, but the possibility of them being granted was next to nil. Stephen controlled the mining operations even more tightly than he controlled the slabs. Webster was on the man's shit list. Either Webster wasn't producing enough or Stephen just didn't like something about him. The boss didn't require a solid reason because he only answered to those fellow slab lords with whom he traded.

Running out in the middle of the night was also out of the question. Stephen had boobytraps planted everywhere that would leave the person bleeding out, carrion for crows. The only safe exit from Stephen's domain was via escort.

There was always the possibility of accepting the consequences of asking for a third extension. The whole idea of extensions was one of Stephen's hilarious notions as no one ever managed to dig themselves out from under a first extension. And if Webster thought his options were limited now, they composed a veritable buffet compared to what he'd face once he was marked. He'd seen those people leaving the slabs, marching the long dirt road with eighty pounds of gear strapped to their back and shoulders. It didn't matter if they were old, young, or some work-worn combination of both—their countenance foretold a swift and impending end as their entire face spoke of their debt to Stephen. The trademark *D* stood in contrast to their cheeks and forehead like a bas-relief, their identity as debtors forever seared onto their flesh. Most of them would die within a few months, down in the stretches of shadeless hills and waterless canyons, their marks forbidding them admission into other slab kingdoms.

No, he couldn't leave, now. Not that he knew about her.

There was a single viable answer.

Webster dug through the trash spread across his floor until he found what he was looking for, then headed for Ying's.

* * *

Before stepping inside, Stephen removed his battered tennis shoes and placed them in the wicker basket sitting beside the entrance flap. The musky smell of patchouli drifted out from the entrance into the still desert air.

If Webster's tent was a hovel, Ying's was a royal palace. There were at least three rooms, two of them separated to the left and right by thick, wool rugs hanging from the ceiling. The main room was three hundred square feet, its floor lined with more soft rugs. A wooden oval table sat near the back, maybe ten inches from the ground, covered with a thin green cloth and with a pair of burning candles sitting in iron stands at each end. Behind the table sat the cross-legged gambler Ying, flipping and shuffling playing cards in his hand, carefully examining the corners of each one.

Webster didn't know how he did it, but Ying's white, collared button-up shirt was always pressed as cleanly as those he'd seen on men in the old magazines. He seemed to wear a new tie every day, today's being yellow with diagonal blue stripes. His sleeves were rolled up to his elbows and his hair was combed back with the sides neatly shaved. One would never guess he worked the mines and that's because he didn't. Ying found a way to get people to work for him. Webster couldn't fathom how he got away with it. Stephen had to have known, but they obviously had an agreement worked out.

To the residents of Stephen's little slab town, Ying was a man of last resorts. Webster remembered how he had barely set up his tent before hearing of Ying's special status. Things didn't always work out when dealing with him. Winning was no guarantee. Still, he was an option to those that had need of money and also had something Ying was willing to play for.

Sitting beside the old gambler was a small girl with wavy, radiant blonde hair flowing down her shoulders and slightly across the sides of her face—a face covered in a thick layer of white powder like that of the old-world Geisha girls. She lay one hand in Ying's lap and the other on her own, palms up as if preparing for meditation. Her age was puzzling as her make-up hid any potential wrinkles but her gray eyes held the air of experience.

Webster had no time to open his mouth before Ying spoke.

"You have nothing to offer me. I suggest you take the mark and leave," he said.

News traveled fast.

"Don't be so sure," Webster said.

Ying laughed. "Unless you hold secrets from me, which I doubt, all I'm willing to give you at this point is a worthless wish of safe journies."

"Ying," he nodded. "Let's play."

Ying gently placed all but one of the cards down face-down on the table and held the remaining one up to a candle to examine it more closely. It was the Queen of Clubs.

"What is it that you think you have that you think I want to play you for?" Ying asked.

Webster reached into the back pocket of his jean-shorts and pulled out a flat, solid item wrapped in an old mechanic's towel. "See for yourself," he said, gently placing it on Ying's table. It connected with a solid thunk.

Ying, still examining the card, nodded absently at the girl. She leaned forward and unraveled the dirty red cloth. Candlelight gleamed off the silver, oversized novelty coin, drawing Ying's attention. He placed the card in his hand on top of the rest and reached for the coin.

"I feel I should be offended, but I like your sense of humor," he said with a smile.

"If you think I handpicked that from a wide selection, you're not as smart of a man as I believed you were," Webster replied. He hoped it was enough to keep the gambler interested.

"Of course," Ying said. "Then maybe it is not you with the sense of humor." He picked up the coin and flipped it back and forth. One side was stamped with a tall building covered by hovering words: *Emperor's Palace*. The other side said *Las Vegas* housed inside a sideways diamond.

"It's cute," Ying said, "but it is not worth nearly what you need."

"Let me worry about that," Webster said.

Ying's shrugged his shoulders. As if the gambler and the girl were of the same mind, she picked up the sitting deck with her delicate hands and began to shuffle.

* * *

The round was over before it started. Even with a pair of Jacks in his hands, Webster had no chance against the full house Ying laid down on the table.

"I'm sorry," Ying said. "Lady Luck is fickle. Maybe we'll meet again under better circumstances." The dismissive look on his face did nothing to convince Webster that that was anything beyond an impossibility.

"Don't be sorry," Webster said, pushing himself to his feet. At least on the spots where callouses had not formed on his soles, the softness of the fuzzy wool felt like heaven. "I didn't actually lose."

Ying began to laugh. Webster watched as the man's right hand slid beneath the table. "It would appear otherwise. The cards speak from themselves."

"Oh, that?" Webster said. He turned his head and neck, working out the kinks. He banked on Ying not having an itchy trigger finger. "Is that the game you thought we were playing?"

Ying's eyes narrowed. Webster was trying hard not to get ahead of himself, but he had Ying exactly where he wanted him.

"You know, your partner has a beautiful face," Webster said. "I'm sure that layer of sugar you have her coated in makes her all the more sweet, eh?"

The girl's eyes darted up and met Webster's, but she quickly dropped them back to the table as demurely as a beaten dog. She was obviously not as well-versed in hiding her emotions as Ying.

"You should leave," Ying said. "Before someone gets hurt." Webster stood strong. He was still gambling, hoping Ying would let him finish before popping off a round or two.

"I bet that if I were to see her without all of that sugar, I wouldn't even recognize her. I might even think she's someone else. There may be some revealing beauty marks, no? Marks that would make it difficult to make one's way in the world."

Despite what were likely his best efforts, Ying's face began to resemble a boiling kettle. Webster decided it was time release a little steam before things went south. "It's a good thing I haven't told anyone my theory yet. Or, wait…" Webster held a finger to his chin. "I may have mentioned something to…" He scratched. "Gee, ya know, I can't remember who I may have told."

Ying slowly turned to the girl and nodded. She rose quickly without saying a word and disappeared into the room on the left.

Ying spoke through gritted teeth. "Even if I give you what you need, you'll be back on Stephen's shit list next month. Don't think that this is going to be a regular installment."

"Let me worry about that," Webster said.

There was plenty to worry about as he wasn't yet done gambling.

* * *

"Where's your pet gorilla?" Webster asked.

"He's handling another case," she said. The notepad was hanging from a silver beaded chain around her neck.

Somehow, with the sun now setting behind her, her beauty seemed to increase ten-fold. She lifted her sunglasses so they rested in her kinked hair like a pair of eggs in a nest, revealing, if Webster wasn't mistaken, eyes that hinted at some semblance of sorrow.

"You have until sunrise tomorrow to report to Stephen's office. Technically, I don't have to let you know this until—"

"Here," he said. He pulled his hand out from a back pocket and waved a stack of scrip in front of her face.

She hesitated but eventually grabbed it. Her eyes left his only long enough to verify that the money was legit.

"How did you get this?" she asked.

"A little bit of work, a little bit of luck," Webster said. She didn't need to know the full story, yet.

"You're very resourceful," she said.

Webster tried to come up with something clever, but instead, he said, "Yeah."

A squawking flock of birds flying overhead filled the gap between drawn-out moments of silence. Webster felt a renewed sense of confidence. Something he hadn't felt in months. Something that he thought had been beaten out of him by the hardships of life in the modern world of dog-eat-dog and slab lord-eat-slab lord.

"You know," he said, "I feel like the two of us could probably accomplish a lot if we weren't tied down to one place."

He wasn't sure how she was going to take that, but at this point, he didn't care. He had nothing to lose.

The woman chuckled under her breath, then extended a hand. "I'm Stella."

A Letter to the Gubamint

Darryl was already agitated when Karrie insisted on digging into him some more.

"You think they care? You're wastin' your time!"

Over the years, Darryl had figured out that holding his tongue and letting his wife air out her feelings was the quickest way to resolution, but by God, she never made it easy.

"Instead of fiddlin' 'round with that, maybe you ought to help me put this diaper on," she continued.

His pencil poked through the paper several times, leaving tiny holes in his anxious words.

"If they do anything, they'll send some men in some suits and sunglasses down here and haul you away. And then how am I s'posed to take care of Kenny?" His wife laughed without taking a breath. "Not that much would change eitherways."

The lead finally snapped off the end of the pencil and Darryl slapped it down on the tiny table extending from the wall of their imitation Airstream trailer.

"Dang it, woman! Don't you think someone with some special

firepower ought to know about this? I ain't got enough ammo to take 'em all on myself. And 'sides, they're probably invincible to the kind of bullets they sell at Walmart."

"They ain't gonna believe you," Karrie replied. She stood a whole three feet from him, hovering over a pot of boiling water, emptying a blue box of macaroni and cheese with one hand and holding Kenny in the other. The boy was squirming and yelping as his feet dangled inches from the hot steam.

"Ha!" he erupted. "Shows what you know. Who do you think knows about 'em if it ain't the gubamint?"

Finally, she shut her lips. Darryl yanked off his green-and-yellow trucker hat, grabbed the back of his neck and twisted his head around to release some tension. He stood and proceeded to pull open every drawer in the place, all three of them, rummaging through while tossing aside expired coupons and Karrie's unread issues of *The Enquirer*.

He slammed the last drawer back into its place. The knob came flying off and bounced onto the floor. "Ain't we got more than one dang pencil in this place?"

"You want to write that letter so gawt-dang bad, go and get one from the *scary* neighbors," she said. "I'm busy puttin' food on the table and takin' care of our son."

* * *

Darryl didn't want to say he was becoming one of those gorephobes—people that shut themselves up and didn't come outside for nothing but what they had to—but he was starting to dread any potential run-ins with the residents of Coconut Groves Mobile Home Park.

If he had to guess, it all started a couple of weeks ago. Wilmer down towards the entrance was the first one Darryl had noticed. Usually hiding in his trailer most days, Wilmer worked nights at Shooter's, a pool hall down the interstate a few miles, but he had since become a regular social moth, full of 'Good morning's and 'How are you today's. Darryl swore Wilmer even said something in French once or twice, but since Darryl didn't speak French, he could only say it *sounded* like French.

By yesterday evening, it seemed almost every other neighbor had taken on airs like they'd hit the lottery. But there was more to it than that and Darryl couldn't quite put a finger on it other than to come to the most logical conclusion—the Grays had come (aliens, to the layman) and they were either controlling the people's minds or had swapped bodies with them completely. Darryl had watched enough episodes of *Ancient Aliens* to be convinced such a thing was not outside the realm of possibility.

He slammed the trailer door shut and was accosted by his nearest neighbor.

"Good morning, Darryl. Marvelous and sublime weather we are having, is it not? Though they say a cold front is moving in, which is a mass of cold air on the edge of a low-pressure system."

As Darryl cleared his front yard in a few steps, the only acknowledgment he gave Little Jim was a squint and a wide berth. The man was five-three and had to be clocking in at around two-fifty, wearing the same stained t-shirt he'd gotten for free at a raffle at Pete's Cars six years ago. There was no telling if the problem was catching, so Darryl held his breath until he made it to the front office and checked in with Debbie.

"Hey Deb," he said, resting his arms on the counter overlooking her desk. Darryl wondered how she could find anything through piles of sun-faded Beanie Babies. "You got a pencil?"

Her chair squeaked as she stood to meet him. She was wearing a tight tank top that showed off her freckled chest and shoulders and her acid-wash shorts seemed like they were cutting off circulation to her dimpled thighs on down.

"I'm sure I have one or two around here for you, Darryl." Behind her glasses, her hazel eyes glowed like those of a man on a diet standing outside Rod's Donut Shop.

"Okay, great," Darryl said. "I been trying to finish this dang letter."

"Oh?" she asked, completely ignoring his request. "Whatcha doin'? Writin' a love letter?"

"No, nothin' like that," he said with all seriousness. "Important stuff. Gubamint stuff."

Debbie raised her eyebrows. "Ooh. Not only are you a handsome man, but you got some intrigue to ya'. That wife of yours better be ap-preciatin' you."

"Hey, you noticed anything funny 'round here?" Daryl asked.

"There ain't a day goes by that I don't notice something funny at Coconut Groves."

"Well, yeah, but I mean somethin' different. Like people actin'... different?"

Debbie's remained motionless.

"Anyway, don't matter," Darryl said. "I'm gonna see it gets taken care of. So you got a pencil or what?"

She gave him a disappointed look. "Yeah, sure, hold on."

Debbie turned around and leaned down to pull open a drawer in the cabinet behind her.

"Gotta be one in here somewhere," she said, looking over her shoulder at Darryl while her butt swayed in the air like one of them ba-boons Darryl had seen on TV the other night.

He was growing impatient. He wanted to get the letter in before the mail lady came, and was about to walk down to Perly's Drug Store and just spend some scratch on a new pencil before Debbie finally shut the drawer and handed him a #2 with an eraser on the end that looked like a watermelon.

"Thanks, Deb."

He was already out the door as she was saying something about calling her anytime he needed help with something, anything at all, be it business or personal, but especially personal because she was certain she could take care of his needs.

Gravel ground beneath Darryl's flip-flops as he headed back to his trailer, but he stopped halfway and decided he'd have a better chance of getting the letter done on a picnic bench in the common area. After five minutes of writing and swatting at mosquitoes, he had the thing finished and sealed in an envelope. Hoping to avoid Debbie, he went the long way around the back of the front office to the mailboxes on the side. Before he slipped it in the outbox, he confirmed he'd gotten the address right:

To the folks dealing with the Grays, Pentagon, Washington.

He was smiling as he walked the hundred yards back home until he was accosted by a skin-and-bones woman with a drooling mutt in tow.

"Darryl, how are you? Is that a new pair of pants? You are looking quite urbane. One might even say, debonair."

Oh no, he thought, not you too, Jolene.

He picked up the pace.

* * *

Darryl and Karrie had spent a couple days back in the routine when, one afternoon, a set of rapid knocks set the whole trailer to rattling.

Kenny stirred in his crib.

Karrie looked at Darryl and he looked back at her. Darryl grabbed the remote and turned the volume down on *Family Feud.*

He spread a section of vinyl mini-blinds beside his chair and spied a man and a woman, both wearing matching dark suits and sunglasses. Two points for Karrie, but Darryl was confident the gubamint wasn't going to take him away. Hell, he was going to be a hero. Images of getting some sort of medal from the President himself flashed through his mind, though he couldn't quite remember who the President was this year, so the face was just a blur.

Darryl was surprised the feds had responded so quickly, but he had a feeling gubamint mail moved faster than people mail, especially when it came to matters of national security.

The door squealed on its rusty hinges as Darryl pushed it open.

"Mr. Shamesworth?" the woman asked. She took off her sunglasses, revealing a pair of eyes bluer than the sky. The man beside her had barely moved, probably due to the fact that he had a gallon of gel holding down his hair. It looked like the kind of mop you'd see on a plastic doll. In his right hand was a leather briefcase.

"The one and only," Darryl replied. "I knew it. I knew you'd come and do somethin' about this." He spoke the words to them but gave a self-satisfied look to Karrie.

The woman squinted and smiled, then looked her partner. The man simply shrugged. "We're here to help," she said. "My name is Candace and this is William. We've come to talk to you about a few things that your neighbors are involved in. May we come in and discuss?"

"Of course!" Darryl said. The two visitors stepped inside the trailer while Darryl gave his wife a big wink. She remained seated and eyed Candace and William with suspicion as they said their hellos.

"You'll have to 'scuse the mess," Darryl said, suddenly embarrassed at the state of the trailer. He swept away little Kenny's dried *Oatie Os* that had fallen across the dining table. "Please, have a seat." Darryl extended his hand toward the booth around the table.

The man and the woman squeezed themselves in, both looking as uncomfortable as a pair of rabbits at a bloodhound convention.

Daryl plopped down across from them and launched into the speech that had been running over and over in his mind since he'd dropped the letter off in the mail.

"Ms. Candace. Mr. William. Now, I'm not sure where you want to start, but I been trying to figure out if there's some sort of pattern here, some—"

"Mr. Shamesworth," she interrupted. "Mrs. Shamesworth," she followed with a nod in Karrie's direction. "How do you feel about your current situation at Coconut Groves?"

Karrie began to speak, "Well, it had been just fine until my husband—"

"Oh, is this a test?" Darryl interrupted. "Ha! Of course, of course. Yup, you gotta make sure we're free and clear. I'll tell you right now, we's still us. I try to stay away from the neighbors and I told Karrie she oughta' do the same until ya'll can get down here and assess the situation."

William finally removed his own sunglasses and pinched the bridge of his nose.

"I'm sure you've seen quite a change in your neighbors, right?" he asked.

"Right!" Darryl replied.

"Would you say that they've come across more...educated?" Candace asked.

"Oh, definitely. It's like they got these fancy brains all of a sudden. Take Odelia, for instance—the gal in space 13-C. I was trying to get to work the other morning and she comes flying at me, waving her arms as if she were in trouble. I asked what it was and she starts babbling at me about how she was going to have a little shindig that night to watch Comet 45P cross Aquila and Hercules and she'd love for the Missus and me to come."

Candace and William smiled at each other.

Darryl continued, "I mean, I knew right then that somethin' was up because only a week prior, she'd been complainin' to Karrie that the light outside her trailer was broken and how was she s'posed to shoot the raccoons that get in her garbage if she couldn't see 'em. Ain't never made a single mention in her life about no comets."

"That's great," William said. "Fantastic!"

Darryl wasn't sure what he said that made the man so happy, but he was beginning to feel confident that he was on the right track and something would be done.

"So what are ya'll gonna do 'bout this?" he asked. "If you can let me know before ya'll drop a bomb or bring in the tanks, I'd 'ppreciate it. I can hitch this trailer right up and park at Island Oasis up the street."

William and Candace threw each other another confused look.

Finally, William undid the latches on his briefcase and opened it up.

"I think you're going to like what we have to offer you. And best of all, it's free."

Darryl looked at Karrie.

"Well, I didn't s'pect to pay nothin' that you ain't already got through my taxes."

"That's right," Candace said, turning the briefcase around so everyone could see what was inside. "The good people of Horsetail County have already paid for these educational CDs."

Except for the sound of cars zooming by on the nearby interstate and Kenny's light snoring, the trailer was silent.

"Educational CDs?" Darryl looked like he'd just been invited to dinner with the pope. "What's that got to do—"

"You get your pick," Candace continued "though most of the neighbors have gotten to the good stuff already. Our apologies, but Horsetail didn't get *that* much taxpayer money." She pulled out a few DVD jewel cases and shuffled through them. "What do you think? Latin 101? Biology? Shakespeare's King Lear? And don't worry if you don't have a CD player, the county can provide one on a payment plan."

"I don't understand," Darryl said. "How's this going to help us deal with the Grays?"

"The Grays?" Candace asked. "I don't think we've met them yet. We've met the Turgensons, the Madgetts,—"

"Oh yeah, they got all the ones on Beethoven's Sonatas," William chimed in.

Darryl jumped to his feet, slamming his knees into the bottom of the table. He tried to hide the sting.

"What's the big idea, here? I write ya'll a letter to help with the Grays and you bring *educational* CDs?"

"Mr. Shamesworth," Candace replied. "I'm not sure what you think we're here for, and we haven't been informed of any correspondence from you, but we work for Horsetail County. We're a part of an educational outreach program for the 'underprivileged,'" she said, flexing her index fingers in the air. "We feel the lack of easily available educational resources is a barrier to improving one's livelihood and career trajectory."

More painful silence, broken up only by a giggle from Karrie.

"I see," Darryl said. "Ya'll are from the gubamint though, right?"

"Well, yes, technically," William replied.

Darryl was silent now as he stared at the two of them and then looked to his wife. Smug airs were written all over face, but he held back any comments.

"We'll take the Shakespeare one!" he shouted, waking up little Kenny. Karrie jumped up to attend to him.

"Are you sure that's the one you want?" Candace asked.

"Yep. Absolutely. I think that will do us just fine," Darryl replied with as big of a smile as possible.

William smiled back. "Shakespeare it is! Now do you need the CD play—"

"Nope, we got one."

"Darryl, we don't—" Karrie said while bouncing Kenny on her shoulder.

"Yeah," Darryl interrupted. "we are ay-okay. Much appreciated."

William placed a jewel case on the table and closed the briefcase. They shook hands with both Darryl and Karrie, then left the trailer.

After a few minutes, when Kenny was lulled back to bed, Darryl slipped on his pair of sandals and walked toward the door.

"Where you goin'?" Karrie asked.

"Headin' down to Perly's to buy us a pencil and get the name of the President."

Karrie shot him a look of confusion. "What for?" she asked.

"He needs to know the Grays have gotten deep into the system."

BRANDED

Though his belly touched the sand, his face was turned slightly up, facing west—the direction of home. Yellow pus streamed from the corner of his left eye onto the bridge of his narrow nose, leaving a noxious stench. Flies buzzed in circles over his open mouth. And then there was the maroon-stained hole punched clean between his shoulder blades, the fabric of his dirty shirt shredded. These signs all added up to one thing.

Jenny Tighe's papa was dead.

It was normal for him to be gone for a few days at a time when checking up on the ranging cattle, and usually, Jenny was with him, learning how to rope and drive. But she had enough to do with keeping the house in order since they lost Mama to consumption earlier in the summer. Scrubbing the splintered floors of their tiny cabin was the last thing Jenny was intent on doing, but she did it because someone had to and she knew it would be one less worry for Papa.

Now, circling buzzards had led her to his body on the dry Mojave Desert floor. Those same vultures were perched, six of them, all waiting patiently on a large pile of tan and gray boulders which sat a half-mile south of the Granite Mountains. Her eyes scanned the nooks and crannies of the surrounding hills while her Winchester 1873 rifle rested in her hands like a familiar tool. Jenny never had to use it on a human before, but Papa had made sure she was ready for anything. She'd been a crackshot with deer in the nearby San Bernardino mountains and was ready to put those skills to use, now that everything had changed.

Nothing seemed to be out there among the thin creosote bushes and tumbleweeds except a few skittering lizards and jackrabbits. Given the state of Papa's body, she figured the culprits were long gone.

She didn't want to get close to him, to rest a hand on his upturned cheek or to shed the tears that were welling up behind her eyes. But she had to lean in to get a closer look at the thing that caught her attention. She rolled his body over to face the sky and his face along with it. Her heart skipped a beat when she saw the five-pointed star branded on his forehead.

* * *

The McLarens weren't just unconcerned if it was discovered that they did this. Seems they *wanted* whoever found Papa to know it was them.

There was no time for pleasantries. As badly as she wanted to dig him a grave, Papa would have been satisfied giving the buzzards the meal of their lives.

Bolt dipped her long head as Jenny approached. Jenny scratched the mare's neck a couple of times, then rummaged through the saddle-

bag, digging past slabs of beef jerky and a half-empty canteen until

she came up with five .44 caliber rounds. Her Winchester was the half-

magazine model, capable of holding six potential shots at a time. It was

already fully loaded, ready for business at a drop of the lever, She didn't

have much extra ammunition, but she hoped not to need it.

She mounted Bolt and galloped east.

* * *

It was nice enough in the greater Mojave. Night temperatures

were mild and the sun's power was dampened by unusual autumn clouds.

Jenny knew every waterhole between her ranch and the McLaren hideout

in Hidden Valley, so she and Bolt were well nourished on the two days

it took to travel the seventy miles from home. Deeper into the desert.

Deeper into danger.

That had to be where they went. Papa had mentioned that it was

the worst kept secret in all of Southern California. She could only imag-

ine now that he brought it up with her just in case something happened.

The long trip had given the fire and fury inside of Jenny time to

become a slow burn. She could be more calculating. Make fewer mis-

takes. The McLarens knew her. Probably knew what had happened to

Mama. Jenny met them once, when Papa and her had a run-in a year ago

when she was only fourteen. They were heading out to dehorn a group

of grazing cattle when Bill McLaren and his brother, Jim, were caught hanging back on a ridge with packs full of rope. They said they'd been searching for their own lost cattle. Papa intimated that he knew what they were up to, but he let them save face.

Stupid. He should have taken care of them then and there.

Bill put on good appearances—he was congenial, handsome even, but she could sense his calculating mind and devious heart. His brother, Jim, on the other hand, was repulsive to the core and seemed not to give a damn about anything. With mussed hair and a reek of whiskey that carried in the wind, he seemed to get a kick out of whistling out of tune and wouldn't stop leering at Jenny until Papa said he'd cut his eyes out right then and there and feed them to the family's bloodhound.

They must have branded Jenny Tighe a girly girl. That she would be too scared to do what she was about to do. Now she was trotting through an arroyo a few miles north of Hidden Valley, chilly without a fire as the sun began to set, ready to put this thing to rest.

* * *

"Get up."

Jim was still snoring. An empty glass bottle laid tipped over on the tent floor beside his cot. Jenny shoved the tip of the rifle barrel into his right nostril and cocked the lever.

Even in the dark, his crusted eyes blinked as he tried to adjust his vision.

"Well, I'll be. What good deed did I do to deserve a visit from an angel?" He started to laugh, but it turned into a phlegm-filled coughing fit. Jenny kept the rifle pointed at his face. She had thought about just pulling the trigger when he was sleeping, but she wanted him to know who was collecting on the debt he owed.

"Do you know who I am?"

"Let me sit up and get a closer look."

She flipped the rifle around like a baton and jammed the butt into his forehead. The crack sent his hands flying to his head.

"Gottdamn! That hurt, you little bitch!"

She swung the barrel of the gun back toward him. "You've only started hurting. Now, get up. Slow."

There had been only one tent in the camp, one cot inside. Remnants of a fire glowed in a ring of stones outside.

"Where's your brother?"

She thought that maybe Bill was out rustling up more cattle. She'd come across a mass of them corralled inside the camp—even recognized a few of them before she even needed to see Papa's brand burnt into their haunches. The plan was to settle up with Jim and then wait until Bill returned. The fire and fury seemed to resurge at the alcohol odor of the younger brother and she knew she was acting more recklessly than she should have been.

She heard a pistol hammer cock behind her.

"You lookin' for me, little lady?"

Jenny's eyes remained on Jim, his black-and-yellow grin bringing her closer to pulling the trigger.

"You may want to think about what it is you intend to do here," Bill said. "My advice? Slowly lay the rifle to the ground."

She wanted to cry. To come so far and make such a foolhardy mistake.

"You killed my papa. I can't let that go unanswered," she said, staring down at Jim the whole time while he slowly climbed out of his canvas sleeping sack, testing her with each move.

The silence in the air was thick. Jenny ran through her options which had narrowed rapidly.

It wasn't as if she could dash out, hop on her horse and make a break for it. She'd left Bolt tied to a yucca tree a half-mile out between the hideout and the arroyo. Besides, if she did get away, contacted the Sheriff, chances are Papa's brand would be converted by the time someone came out here. And that was assuming the McLaren's were even in Hidden Valley at that point.

Jim appeared to be having trouble standing on his own two feet, swaying side-to-side a little. Jenny's gun was still pointed at him, but now at his chest.

"We both know you ain't gonna shoot," he said, placing one hand on the barrel of the gun and the other on her cheek. Jenny felt him pushing the rifle gently to the side. He began to stroke her face. "So just do what my bro—"

In one swift motion, her finger crushed the trigger and she quickly kicked her left boot back, connecting with what she hoped was Bill's private parts. Her ears went ringing while the scent of gunpowder shot up her nose. Jim flew backward, ripping a gash in the tent wall before coming to rest on the ground. Something wet had splashed against her face which left a ferrous taste in her open mouth. As if she didn't care if she died now, Jenny turned without haste to look at Bill. She saw what looked to be the outline of a pistol in the dark ground. next to her feet, and a man crumpled up like a curlicue, his hands tucked into his crotch. She grabbed the pistol and listened to Bill's muffled whimpered for a few seconds.

"You're gonna pay for what you done," she said.

"You can't prove anything," Bill spat out between heavy breaths. "You're gonna hang, girl."

Jenny pocketed the pistol and pointed her rifle at Bill's head.

"Get up."

* * *

The coals were still warm. She picked up the five-point-star brand she'd left resting in the fire pit. Bill lay on the ground now, hogtied tied just as Papa had shown her when they were busting steer.

"Seems to me there ain't much left for me here," Jenny said. "So, I don't need to prove nothin' to nobody. This will be the last time you see me. This will make sure you don't forget your deeds."

She pressed the glowing pattern into his forehead and his scream echoed across the desert valley.

ƑANTASTIC ȘHORTS

I hope you enjoyed these stories. Reviews are always welcome! If you'd like to read more fantastic fiction by Phillip McCollum:

Fantastic Shorts - Volume 2

52 Stories in 52 Weeks: One writer's journey in tackling, shackling, and shooting his inner critic

About the Author

From 2017 to 2018, Phillip McCollum spent 52 weeks writing 52 short stories in an effort to prove to himself that he might be cut out for this writing thing after all. He hails from Southern California where he shares living quarters with his wife, son, an old cat, and young betta fish.

If you'd like to hear about his latest work, please sign up for the newsletter on his website (phillipmccollum.com). He also pokes his head up on Twitter once in a while.